Aubrey De Vere

Legends of the Saxon saints

Aubrey De Vere

Legends of the Saxon saints

ISBN/EAN: 9783337202262

Printed in Europe, USA, Canada, Australia, Japan

Cover: Foto ©Andreas Hilbeck / pixelio.de

More available books at **www.hansebooks.com**

LEGENDS

OF THE

SAXON SAINTS

BY

AUBREY DE VERE

'Hic sunt in fossa Bedæ Venerabilis ossa

(Old Inscription

LONDON
MACMILLAN & CO.
1893
MᶜN

VENERABLE BEDE

'Mid quiet vale or city lulled by night
Well-pleased the wanderer, wakeful on his bed,
Hears from far Alps on fitful breeze the sound
Of torrents murmuring down their rocky glens,
Strange voice from distant regions, alien climes :—
Should these far echoes from thy legend-roll
Delight of loftier years, these echoes faint,
Thus waken, thus make calm, one restless heart
In our distempered day, to thee the praise,
Voice of past times, O Venerable Bede !

PREFACE.

MANY YEARS AGO a friend remarked to me on the strangeness of the circumstance that the greatest event in the history of a nation, its conversion to Christianity, largely as it is often recorded in national legends, has never been selected as a theme for poetry. That event may indeed not supply the materials necessary for an Epic or a Drama, yet it can hardly fail to abound in details significant and pathetic, which especially invite poetic illustration. With the primary interest of that great crisis, many others, philosophical, social, and political, generally connect themselves. Antecedent to a nation's conversion, the events of centuries have commonly either conduced to it, or thrown obstacles in its way; while the history as well as the character of that nation in the

subsequent ages is certain to have been in a principal
measure modified by that event. Looking back
consequently on that period in which the moral
influences of ages, early and late, are imaged, a
people recognises its own features as in a mirror,
but sees them such as they were when their expres-
sion was still undetermined ; and it may well be
struck by the resemblance at once to what now
exists, and also by the dissimilitude. Many countries have unhappily lost almost all authentic
records connected with their conversion. Such
would have been the fate of England also, had it
not been for a single book, ' Bede's Ecclesiastical
History.' In the following poems I have endea-
voured to walk in the footsteps of that great master.
Their scope will best be indicated by some remarks
upon the character of that wonderful age which
he records.

St. Augustine landed in the Isle of Thanet
A.D. 597, and Bede died A.D. 735. The inter-
vening period, that of his chronicle, is the golden
age of Anglo-Saxon sanctity. Notwithstanding
some twenty or thirty years of pagan reaction, it

was a time of rapid though not uninterrupted progress, and one of an interest the more touching when contrasted with the calamities which followed so soon. Between the death of Bede and the first Danish invasion, were eighty years, largely years of decline, moral and religious. Then followed eighty years of retribution, those of the earlier Danish wars, till, with the triumph of Alfred, England's greatest king, came the Christian restoration. Once more periods of relaxed morals and sacrilegious princes alternated with intervals of reform ; again and again the Northmen over-swept the land. The 460 years of Anglo-Saxon Christianity constituted a period of memorable achievements and sad vicissitudes ; but that period included more than a hundred years of high sanctity, belonging for the most part to the seventh century, a century to England as glorious as was the thirteenth to Mediæval Europe.

Within that century the kingdoms of the Heptarchy successively became Christian, and those among them which had relapsed returned to the Faith. Sovereigns, many of whom had boasted a descent from Odin himself, stood as interpreters beside the missionaries when they preached, and rivalled each other in the zeal with which they built churches, some of which were founded on the sites of ancient temples, though, in other cases, with a charitable prudence, the existing fanes were spared, purified, and adapted to Christian worship. At Canterbury and York, cathedrals rose, and on many a site besides; and when the earlier had been destroyed by fire, or had fallen through decay, fabrics on a vaster scale rose above their ruins, and maintained a succession which lasts to this day. Monasteries unnumbered lifted their towers above the forests of a land in which the streams still ran unstained and the air of which had not yet been dimmed by smoke, imparting a dignity to fen and flat morass. Round them ere long cities gathered, as at St. Albans, Malmesbury, Sherborne, and Wimborne ; the most memorable of those monasteries being that at Canterbury, and that at Westminister, dedicated to St. Peter, as the cathedral church near it had been dedicated to St. Paul. In the North they were at least as numerous. The University of Oxford is also associated with that early age. It was beside the Isis that St. Frideswida raised her convent, occupied at a later date by canons regular, and ultimately transformed into Christ Church by Cardinal Wolsey— becoming thus the chief, as it had been the earliest, among the schools in that great seat of learning which within our own days has exercised a religious influence over England not less remarkable than that which belonged to its most palmy preceding period.

During that century England produced most of those saintly kings and queens whose names still enrich the calendar of the Anglo-Saxon Church, sovereigns who ruled their kingdoms with justice, lived in mortification, went on pilgrimages, died in cloisters. The great missionary work had also begun. Within a century from the death of St. Augustine, apostles from England had converted multitudes in Germany, and St. Wilfrid had preached to the inhabitants of Friesland. Something, moreover, had been done to retrieve the past. The Saxon kings made amends for the wrongs inflicted by their ancestors upon the British Celts, endowing with English lands the churches and convents founded by them in Brittany. King Kenwalk of Wessex showed thus also a royal munificence to the Celtic monastery of Glastonbury, only stipulating in return that the British monks there, condoning past injuries, should offer a prayer for him when they knelt at the tomb of King Arthur.

The England of the seventh century had been very gradually prepared for that drama of many ages which had then its first rehearsal. In it three races had a part. They were those of the native Britons, the Saxons who had over-run the land, and the Irish missionaries. Rome, the last and greatest of the old-world empires, had exercised more of an enfeebling and less of an elevating influence among the British than among her other subject races ; but her great military roads still remained the witnesses of her military genius ; and many a city, some in ruin, were records of her wealth and her arts. The Teutonic race in England, which for centuries had maintained its independence against Rome, could not forgive the Britons for having submitted to their hated foe, and trampled on them the more ruthlessly because they despised them. Yet they at least might well have learned to respect that race. It has been well remarked that if the Britons submitted easily to Rome, yet of all her subject races they made far the most memorable fight against that barbaric irruption which swept over the ruins of her empire. For two centuries that race had fought on. It still retained the whole of Western Britain, Cornwall, Wales, and Strathclyde; while in other parts of England it possessed large settlements. On the other hand, in matters of spiritual concern the British race contrasted unfavourably with the other races subjected by the barbarians. In France, Spain, and Italy, the conquered had avenged a military defeat by a spiritual victory, bringing over their conquerors to Christianity; and, as a consequence, they had often risen to equality with them. In those parts of England, on the contrary, where the British had submitted to the Pagan conquerors, they by degrees abandoned their Christian faith;[1] and where they retained their independence, they hated the Saxon conquerors too much to share their

[1] See Montalembert's 'Moines de l'Occident,' vol. iii. p. 343; and also Burke: 'On the Continent the Christian religion, after the northern irruptions, not only remained but flourished. . . . In England it was so entirely extinguished that when Augustine undertook his mission, it does not appear that among all the Saxons there was a single person professing Christianity.'

Christianity with them. Far from desiring their conversion, they resisted all the overtures made to them by the Roman missionaries who ardently desired their aid ; and as a consequence of that refusal, they eventually lost their country. The chief cause of that refusal was hatred of the invader. The Irish as well as the British had a passionate devotion to their own local traditions in a few matters not connected with doctrine ; but they notwithstanding worked cordially with the Benedictines from St. Gregory's convent for the spread of the Christian Faith. Had the Britons converted the Anglo-Saxon race they would probably have blended with them, as at a later time that race blended with their Norman conquerors. Three successive waves of the Teuton-Scandinavian race swept over their ancient land, the Anglo-Saxon, the Danish, and the Norman : against them all the British Celts fought on. They fell back toward their country's western coasts, like the Irish of a later day ; and within their Cambrian mountains they maintained their independence for eight centuries.

Yet the Anglo-Saxons' victory was not an

unmixed one. Everywhere throughout England they maintained during the seventh century two different battles, a material and a spiritual one, and with opposite results. Year by year that race pushed further its military dominion; but yearly the Christian Faith effected new triumphs over that of Odin. For this there were traceable causes. The character of the Teutonic invader included two very different elements, and the nobler of these had its affinities with Christianity. If, on the one hand, that character was fierce, reckless, and remorseless, and so far in natural sympathy with a religion which mocked at suffering and till the ninth century offered up human sacrifices, it was marked no less by robustness, simplicity, honesty, sincerity, an unexcitable energy and an invincible endurance. It possessed also that characteristic which essentially contradistinguishes the *ordo equestris* from the *ordo pedestris* in human character, viz., the spirit of reverence. It had aspirations; and, as a background to all its musings and all its hopes there remained ever the idea of the Infinite. As a consequence, it retained a large measure of self-respect, purity, and that veneration for household ties attri-

buted to it by the Roman historian[1] at a time
when that virtue was no longer a Roman one.
Such a character could not but have its leanings
toward Christianity; and, when brought under
its influences, it put forth at once new qualities, like a wild flower which, on cultivation,
acquires for the first time a perfume. Its spirit
of reverence developed into humility, and its
natural fortitude into a saintly patience; while its
fierceness changed into a loyal fervour; and the
crimes to which its passions still occasionally
hurried it were voluntarily expiated by penances
as terrible. Even King Penda, the hater of Christianity, hated an insincere faith more. 'Of all men,'
he said, 'he that I have ever most despised is the
man who professes belief in some God and yet does
not obey his laws.' Such was that character destined
to produce under the influences of faith such noble
specimens of Christian honour and spiritual heroism.
From the beginning its greatness was one

> True to the kindred points of Heaven and Home;

[1] Tacitus. The German's wife might well be called his 'help-
mate.' His wedding gift to his bride consisted of a horse, a yoke of
oxen, a lance and a sword.

and in later ages it became yet more eminently domestic, combining household ties with the pursuit of letters and science in colleges which still preserved a family life. Its monks had no vocation to the life of the desert ; in this unlike the Irish saints, who, like those of Eastern lands, delighted in the forest hermitage and the sea-beat rock.

The Anglo-Saxon race was but a branch of that great Teuton-Scandinavian race, generically one whether it remained in the German forests or wandered on to the remoter coasts of Denmark, Sweden and Norway. It was the race which the Romans called 'the Barbarians,' but which they could never conquer. A stern history had trained it for a wonderful destiny. Christianity in mastering the Greek had possessed itself of the intellect of the world, and in mastering Rome had found access to all those vast regions conquered by Roman arms, opened out by Roman roads, governed by Roman law, and by it helped to the conception of a higher law. But the Greek and the Roman civilisations had, each of them, corrupted its way, and yielded to the seductions of pride, sense, and material prosperity ; and, as a consequence, both had become

a

incapable of rendering full justice to much that is highest in Christianity. That which they lacked the 'Barbaric' race alone was capable of supplying. In its wanderings under darkened skies and amid pitiless climates it had preserved an innocence and simplicity elsewhere lost. Enriched by the union of the new element, thus introduced, with what it had previously derived from Greek thought and Roman law, that authentic Religion which had been prospectively sown within the narrow precinct of Judea extended its branches over the world. Had the Barbaric race shared in the Greek sciences and arts, and clothed itself in the Roman civilisation, it must have learned their corruptions. The larger destiny of man could thus, humanly speaking, never have been accomplished, and neither the mediæval world, the modern world, nor that yet higher order of human society which doubtless lies beyond both, could have existed. It was necessary that in some region, exacting, yet beneficent, civilisation should be retarded, that a remedy might be found for the abuses of civilisation; and races whose present backward condition we are accustomed to deplore may likewise be intended for a similar purpose.

Plants are thus kept in the dark in order to re-serve their fruitage for a fitter season.

But what had been the earlier history of a race before which such destinies lay? What training had prepared it for its work—the last that might have been expected from it? On this subject there remains a tradition, the profoundly significant cha-racter of which ought to have made it more widely known. Mallet, in his 'Northern Antiquities,' translated by Bishop Percy, to whom our ballad literature is so deeply indebted, records it thus:—
' A celebrated tradition, confirmed by the poems of all the northern nations, by their chronicles, by institutions and customs, some of which subsist to this day, informs us that an extraordinary person named Odin formerly reigned in the north. . . . All their testimonies are comprised in that of Snorri, the ancient historian of Norway, and in the com-mentaries and explications which Torphæus added to his narrative. The Roman Commonwealth was arrived at the highest pitch of power, and saw all the then known world subject to its laws, when an unforeseen event raised up enemies against it from the very bosom of the forests of Scythia and on the

banks of the Tanais. Mithridates by flying had drawn Pompey after him into those deserts. The King of Pontus sought there for refuge and new means of vengeance. He hoped to arm against the ambition of Rome all the barbarous nations his neighbours, whose liberty she threatened. He succeeded in this at first, but all those peoples, ill united as allies, ill armed as soldiers, and still worse disciplined, were forced to yield to the superior genius of Pompey. Odin is said to have been of their number. . . . Odin commanded the Æsir, whose country must have been situated between the Pontus Euxinus and the Caspian Sea. Their principal city was Asgard. The worship there paid to their supreme God was famous throughout the circumjacent countries. Odin, having united under his banners the youth of the neighbouring nations, marched towards the north and west of Europe, subduing, as we are told, all the people he found in his passage, and giving them to one or other of his sons for subjects. Many sovereign families of the North are said to be descended from these princes. Thus Horsa and Hengist, the chiefs of those Saxons who conquered Britain in the fifth century, counted

Odin or Wodin in the number of their ancestors; it was the same with the other Anglo-Saxon princes as well as the greatest part of those of lower Germany and the North.'[1]

Gibbon refers to this ancient tradition, though not as accepting it for a part of ascertained history, yet in a spirit less sceptical than was usual to him. He writes thus: 'It is supposed that Odin was chief of a tribe of barbarians which dwelt on the banks of the lake Mœotis, till the fall of Mithridates and the arms of Pompey menaced the north with servitude. That Odin, yielding with indignant fury to a power which he was unable to resist, conducted his tribe from the frontiers of the Asiatic Sarmatia into Sweden, with the great design of forming, in that inaccessible retreat of freedom, a religion and a people which, in some remote age, might be subservient to his immortal revenge; when his invincible Goths, armed with martial fanaticism, should issue in numerous swarms from the neighbourhood of the Polar circle to chastise the oppressors of

[1] Mallet's *Northern Antiquities*, pp. 79, 80. (Bell and Daldy, 1873.) Burke records this tradition with an entire credence. See note in p. 288.

mankind. . . . Notwithstanding the mysterious obscurity of the Edda, we can easily distinguish two persons confounded under the name of Odin; the god of war, and the great legislator of Scandinavia. The latter, the Mahomet of the north, instituted a religion adapted to the climate and to the people. Numerous tribes on either side of the Baltic were subdued by the invincible valour of Odin, by his persuasive eloquence, and by the fame which he acquired of a most skilful magician. The faith that he had propagated during a long and prosperous life he confirmed by a voluntary death. Apprehensive of the ignominious approach of disease and infirmity, he resolved to expire as became a warrior. In a solemn assembly of the Swedes and Goths he wounded himself in nine mortal places, hastening away (as he asserted with his dying voice) to prepare the feast of heroes in the palace of the great god of war.'[1]

In a note Gibbon adds, referring to the Roman and Oriental part of the legend: 'This wonderful expedition of Odin, which, by deducing the enmity of the Goths and Romans from so memorable a

---

[1] *Decline and Fall of the Roman Empire*, chap. x.

cause, might supply the noble groundwork of an epic poem, cannot safely be received as authentic history. According to the obvious sense of the Edda, and the interpretation of the most skilful critics, Asgard, instead of denoting a real city of the Asiatic Sarmatia, is the fictitious appellation of the mystic abode of the gods, the Olympus of Scandinavia.' Whether the emigration of the Barbaric race from the East be or be not historical, certainly the grounds upon which Gibbon bases his distrust of it are slender. He forgot that there might well have been both an earthly Asgard and also, according to the religion of the north, an Asgard in heaven, the destined abode of warriors faithful to Odin. Those who after his death changed their king into a god would, by necessity, have provided him with a celestial mansion ; nor could they have assigned to it a name more acceptable to a race which blended so closely their religion with their patriotic love than that of their ancient capital, from which their great deliverer and prophet had led them forth in pilgrimage. Let us hope that Gibbon's remark as to the fitness of this grand legend for the purposes of epic poetry may yet prove prophecy. It has had one chance already : for we learn from the first book of *The Prelude* that the theme was one of those on which the imagination of Wordsworth rested in youth, when he was seeking a fit subject for epic song.

It is difficult to imagine a historical legend invested with a greater moral weight or dignity than belongs to this one. The mighty Republic was soon to pass into an Empire mightier and more ruthless still, the heir of all those ancient empires which from the earliest had represented a dominion founded on the pride of this world, and had trampled upon human right. A race is selected to work the retribution. It is qualified for its work by centuries of adversity, only to be paralleled by the prosperity of its rival. Yet when at last that retribution comes, it descends more in mercy than in judgment! Great changes had prepared the world for a new order of things. The centre of empire had moved eastward from Rome to Constantinople : the spiritual centre had moved westward from Jerusalem to Rome. The empire had herself become Christian, and was allowed after that event nearly a century more of gradual decline.

The judgment was not thus averted; but it was ennobled. Her children were enabled to become the spiritual instructors of those wild races by which the '*State* Universal' had been over-whelmed. That empire indeed, was not so much destroyed as transformed and extended, a grace rendered possible by her having submitted to the yoke of Christ; the new kingdoms which consti-tuted the Christian '*Orbis Terrarum*' being, for the most part, fragments of it, while its laws made way into regions wider far, and exercised over them a vast though modified authority not yet extinct. Here, if anywhere, we catch glimpses of a hand flashing forth between the clouds, pointing their way to the nations, and con-ducting Humanity forward along its arduous and ascending road. There is a Providence or there could be no Progress.

For the fulfilment of that part assigned to the 'Barbarians' in this marvellous drama of the ages, it was necessary that many things should combine; an exemption from the temptations which had ma-terialised the races of the south; the severe life that perfects strength; a race endowed with the physical

strength needed to render such sufferings endurable;
and lastly, an original spiritual elevation inherent
in that race, and capable of making them understand the lesson, and accept their high destiny. The
last and greatest of these qualifications had not
been wanting. Much as the religion of the Barbaric race had degenerated by the time when it
deified its great deliverer, it had inherited the
highest traditions of the early world. Mallet
thus describes their religion in its purity: 'It
taught the being of a " Supreme God, master of the
universe, to whom all things are submissive and
obedient." Such, according to Tacitus, was the
supreme God of the Germans. The ancient Icelandic mythology calls him "the Author of everything that existeth; the eternal, the ancient, the
living and awful Being, the searcher into concealed
things, the Being that never changeth." This
religion attributed to the Supreme Deity "an
infinite power, a boundless knowledge, an incor-
ruptible justice," and forbade its followers to repre-
sent Him under any corporeal form. They were
not even to think of confining Him within the
enclosure of walls, but were taught that it was

within woods and consecrated forests that they could serve Him properly. There He seemed to reign in silence, and to make Himself felt by the respect which He inspired.[1] . . . From this Supreme God were sprung (as it were emanations from His divinity) an infinite number of subaltern deities and genii, of which every part of the visible world was the seat and the temple. . . . To serve this divinity with sacrifices and prayers, to do no wrong to others, and to be brave and intrepid in themselves, were all the moral consequences they derived from these doctrines. Lastly, the belief of a future state cemented and completed the whole building.[2] . . . Perhaps no religion ever attributed so much to a Divine Providence as that of the northern nations.'[3]

It was not among the Scandinavians only that the religion of the North retained long these vestiges of its original purity, and elevation. 'All the Teutonic nations held the same opinions, and it was upon these that they founded the obligation of serving the gods, and of being valiant

---

[1] Mallet's *Northern Antiquities*, pp. 88, 89.
[2] P. 89.   [3] P. 100.

in battle. . . . One ought to regard in this respect the Icelandic mythology as a precious monument, without which we can know but very imperfectly this important part of the religion of *our fathers*.'[1]

The earlier and purer doctrine seems to have long survived the incrustations of later times in the case of a select few. Harold Harfraga, the first king of all Norway, thus addressed an assembly of his people: 'I swear and protest in the most sacred manner that I will never offer sacrifice to any of the gods adored by the people, but to Him only who hath formed this world, and everything we behold in it.' A belief in the divine Love, as well as the divine power, knowledge and justice, though probably not held by the many at a later day, is yet distinctly expressed, as well as the kindred belief in an endless reign of peace, by the earliest and most sacred document of the Northern religion, viz. the 'Völuspá Prophecy.' That prophecy, after foretelling the destruction of all things, including the Odin gods themselves, by the Supreme God and His ministers, proceeds: 'There will arise out of the sea, another earth

[1] Mallet's *Northern Antiquities*, p. 103.

most lovely and verdant with pleasant fields where the grain shall grow unsown. Vidar and Vali, shall survive; neither the flood nor Surtur's fire shall harm them. They shall dwell on the plain of Ida *where Asgard formerly stood.* . . . Baldur and Hödur shall also repair thither from the abode of death. There they shall sit and converse together, and call to mind their former knowledge and the perils they underwent.'[1]

The similarity between the higher doctrines of the northern faith and the religion of ancient Persia is at once accounted for by the tradition of the Odin migration from the East. A writer the reverse of credulous expresses himself thus on that subject: 'We know that the Scandinavians came from some country of Asia. . . . This doctrine was in many respects the same with that of the Magi. Zoroaster had taught that the conflict between Ormuzd and Ahriman (*i.e.* light and darkness, the Good and Evil Principle) should continue to the last day; and that then the Good Principle should be reunited to the Supreme God, from whom it had first issued; the Evil should be overcome and subdued;

[1] *The Prose Edda.*

darkness should be destroyed; and the world, purified by a universal conflagration, should become a luminous and shining abode, into which evil should never be permitted to enter.'[1] The same writer continues thus: 'Odin and the Æsir may be compared to Ormuzd and the Amshaspands; Loki and his evil progeny, the Wolf Fenrir and the Midgard Serpent, together with the giants and monsters of Jötunheim and Hvergelmir, to Ahriman and the Devs.[2] . . . We will not deny that some of these doctrines may have been handed down by oral tradition to the pontiff-chieftains of the Scandinavian tribes, and that the Skalds who composed the mythic poems of the elder Edda may have had an obscure and imperfect knowledge of them. Be this as it may, we must not forget that the higher doctrines of the Scandinavian system were confined to the few, whereas those of the Zendavesta were the religious belief of the whole nation.[3] . . . The Persian system was calculated to form an energetic, intellectual and highly moral people; the Scandinavian a semi-barbarous troop of crafty and re-

---

[1] *Northern Antiquities:* the Editor, T. A. Blackwell.
　　　[2] P. 474.　　　　　[3] P. 475.

morseless warriors. . . . Yet, such as they were, these Scandinavians seemed to have been destined by the inscrutable designs of Providence to invigorate at least one of the nations of which they were for centuries the scourge, in order, as we previously had occasion to observe, that the genial blending of cognate tribes might form a people the most capable of carrying on the great work of civilisation, which in some far distant age may finally render this world that abode of peace and intellectual enjoyment dimly shadowed forth in ancient myths as only to be found in a renovated and fresh emerging universe.'[1]

The inferiority of the later Scandinavian to the earlier Persian religion may be sufficiently accounted for by the common process of gradual degeneration. That degeneration was not confined to the great emigrant race. Centuries before Odin had left the East, the Persian religion had degenerated upon its native soil. Its Magi retained a pure doctrine, which led them later to the Bethlehem crib; but its vulgar had in part yielded to the seduction of Greek poets, and worshipped in temples like theirs.

[1] T. A. Blackwell. See Mallet's *Northern Antiquities*, p. 476.

It is remarkable that that 'one of the nations' with which the hopes of the future are so singularly connected is that one upon which the discipline of adversity had fallen with double force. When the ancient enemy of the 'Barbaric races,' Rome, had passed away, a new enemy, and one to it more formidable, rose up against England in her own kinsfolk, the Scandinavian branch of the same stock. The Danish invaders expected to set kingdom against kingdom throughout the Heptarchy, and subject them all to the sceptre of Odin. On the contrary, it united them in one; and that union was facilitated by the bond of a common Christianity.[1]

That the belief of the Anglo-Saxons, though less developed by poetry and romance, was substantially the same as that recorded in the Scandinavian Edda, appears to be certain. It is thus that Mr. Kemble speaks:

'On the Continent as well as in England, it is only by the collection of minute and isolated facts —often preserved to us in popular superstitions,

---

[1] 'This (Christianity), as it introduced great mildness into the tempers of the people, made them less warlike, and consequently prepared the way to their forming one body.'—Burke, *An Abridgment of English History*, book ii. chap. iii.

legends, and even nursery tales—that we can render probable the prevalence of a religious belief identical in its most characteristic features with that which we know to have been entertained in Scandinavia. Yet whatsoever we can thus recover proves that, in all main points, the faith of the Island Saxons was that of their Continental brethren.' ' The early period at which Christianity triumphed in England, adds to the difficulties which naturally beset the subject. Norway, Sweden, and Denmark, had entered into public relations with the rest of Europe long before the downfall of their ancient creed ; here the fall of heathendom, and the commencement of history were contemporaneous. We too had no Iceland to offer a refuge to those who fled from the violent course of a conversion.' [1]

Among the proofs of identity between the Anglo-Saxon and the Scandinavian religion, Mr. Kemble refers to the fact that ' genealogies of the Anglo-Saxon kings contain a multitude of the ancient gods, reduced indeed into the family relations, but still capable of identification with the deities of the North, and of Germany. In this relation we

[1] *Saxons in England*, vol. i. p. 330.

b

find Odin, Bœldœg, Géat, Wig, and Frea. The days of the week, also dedicated to gods, supply us further with the names of Tiw, Dunor, Friege, and Sœtere; and the names of places in all parts of England attest the wide dispersion of the worship.[1]

Mr. Kemble shows also that among the Anglo-Saxons and the Scandinavians there existed a common belief respecting monsters, especially the wolf Fenrir, the Midgard snake, evil spirits and giants; respecting Loki, the accursed spirit, and Hela, the queen of Hades. To the same effect Mr. Sharon Turner speaks: ' The Voluspá and the Edda are the two great repositories of the oldest and most venerated traditions of pagan Scandinavia. The Voluspá opens abruptly, and most probably represents many of the ancient *Saxon* traditions or imaginations.'[2] The authority of these eminent writers accounts for and justifies the frequent references to the Scandinavian mythology in the following 'Saxon Legends.'

We have thus seen that in the religion of the 'Barbaric' race there were blended two different elements: a higher one derived from its eastern

[1] *Saxons in England*, vol. i. p. 335.
[2] *History of the Anglo-Saxons*, vol. i. p. 241.

origin, and a lower one the result of gradual de-generation. We had previously seen that a re-markable duality was to be found in the character of that race ; and without understanding this duality and its root in their religion, no just conception can be formed of the relations of that race with Christianity. Had the 'Barbarians' possessed nothing deeper than is indicated by their fiercer traits, the history of the seventh century in England must have been very different. It was characterised by rapid conversions to Christianity on a large scale, and often, after the lapse of a few years, by sanguinary revolts against the Faith. The chief reason of such fluctuation seems to have been this, viz. because all that was profound, and of venerable antiquity in the Northern religion, was in sympathy with Christianity, as the religion of sanctity and self-sacrifice ; while all that was savage in it opposed itself to a religion of humility and of charity. The Northern religion was an endless warfare, and so was that early Persian religion from which its higher element was derived ; but by degrees that warfare had, for the many, ceased to be the warfare between light and dark-

ness, between Good and Evil. To the specu-
lative it had become a conflict between all the
wild and illimitable forces of Nature and some
unknown higher Law ; but to the common herd it
meant only an endless feud between race and race.
Thus understood it could have no affinities with
Christianity, either in her militant character, or
as the religion of peace.

In explanation of the frequent outbreaks against
Christianity on the part of the Anglo-Saxons,
after their conversion, Montalembert assigns another cause, viz. that the Roman missionaries had
sometimes relied too much upon the converted
kings, and their authority over their subjects. The
work had in such cases to be done again ; and it
was largely done by Irish missionaries, who had left
Iona only to seek as lonely a retreat in Lindisfarne.
They shunned cities, drew the people to them, and
worked upwards through that people to the great.

The Irish mission in England during the seventh
century was one among the great things of history,
and has met with an inadequate appreciation.
The ancient name of the Irish, ' Scoti,' commemo-
rative of their supposed Scythian origin, the name

by which Bede always designates them, had been
frequently translated 'Scottish' by modern his-
torians ; and those who did not know that an Irish
immigrant body had entered Scotland, then called
Alba, about the close of the second century, had
conquered its earlier inhabitants, the Picts, after a
war of centuries, and had eventually given to that
heroic land, never since subdued, its own name and
its royal house, naturally remained ignorant that
those 'Scottish' missionaries were Irish.   A glance
at Bede,[1] or such well known recent works as Sir W.
Scott's ' History of Scotland,'[2] makes this matter
plain ; yet the amount of work done in England
by those Irish missionaries is still known to few.

They came from a country the fortunes, the
character, and the institutions of which were singu-

[1] In process of time, Britain, besides the Britons and Picts,
received a third nation, the Scots, who migrating from Ireland,
under their leader Reuda, either by fair means or by force of arms
secured to themselves those settlements among the Picts which they
still possess.'—Bede's *Ecclesiastical Hist.* book i. cap. i.

[2] 'In the fifth century there appear in North Britain two powerful
and distinct tribes, who are not before named in history. These
are the Picts and the Scots. . . . The Scots, on the other hand,
were of Irish origin ; for, to the great confusion of ancient history,
the inhabitants of Ireland, those at least of the conquering and
predominating caste, were called Scots. A colony of these Irish

larly unlike those of England ; one in which ancient
Rome had had no part ; which, in the form of clan-
life, retained as its social type the patriarchal
customs of its native East, all authority being an
expansion of domestic authority, and the idea of a
family, rather than that of a state, ruling over the
hearts of men. About two centuries previously, Ireland had become Christian ; and an image of its immemorial clan-system was reproduced in the vast
convents which ere long covered the land, and sent
forth their missionaries over a large part of Europe.
It might well have been thought doubtful whether

Scots, distinguished by the name of Dalriads, or Dalreudini, natives
of Ulster, had early attempted a settlement on the coast of Argyle-
shire ; they finally established themselves there under Fergus, the
son of Eric, about the year 503, and, recruited by colonies from
Ulster, continued to multiply and increase until they formed a
nation which occupied the western side of Scotland.'—Sir Walter
Scott's *History of Scotland,* vol. i. p. 7. Scott proceeds to record
the eventual triumph of the Irish or Scotic race over the Pictish in
the ninth century. 'So complete must have been the revolution
that the very language of the Picts is lost. . . . The country united
under his sway (that of Kenneth Mac Alpine) was then called for
the first time Scotland.' The same statement is made by
Burke : 'The principal of these were the Scots, a people of ancient
settlement in Ireland, and who had thence been transplanted into
the northern part of Britain, which afterwards derived its name from
that colony.'—Burke, *Abridgment of English History,* book i.
cap. iv.

these were likely to work successfully among a race so dissimilar as the Anglo-Saxon ; but the event proved that in this instance dissimilar qualities meant qualities complemental to each other, and that sympathy was attracted by unlikeness.

The Irish mission in England began at a critical time, just when the reaction against the earlier successes of the Roman mission had set in. At York, under Paulinus, Christianity had triumphed ; but eight years after that event Edwin, the Christian king of Dëira, perished in battle, and northern England was forced back by king Penda into paganism. Southern England, with the exception of Canterbury and a considerable part of Kent, had also lost the Gospel, after possessing it for thirty years. Nearly at the same time East Anglia and Essex, at the command of pagan-kings, had discarded it likewise. It was then that Oswald, on recovering his kingdom of Northumbria, besought the Irish monks of Iona to reconvert it, or rather to complete a conversion which had been but begun. Their work prospered ; by degrees the largest kingdom of the Heptarchy became solidly and permanently Christian, its See being fixed in the Island of Lindisfarne, whence the huge diocese of the north was ruled successively by three of St. Columba's order, Aidan, Finan, and Colman. But the labours of St. Columba's sons were not confined to the north. In East Anglia an Irish monk, St. Fursey, founded on the coast of Suffolk the monastery of Burghcastle, in which King Sigebert became a monk. An Irish priest, Maidulphus, built that of Malmesbury in Wessex. Glastonbury was an older Celtic monastery inhabited partly by Irish monks, and partly by British. Peada, king of Mercia, son of the terrible Penda, was baptized by St. Finan close to the Roman Wall, as was also Sigebert, king of the East Saxons. Diama, an Irish monk, was first bishop of all Mercia, its second, Céolach, being Irish also, and also its fourth.

Montalembert, in his *Moines d'Occident*, has given us the most delightful history that exists of the conversion of Anglo-Saxon England, a work combining the depth of a Christian philosopher with the sagacity of a statesman, and a dramatist's appreciation of character, while in it we miss nothing of that picturesque vividness and engaging simplicity

which belong to our early chroniclers ; thus confer-
ring upon England a boon if possible greater than
that bestowed upon Ireland in his lives of St. Columba, St. Columbanus and other saints. It is thus
that he apportions the share which the Irish missionaries and the Roman had in that great enterprise.

'En résumant l'histoire des efforts tentés pendant
les soixante ans écoulés depuis le débarquement
d'Augustin jusqu'à la mort de Penda, pour introduire
le Christianisme en Angleterre, on constate les
résultats que voici. Des huit royaumes de la
confédération Anglo-Saxonne, celui de Kent fut
seul exclusivement conquis et conservé par les
moines romains, dont les premières tentatives,
chez les Est-Saxons et les Northumbriens, se
terminèrent par un échec. En Wessex et en Est-
Anglie les Saxons à l'ouest et les Angles à l'est
furent convertis par l'action combinée de mission-
naires continentaux et de moines celtiques. Quant
aux deux royaumes Northumbriens' (Dëira and
Bernicia), 'à l'Essex et à la Mercie, comprenant
à eux seuls plus de deux tiers du territoire occupé
par les conquérants germains, ces quatre pays
durent leur conversion définitive exclusivement à

l'invasion pacifique des moines celtiques, qui n'avaient pas seulement rivalisé de zèle avec les moines
romains, mais qui, une fois les premiers obstacles
surmontés, avaient montré bien plus de persévé-
rance et obtenu bien plus de succès.'[1]   The only
effort made at that early period to introduce
Christianity into the kingdom of the South-Saxons
was that of an Irish monk, Dicul, who founded a
small monastery at Bosham.   It did not however
prove successful.

There is something profoundly touching in the
religious ties which subsisted between England and
Ireland during the seventh century, when compared
with the troubled relations of those two countries
during many a later age.   If the memory of
benefits received produces a kindly feeling on the
part of the recipient, that of benefits conferred
should exert the same influence on the heart of the
bestower.   To remember the past, however disastrous or convulsed, is a nation's instinct, and its duty
no less, since a tribute justly due is thus paid to
great actions and to great sufferings in times gòne
by ; nor among the wise and the generous can the

---

[1] *Moines d'Occident,* vol. iv. pp. 127-8.   Par le Comte de
Montalembert.

discharge of that patriotic duty ever engender an
enmity against the living: but there is a special
satisfaction in turning to those recollections with
which no human infirmity can connect any feeling
save that of good will; and it is scarcely possible
to recall them in this instance without a hope that
the sacred bonds which united those two countries
at that remote period may be a pledge for recipro-
cated benefits in the ages yet before us. For both
countries that early time was a time of wonderful
spiritual greatness. In noble rivalry with Ireland
England also sent her missionaries to far lands;
and a child of Wessex, St. Boniface, brought the
Faith to Germany, by which it was eventually
diffused over Scandinavia, thus, by anticipation,
bestowing the highest of all gifts on that terrible
race the Northmen, in later centuries the scourge of
his native land.

At home both islands were filled with saints
whose names have ever since resounded throughout
Christendom. Both islands, as a great writer [1]
has told us, 'had been the refuge of Christianity, for a time almost exterminated in Christendom, and the centres of its propagation in

countries still heathen. Secluded from the rest
of Europe by the stormy waters in which they lay,
they were converted just in time to be put in
charge with the sacred treasures of Revelation, and
with the learning of the old world, in that dreary
time which intervened between Gregory and Charle-
magne. They formed schools, collected libraries,
and supplied the Continent with preachers and
teachers.' He remarks also that 'There was a
fitness in the course of things that the two peoples
who had rejoiced in one prosperity should drink
together the same cup of suffering : *Amabiles, et
decori in vitâ suâ, in morte non divisi ;*' and he
proceeds to remind us that, immediately after
their participation in that common religious greatness, they partook also a tragic inheritance. In
England for two centuries and a half, in Ireland
for a longer period, the Northmen were repulsed
but to reappear. Again and again the sons of
Odin blackened the river-mouths of each land with
their fleets ; wherever they marched they left
behind them the ashes of burned churches and

---

[1] Cardinal Newman's *Historical Sketches*, vol. i. p. 266 : *The
Northmen and Normans in England and Ireland.*

monasteries, till, in large parts of both, Christianity
and learning had well nigh perished, and barbarism
had all but returned. In both countries domestic
dissensions had favoured the invader; eventually
in both the Danish power broke down; but in
both and in each case claiming a spiritual sanction
—another branch of the same Scandinavian stock
succeeded to the Dane, viz. the only one then
Christianised, the Norman. In that seventh
century how little could Saxon convert or Irish
missionary have foreseen that the destinies of their
respective countries should be at once so unlike yet
so like, so antagonistic yet so interwoven!

The aim of the 'Legends of Saxon Saints,' as
the reader will perhaps have inferred from the
preceding remarks, is to illustrate England, her
different races and predominant characteristics,
during the century of her conversion to Christianity,
and in doing this to indicate what circumstances
had proved favourable or unfavourable to the
reception of the Faith. It became desirable thus to
revert to the early emigration of that 'Barbaric'
race of which the Anglo-Saxon was a scion, making

the shadow of Odin pass in succession over the background of the several pictures presented (the Heroic being thus the unconscious precursor of the Spiritual), and to show how the religion which bore his name was fitted at once to predispose its nobler votaries to Christianity and to infuriate against it those who but valued their faith for what it contained of degenerate. It seemed also expedient to select for treatment not only those records most abounding in the picturesque and poetic, but likewise others useful as illustrating the chief representatives of a many-sided society; the pagan king and the British warrior, the bard of Odin and the prophetess of Odin, the Gaelic missionary and the Roman missionary, the poet and the historian of Anglo-Saxon Christianity. In a few instances, as in the tales of Oswald and of Oswy, where the early chronicle was copious in detail, it has been followed somewhat closely; but more often, where the original record was brief, all except the fundamental facts had to be supplied. On these occasions I found encouragement in the remark of a writer at once deep and refined. 'Stories to be versified should not be already nearly complete, having the beauty in themselves, and gaining from the poet but a garb. They should be rough, and with but a latent beauty. The poet should have to supply the features and limbs as well as the dress.'[1]

Bede has been my guide. His records are, indeed, often 'rough,' as rough as the crab-tree, but, at the same time, as fresh as its blossom. Their brief touches reveal all the passions of the Barbaric races ; but the chief human affections, things far deeper than the passions, are yet more abundantly illustrated by them.[2] It was a time when those affections were not frozen by conventionalities and forced to conceal themselves until they forgot to exist. In the narrative of Bede we find also invaluable illustrations of a higher but not less real range of human affections, viz. the affections of 'Christianised Humanity,' affections grounded on divine truths and heavenly hopes, and yet in entire harmony with affections of a merely human order, which lie beneath them in a parallel plane. Occasionally the two classes enter into conflict, as

[1] Sara Coleridge.

[2] As the illustration of an Age, Bede's *History* has been well compared by Cardinal Manning with the *Fioretti di S. Francesco*, that exquisite illustration of the thirteenth century.

in the case of the monks of Bardeney who found it so difficult to reconcile their reverence for a Saint with their patriotic hatred of a foreign invader; but almost invariably the earthly and the heavenly emotions are mutually supplemental, as in those tender friendships of monk with monk, of king and bishop, grounded upon religious sympathy and co-operation; so that the lower sentiment without the higher would present, compared with the pictures now bequeathed to us, but an unfinished and truncated image of Humanity. Here, again, the semibarbaric age described by Bede rendered the delineation more vivid. In ages of effeminate civilisation the Christian emotions, even more than those inherent in unassisted human nature, lose that ardour which belongs to them when in a healthy condition—an ardour which especially reveals itself during that great crisis, a nation's conversion, when, beside a throng of new feelings and new hopes, a host of new Truths has descended upon the intelligence of a whole people, and when a sense of new knowledge and endless progress is thus communicated to it, far exceeding that which is the boast of nations devoted chiefly to physical science. The sense of progress, indeed, when such a period reaches its highest, is a rapture. It is as though the motion of the planet which carries us through space, a motion of which we are cognisant but which we yet cannot feel, could suddenly become, like the speed of a racehorse, a thing brought home to our consciousness.

Such ardours are scarcely imaginable in the later ages of a nation; but in Bede's day a people accepting the 'glad tidings' was glad; and, unambitious as his style is of the ornamental or the figurative, it is brightened by that which it so faithfully describes. His chronicle is often poetry, little as he intended it to be such; nay, it is poetry in her 'humanities' yet more than in her distinctively spiritual province, and better poetry than is to be found in the professed poetry of a materialistic age, when the poet is tempted to take refuge from the monotony of routine life, either amid the sensational accidents to be found on the byeways, not the highways, of life, or in some sickly dreamland that does not dare to deal with life, and belongs neither to the real nor to the ideal. In nothing is Bede's history of that great age, to which our own owes all that it possesses of real greatness, more striking than in that spirit of unconscious elevation and joyousness which belongs to the Christian life it records, a joyousness often so strikingly contrasted with the sadness—sometimes a heroic sadness—to be found in portions of his work describing pagan manners. With all its violences and inconsistencies, the seventh century was a noble age—an age of strong hearts which were gentle as well as strong, of a childhood that survived in manhood, of natures that had not lost their moral unity, of holy lives and of happy deaths. Bede's picture of it is a true one; and for that reason it comes home to us.

To some it may seem a profaneness to turn those old legends into verse. I should not have attempted the enterprise if they were much read in prose. The verse may at least help to direct the attention of a few readers to them. From them the thoughtful will learn how to complete a 'half-truth' often reiterated. Those who have declared that 'the wars of the Heptarchy are as dull as the battles of kites and crows,' have not always known that the true interest of her turbulent days belonged to peace, not to war, and is to be found in the spiritual development of the Anglo-Saxon race.

CONTENTS.

————◆◆————

	PAGE
ODIN THE MAN	1
KING ETHELBERT OF KENT AND ST. AUGUSTINE .	13
THE CONSECRATION OF WESTMINSTER ABBEY .	32
THE PENANCE OF ST. LAURENCE . . .	47
KING SIGEBERT OF EAST ANGLIA, AND HEIDA THE PROPHETESS	66
KING SIGEBERT OF ESSEX, OR A FRIEND AT NEED	84
KING OSWALD OF NORTHUMBRIA, OR THE BRITON'S REVENGE	100
CEADMON THE COWHERD, THE FIRST ENGLISH POET	117
KING OSWY OF NORTHUMBRIA, OR THE WIFE'S VICTORY	142
THE VENGEANCE OF THE MONKS OF BARDENEY .	162
HOW SAINT CUTHBERT KEPT HIS PENTECOST AT CARLISLE	176

PAGE

SAINT FRIDESWIDA, OR THE FOUNDATIONS OF
OXFORD 2c8

THE BANQUET HALL OF WESSEX, OR THE KING
WHO COULD SEE 223

EPILOGUE: BEDE'S LAST MAY . . . 259

NOTES 283

PROLOGUE.

ODIN, THE MAN.

Odin, a Prince who reigned near the Caspian Sea, after a vain resistance to the Roman arms, leads forth his people to the forests north of the Danube, that, serving God in freedom on the limits of the Roman Empire, and being strengthened by an adverse climate, they may one day descend upon that empire in just revenge; which destiny was fulfilled by the sack of Rome, under Alaric, Christian King of the Goths, a race derived, like the Saxon, from that Eastern people.

FORTH with those missives, Chiron, to the Invader !
Hence, and make speed : they scathe mine eyes like fire :
Pompeius, thou hast conquered ! What remains ?
Vengeance ! Man's race has never dreamed of such ;
So slow, so sure. Pompeius, I depart :
I might have held these mountains yet four days :
The fifth had seen them thine—

I look beyond the limit of this night :
Four centuries I need; then comes mine hour.

What saith the Accursed One of the Western World?
I hear even now her trumpet!   Thus she saith :
'I have enlarged my borders : iron reaped
Earth's field all golden.   Strenuous fight we fought :
I left some sweat-drops on that Carthage shore,
Some blood on Gallic javelins.   That is past !
My pleasant days are come : my couch is spread
Beside all waters of the Midland Sea ;
By whispers lulled of nations kneeling round ;
Illumed by light of balmiest climes ; refreshed
By winds from Atlas and the Olympian snows :
Henceforth my foot is in delicious ways ;
Bathe it, ye Persian fountains !   Syrian vales,
All roses, make me sleepy with perfumes !
Caucasian cliffs, with martial echoes faint
Flatter light slumbers ; charm a Roman dream !
I send you my Pompeius ; let him lead
Odin in chains to Rome !'   Odin in chains !
Were Odin chained, or dead, that God he serves
Could raise a thousand Odins—
Rome's Founder-King beside his Augur standing
Noted twelve ravens borne in sequent flight
O'er Alba's crags.   They emblem'd centuries twelve,

The term to Rome conceded. Eight are flown ;
Remain but four. Hail, sacred brood of night !
Hencefore my standards bear the Raven Sign,
The bird that hoarsely haunts the ruined tower ;
The bird sagacious of the field of blood
Albeit far off. Four centuries I need :
Then comes my day. My race and I are one.
   O Race beloved and holy ! From my youth
Where'er a hungry heart impelled my feet,
Whate'er I found of glorious, have I not
Claimed it for thee, deep-musing? Ignorant, first,
For thee I wished the golden ingots piled
In Susa and Ecbatana :—ah fool !
At Athens next, treading where Plato trod,
For thee all triumphs of the mind of man,
And Phidian hand inspired ! Ah fool, that hour
Athens lay bound, a slave ! Later to Rome
In secrecy by Mithridates sent
To search the inmost of his hated foe,
For thee I claimed that discipline of Law
Which made her State one camp. Fool, fool once more !
Soon learned I what a heart-pollution lurked
Beneath that mask of Law. As Persia fell,
By softness sapped, so Rome. Behold, this day,
Following the Pole Star of my just revenge,
I lead my people forth to clearer fates

Through cloudier fortunes.　They are brave and strong :
'Tis but the rose-breath of their vale that rots
Their destiny's bud unblown.　I lead them forth,
A race war-vanquished, not a race of slaves ;
Lead them, not southward to Euphrates' bank,
Not Eastward to the realms of rising suns,
Not West to Rome, and bondage.　Hail, thou North !
Hail, boundless woods, by nameless oceans girt,
And snow-robed mountain islets, founts of fire !
　　　　　Four hundred years !　I know that awful North :
I sought it when the one flower of my life
Fell to my foot.　That anguish set me free :
It dashed me on the iron side of life :
I woke, a man.　My people too shall wake :
They shall have icy crags for myrtle banks,
Sharp　rocks　for　couches.　Strength !　I　must　have
　　　strength ;
Not splenetic sallies of a woman's courage,
But hearts to which self-pity is unknown :
Hard life to them must be as mighty wine
Gladdening the strong : the death on battle fields
Must seem the natural, honest close of life ;
Their fear must be to die without a wound
And miss Life's after-banquet.　Wooden shield
Whole winter nights shall lie their covering sole :
Thereon the boy shall stem the ocean wave ;

Thereon the youth shall slide with speed of winds
Loud-laughing down the snowy mountain-slope :
To him the Sire shall whisper as he bleeds,
' Remember the revenge ? Thy son must prove
More strong, more hard than thou ! '

Four hundred years !

Increase is tardy in that icy clime,
For Death is there the awful nurse of Life :
Death rocks the cot. Why meet we there no wolf
Save those huge-limbed ? Because weak wolf-cubs die.
'Tis thus with man ; 'tis thus with all things strong :—
Rise higher on thy northern hills, my Pine !
That Southern Palm shall dwindle.

House stone-walled—

Ye shall not have it ! Temples cedar-roofed—
Ye shall not build them ! Where the Temple stands
The City gathers. Cities ye shall spurn :
Live in the woods; live singly, winning each,
Hunter or fisher by blue lakes, his prey :
Abhor the gilded shrine : the God Unknown
In such abides not. On the mountain's top
Great Persia sought Him in her day of strength :
With her ye share the kingly breed of Truths,
The noblest inspirations man hath known,
Or can know—ay, unless the Lord of all
Should come, Man's Teacher. Pray as Persia prayed ;

And see ye pray for Vengeance ! Leave till then
To Rome her Idol fanes and pilfered Gods.

I see you, O my People, year by year
Strengthened by sufferings ; pains that crush the weak,
Your helpers. Men have been that, poison-fed,
Grew poison-proof: on pain and wrong feed ye !
The wild-beast rage against you ! frost and fire
Rack you in turn ! I'll have no gold among you ;
With gold come wants; and wants mean servitude.
Edge, each, his spear with fish-bone or with flint,
Leaning for prop on none. I want no Nations !
A Race I fashion, playing not at States:
I take the race of Man, the breed that lifts
Alone its brow to heaven : I change that race
From clay to stone, from stone to adamant
Through slow abrasion, such as leaves sea-shelves
Lustrous at last and smooth. To *be*, not *have*,
A man to be ; no heritage to clasp
Save that which simple manhood, at its will,
Or conquers or re-conquers, held meanwhile
In trust for Virtue ; this alone is greatness.
Remain ye Tribes, not Nations ; led by Kings,
Great onward-striding Kings, above the rest
High towering, like the keel-compelling sail
That takes the topmost tempest. Let them die,

Each for his people! I will die for mine
Then when my work is finished ; not before.
That Bandit King who founded Rome, the Accursed,
Vanished in storm. My sons shall see me die,
Die, strong to lead them till my latest breath,
Which shall not be a sigh ; shall see and say,
'This Man far-marching through the mountainous world,
No God, but yet God's Prophet of the North,
Gave many crowns to others : for himself
His people were his crown.'

                        Four hundred years—
Ye shall find savage races in your path :
Be ye barbaric, ay, but savage not :
Hew down the baser lest they drag you down ;
Ye cannot raise them : they fulfil their fates :
Be terrible to foes, be kind to friend :
Be just; be true. Revere the Household Hearth;
This knowing, that beside it dwells a God :
Revere the Priest, the King, the Bard, the Maid,
The Mother of the heroic race—five strings
Sounding God's Lyre. Drive out with lance for goad
That idiot God by Rome called Terminus,
Who standing sleeps, and holds his reign o'er fools.
The earth is God's, not Man's: that Man from Him
Holds it whose valour earns it. Time shall come,
It may be, when the warfare shall be past,

The reign triumphant of the brave and just
In peace consolidated.   Time may come
When that long winter of the Northern Land
Shall find its spring.   Where spreads the black morass
Harvest all gold may glitter ; cities rise
Where roamed the elk; and nations set their thrones ;
Nations not like those empires known till now,
But wise and pure.   Let such their temples build
And worship Truth, if Truth should e'er to Man
Show her full face.   Let such ordain them laws
If Justice e'er should mate with laws of men.
Above the mountain summits of Man's hope
There spreads, I know, a land illimitable,
The table land of Virtue trial-proved,
Whereon one day the nations of the world
Shall race like emulous Gods.   A greater God
Served by our sires, a God unknown to Rome,
Above that shining level sits, high-towered :
Millions of Spirits wing His flaming light,
And fiery winds among His tresses play :
When comes that hour which judges Gods and men,
That God shall plague the Gods that filched His name,
And cleanse the Peoples.

                When ye hear, my sons,
That God uprising in His judgment robes
And see their dreadful crimson in the West,

Then know ye that the knell of Rome is nigh ;
Then stand, and listen !   When His Trumpet sounds
Forth from your forests and your snows, my sons,
Forth over Istér, Rhenus, Rhodonus,
To Mœsia forth, to Thrace, Illyricum,
Iberia, Gaul ; but, most of all, to Rome !
Who leads you thither leads you not for spoil :
A mission hath he, fair though terrible ;—
He makes a pure hand purer, washed in blood :
On, Scourge of God ! the Vengeance Hour is come.
   I know that hour, and wait it.   Odin's work
Stands then consummate.   Odin's name thenceforth
Goes down to darkness.
                    Farewell, Ararat !
How many an evening, still and bright as this,
In childhood, youth, or manhood's sorrowing years,
Have I not watched the sunset hanging red
Upon thy hoary brow !   Farewell for ever !
A legend haunts thee that the race of man
In earliest days, a sad and storm-tossed few,
From thy wan heights descended, making way
Into a ruined world.   A storm-tossed race,
But not self-pitying, once again thou seest
Into a world all ruin making way
Whither they know not, yet without a fear.
This hour—lo, there, they pass yon valley's verge !—

In sable weeds that pilgrimage moves on,
Moves slowly like thy shadow, Ararat,
That eastward creeps.   Phantom of glory dead !
Image of greatness that disdains to die !
Move Northward thou !   Whate'er thy fates decreed,
At least that shadow shall be shadow of man,
And not of beast gold-weighted !   On, thou Night
Cast by my heart !   Thou too shalt meet thy morn !

LEGENDS

KING ETHELBERT OF KENT AND SAINT AUGUSTINE.

Ethelbert, King of Kent, converses first with his Pagan Thanes, and next with Saint Augustine, newly landed on the shores of Thanet Island. The Saint, coming in sight of Canterbury, rejoices greatly, and predicts the future greatness of that city.

FAR through the forest depths of Thanet Isle,
That never yet had heard the woodman's axe,
Rang the glad clarion on the May-day morn,
Blent with the cry of hounds. The rising sun
Flamed on the forests' dewy jewelry,
While, under rising mists, a host with plumes
Rode down a broad oak alley t'wards the sea.

King Ethelbert rode first : he reigned in Kent,
Least kingdom of the Seven yet Head of all
Through his desert. That morn the royal train,
While sang the invisible lark her song in heaven,
Pursued the flying stag. At times the creature,

As though he too had pleasure in the sport,
Vaulted at ease through sunshine and through shade,
Then changed his mood, and left the best behind him.
Five hours they chased him ; last, upon a rock,
High up in scorn he held his antlered front,
Then took the wave and vanished.

                         Many a frown
Darkened that hour on many a heated brow ;
And many a spur afflicted that poor flank
Which panted hard and smoked.   The King alone
Laughed at mischance.   'The stag, with God to aid,
Has left our labour fruitless !   Give him joy !
He lives to yield us sport some later morn :
So be it !   Waits our feast, and not far off :
On to the left, 'twixt yonder ash and birch !'

    He spake, and anger passed : they praised their sport ;
And many an outblown nostril seemed to snuff
That promised feast.   They rode through golden furze
So high the horsemen only were descried ;
And glades whose centuried oaks their branches laid
O'er violet banks ; and fruit trees, some snow-veiled
Like bridesmaid, others like the bride herself
Behind her white veil blushing.   Glad, the thrush
Carolled ; more glad, the wood-dove moaned ; close by
A warbling runnel led them to the bay :

Two chestnuts stood beside it snowy-coned :
The banquet lay beneath them.

Feasting o'er,
The song succeeded.   Boastful was the strain,
Each Thane his deeds extolling, or his sire's ;
But one, an aged man, among them scoffed :
'When I was young ; when Sigbert on my right
To battle rode, and Sefred on my left ;
That time men stood not worsted by a stag !
Not then our horses swerved from azure strait
Scared by the ridged sea-wave !'   Next spake a chief,
Pirate from Denmark late returned : ' Our skies,
Good friends, are all too soft to build the man !
We fight for fame : the Northman fights for sport ;
Their annals boast they fled but once :—'twas thus :
In days of old, when Rome was in her pride,
Huge hosts of hers had fallen on theirs, surprised,
And way-worn : long they fought : a remnant spent,
Fled to their camp.   Upon its walls their wives
Stood up, black-garbed, with axes heaved aloft,
And fell upon the fugitives, and slew them ;
Slew next their little ones; slew last themselves,
Cheating the Roman Triumph.   Never since then
Hath Northman fled the foemen.'

Egfrid rose :
'Who saith our kinsfolk of the frozen North

One stock with us, one faith, one ancient tongue,
Pass us in valour?   Three days since I saw
Crossing the East Saxon's border and our own
Two boys that strove.   The Kentish wounded fell;
The East Saxon on him knelt; then made demand :
" My victim art thou by the laws of war !
Yonder my dagger lies ;—till I return
Wilt thou abide ?" The vanquished answered, " Yea ! "
A minute more, and o'er that dagger's edge
His life-blood rushed.'   The pirate chief demurred ; ·
' A gallant boy !   Not less I wager this,
The glitter of that dagger ere it smote
Made his eye blink.   Attend !   Three years gone by,
Sailing with Hakon on Norwegian fiords
We fought the Jomsburg Rovers, at their head
Sidroc, oath-pledged to marry Hakon's child
Despite her father's best.   In mist we met :
Instant each navy at the other dashed
Like wild beast, instinct-taught, that knows its foe ;
Chained ship to ship, and clashed their clubs all day,
Till sank the sun : then laughed the white peaks forth,
And reeled, methought, above the reeling waves !
The victory was with us.   Hakon, next morn,
Bade slay his prisoners.   Thirty on one bench
Waited their doom : their leader died the first ;
He winked not as the sword upon him closed !

No, nor the second! Hakon asked the third,
"What think'st thou, friend, of Death?" He tossed his
    head:
"My Father perished; I fulfil my turn."
The fourth, "Strike quickly, Chief! An hour this morn
We held contention if, when heads are off,
The hand can hold its dagger: I would learn."
The dagger and the head together fell.
The fifth, "One fear is mine—lest yonder slave
Finger a Prince's hair! Command some chief,
Thy best beloved, to lift it in his hands;
Then strike and spare not!" Hakon struck. That youth,
Sigurd by name, his forehead forward twitched,
Laughing, so deftly that the downward sword
Shore off those luckless hands that raised his hair.
All laughed; and Hakon's son besought his sire
To loosen Sigurd's bonds: but Sigurd cried,
"Unless the rest be loosed I will not live!"
Thus all escaped save four.'

               In graver mood
That chief resumed: 'A Norland King dies well!
His bier is raised upon his stateliest ship;
Piled with his arms; his lovers and his friends
Rush to their monarch's pyre, resolved with him
To share in death, and with becoming pomp
Attend his footsteps to Valhalla's Hall.

                  c

The torch is lit : forth sails the ship, black-winged,
Facing the midnight seas.   From beach and cliff
Men watch all night that slowly lessening flame :
Yet no man sheds a tear.'
                              Earconwald,
An aged chief, made answer, 'Tears there be
Of divers sorts : a wise and valiant king
Deserves that tear which praises, not bewails,
Greatness gone by.'   The pirate shouted loud,
'A land it is of laughter, not of tears ! '
Know ye the tale of Harald ?   He had sailed
Round southern coasts and eastern—sacked or burned
A hundred Christian cities.   One he found
So girt with giant walls and brazen gates
His sea-kings vainly dashed themselves thereon,
And died beneath them, frustrate.   Harald sent
A herald to that city proffering terms :
"Harald is dead : Christian was he in youth :
He sends you spoils from many a city burnt,
And craves interment in your chiefest church."
Next day the masked procession wound in black
Through streets defenceless.   When the church was
      reached
They laid their chief before the altar-lights :
Anon to heaven rang out the priestly dirge,
And incense-smoke upcurled.   Forth from its cloud

Sudden upleaped the dead man, club in hand,
Spurning his coffin's gilded walls, and smote
The hoary pontiff down, and brake his neck ;
And all those maskers doffed their weeds of woe
And showed the mail beneath, and raised their swords,
And drowned that pavement in a sea of blood,
While raging rushed their mates through portals wide,
And, since that city seemed but scant of spoil,
Fired it and sailed.   Ofttimes old Harald laughed
That tale recounting.'

      Many a Kentish chief
Re-echoed Harald's laugh ;—not Ethelbert :
The war-scar reddening on his brow he rose
And spake : ' My Thanes, ye laugh at deeds accurst !
An old King I, and make my prophecy
One day that northern race which smites and laughs,
Our kith and kin albeit, shall smite our coasts :
That day ye will not laugh ! ' Earconwald,
Not rising, likewise answer made, heart-grieved :
' Six sons had I : all these are slain in war ;
Yet I, an unrejoicing man forlorn,
Find solace ofttimes thinking of their deeds :
They laughed not when they smote.   No God, be sure,
Smiles on the jest red-handed.' Egfrid rose,
And three times cried with lifted sword unsheathed,
' Behold my God !   No God save him I serve !'

While thus they held discourse, where blue waves
    danced
Not far from land, behold, there hove in sight,
Seen 'twixt a great beech silky yet with Spring
And pine broad-crested, round whose head old storms
Had wov'n a garland of his own green boughs,
A bark both fair and large ; and hymn was heard.
Then laughed the King, ' The stag-hunt and our songs ,
So drugged my memory, I had nigh forgotten
Why for our feast I chose this heaven-roofed hall :
Missives I late received from friends in France ;
They make report of strangers from the South
Who, tarrying in their coasts have learned our tongue,
And northward wend with tidings strange and new
Of some celestial Kingdom by their God
Founded for men of Faith.   Nor churl am I
To frown on kind intent, nor child to trust
This sceptre of Seven Realms to magic snare
That puissance hath—who knows not ?—greater thrice
In house than open field.   I therefore chose
For audience hall this precinct.'
                      Muttered low
Murdark, the scoffer with the cave-like mouth
And sidelong eyes, ' Queen Bertha's voice was that !
A woman's man !   Since first from Gallic shores
That dainty daughter of King Charibert

Pressed her small foot on England's honest shore
The whole land dwindles ! '

      In seraphic hymns
Ere long that serpent hiss was lost : for soon,
In raiment white, circling a rocky point,
O'er sands still glistening with a tide far-ebbed,
On drew, preceded by a silver Cross,
A long procession. Music, as it moved,
Floated on sea-winds inland, deadened now
By thickets, echoed now from cliff or cave :
Ere long before them that procession stood.
The King addressed them : ' Welcome, Heralds sage !
And if from God I welcome you the more,
Since great is God, and therefore great His gifts :
God grant He send them daily, heaped and huge !
Speak without fear, for him alone I hate
Who brings ill news, or makes inept demand
Unmeet for Kings. I know that Cross ye bear ;
And in my palace sits a Christian wife,
Bertha, the sweetest lady in this land ;
Most gracious in her ways, in heart most leal.
I knew her yet a child : she knelt whene'er
The Queen, her mother, entered : then I said,
A maid so reverent will be reverent wife,
And wedded her betimes. Morning and eve
She in her wood-girt chapel sings her prayer,

Which wins us kindlier harvest, and, some think,
Success in war.   She strives not with our Gods :
Confusion never wrought she in my house,
Nor minished Hengist's glory.   Had her voice,
Clangorous or strident, drawn upon my throne
Deserved opprobrium '— here the monarch's brows
Flushed at the thought, and fire was in his eyes—
' The hand that clasps this sceptre had not spared
To hunt her forth, an outcast in the woods,
. Thenceforth with beasts to herd !   More lief were I
To take the lioness to my bed and board
Than house a rebel wife.'   Remembering then
The mildness of his Queen, King Ethelbert
Resumed, appeased, for placable his heart ;
' But she no rebel is, and this I deem
Fair auspice for her Faith.'
                              A little breeze
Warm from the sea that moment softly waved
The standard from its staff, and showed thereon
The Child Divine.   Upon His mother's knee
Sublime He stood.   His left hand clasped a globe
Crowned with a golden Cross ; and with His right,
Two fingers heavenward raised, o'er all the earth
He sent His Blessing.
                              Of that band snow-stoled
One taller by the head than all the rest

Obeisance made ; then, pointing to the Cross,
And forward moving t'ward the monarch's seat,
Opened the great commission of the Faith :—
' Behold the Eternal Maker of the worlds !
That Hand which shaped the earth and blesses earth
Must rule the race of man ! '

                      Majestic then
As when, far winding from its mountain springs,
City and palm-grove far behind it left,
Some Indian river rolls, while mists dissolved
Leave it in native brightness unobscured,
And kingly navies share its sea-ward sweep,
Forward on-flowed in Apostolic might
Augustine's strong discourse.   With God beginning,
He showed the Almighty All-compassionate,
Down drawn from distance infinite to man
By the Infinite of Love.   Lo, Bethlehem's crib !
There lay the Illimitable in narrow bound :
Thence rose that triumph of a world redeemed !
Last, to the standard pointing, thus he spake :
' Yon Standard tells the tale !   Six hundred years
Westward it speeds from subject realm to realm :
First from the bosom of God's Race Elect,
His People, till they slew Him, mild it soared :
Rejected, it returned.   Above their walls
While ruin rocked them, and the Roman fire,
Dreadful it hung.   When Rome had shared that guilt,

Mocking that Saviour's Brethren, and His Bride,
Above the conquered conqueror of all lands
In turn this Standard flew.   Who raised it high?
A son of this your island, Constantine!
In these, thine English oakwoods, Helena,
'Twas thine to nurse thy warrior.   He had seen
Star-writ in heaven the words this Standard bears,
" Through Me is victory."   Victory won, he raised
High as his empire's queenly head, and higher,
This Standard of the Eternal Dove thenceforth
To fly where eagle standard never flew,
God's glory in its track, goodwill to man.
Advance for aye, great Emblem!   Light as now
Famed Asian headlands, and Hellenic isles!
O'er snow-crowned Alp and citied Apennine
Send forth a breeze of healing ſ   Keep thy throne
For ever on those western peaks that watch
The setting sun descend the Hespereau wave,
Atlas and Calpe!   These, the old Roman bound,
Build but the gateway of the Rome to be;
Till Christ returns, thou Standard, hold them fast:
But never till the North, that, age by age,
Dashed back the Pagan Rome, with Christian Rome
Partakes the spiritual crown of man restored,
From thy strong flight above the world surcease,
And fold thy wings in rest!'

Upon the sod
He knelt, and on that Standard gazed, and spake,
Calm-voiced, with hand to heaven : ' I promise thee,
Thou Sign, another victory, and thy best—
This island shall be thine ! '

Augustine rose
And took the right hand of King Ethelbert,
And placed therein the Standard's staff, and laid
His own above the monarch's, speaking thus :
' King of this land, I bid thee know from God
That kings have higher privilege than they know,
The standard-bearers of the King of kings.'

Long time he clasped that royal hand ; long time
The King, that patriarch's hand at last withdrawn,
His own withdrew not from that Standard's staff
Committed to his charge.   His hand he deemed
Thenceforth its servant vowed.   With large, meek eyes
Fixed on that Maid and Babe, he stood as child
That, gazing on some reverent stranger's face,
Nor loosening from that stranger's hold his palm,
Listens his words attent.

The man of God
Meantime as silent gazed on Thanet's shore
Gold-tinged, with sunset spray to crimson turned
In league-long crescent.   Love was in his face,
That love which rests on Faith.   He spake : ' Fair land,

I know thee what thou art, and what thou lack'st !
The Master saith, " I give to him that hath :"
Thy harvest shall be great.'　Again he mused,
And shadow o'er him crept.　Again he spake :
' That harvest won, when centuries have gone by,
What countenance wilt thou wear?　How oft on brows
Brightened by Baptism's splendour, sin more late
Drags down its cloud !　The time may come when thou
This day, though darkling, yet so innocent,
Barbaric, not depraved, on greater heights
May'st sin in malice—sin the great offence,
Changing thy light to darkness, knowing God,
Yet honouring God no more ; that time may come
When, rich as Carthage, great in arms as Rome,
Keen-eyed as Greece, this isle, to sensuous gaze
A sun all gold, to angels may present
Aspect no nobler than a desert waste,
Some blind and blinding waste of sun-scorched sands,
Trod by a race of pigmies not of men,
Pigmies by passions ruled ! '
　　　　　　　　　　　　Once more he mused ;
Then o'er his countenance passed a second change ;
And from it flashed the light of one who sees,
Some hill-top gained, beyond the incumbent night
The instant foot of morn.　With regal step,
Martial yet measured, to the King he strode,

And laid a strong hand on him, speaking thus :
' Rejoice, my son, for God hath sent thy land
This day Good Tidings of exceeding joy,
And planted in her breast a Tree divine
Whose leaves shall heal far nations.   Know besides,
Should sickness blight that Tree, or tempest mar,
The strong root shall survive : the winter past,
Heavenward once more shall rush both branch and bough,
And over-vault the stars.'
                      He spake, and took
The sacred Standard from that monarch's hand,
And held it in his own, and fixed its point
Deep in the earth, and by it stood.   Then lo !
Like one disburthened of some ponderous charge,
King Ethelbert became himself again,
And round him gazed well pleased.   Throughout his train
Sudden a movement thrilled : remembrance had
Of those around, his warriors and his thanes,
That ever on his wisdom waiting hung,
Thus he replied discreet : ' Stranger and friend,
Thou bear'st good tidings !   That thou camest thus far
To fool us, knave and witling may believe :
I walk not with their sort ; yet, guest revered,
Kings are not as the common race of men ;
Counsel they take, lest honour heaped on one
Dishonour others.   Odin holds on us

Prescriptive right, and special claims on me,
The son of Hengist's grandson.   Preach your Faith !
The man who wills I suffer to believe :
The man who wills not, let him moor his skiff
Where anchorage likes him best.   The day declines :
This night with us you harbour, and our Queen
Shall lovingly receive you.'
                              Staid and slow
The King rode homewards, while behind him paced
Augustine and his Monks.   The ebb had left
'Twixt Thanet and the mainland narrow space
Marsh-land more late :   beyond the ford there wound
A path through flowery meads ; and, as they passed,
Not herdsmen only, but the broad-browed kine
Fixed on them long their meditative gaze ;
And oft some blue-eyed boy with flaxen locks
Ran, fearless, forth, and plucked them by the sleeve,
Some boy clear-browed as those Saint Gregory marked,
Poor slaves, new-landed on the quays of Rome,
That drew from him that saying, ' " Angli "—nay,
Call them henceforward " Angels " ! '
                              From a wood
Issuing, before them lustrous they beheld
King Ethelbert's chief city, Canterbury,
Strong-walled, with winding street, and airy roofs,
And high o'er all the monarch's palace pile

Thick-set with towers.   Then fire from God there fell
Upon Augustine's heart; and thus he sang
Advancing ; and the brethren sang ' Amen ' :

' Hail, City loved of God, for on thy brow
Great Fates are writ.   Thou cumberest not His earth
For petty traffic reared, or petty sway ;
I see a heavenly choir descend, thy crown
Henceforth to bind thy brow.   Forever hail !

' I see the basis of a kingly throne
In thee ascending !   High it soars and higher,
Like some great pyramid o'er Nilus kenned
When vapours melt—the Apostolic Chair !
Doctrine and Discipline thence shall hold their course,
Like Tigris and Euphrates, through all lands
That face the Northern Star.   Forever hail !   ·

' Where stands yon royal keep, a church shall rise
Like Incorruption clothing the Corrupt
On the resurrection morn !   Strong House of God,
To Him exalt thy walls, and nothing doubt,
For lo ! from thee like lions from their lair
Abroad shall pace the Primates of this land :—
They shall not lick the hand that gives and smites,
Doglike, nor snakelike on their bellies creep

In indirectness base.   They shall not fear
The people's madness, nor the rage of kings
Reddening the temple's pavement.   They shall lift
The strong brow mitred, and the crosiered hand
Before their presence sending Love and Fear
To pave their steps with greatness.   From their fronts
Stubborned with marble from Saint Peter's Rock
The sunrise of far centuries forth shall flame:
He that hath eyes shall see it, and shall say,
" Blessed who cometh in the name of God ! " '

   Thus sang the Saint, advancing ; and, behold,
At every pause the brethren sang ' Amen ! '
While down from window and from roof the throng
Eyed them in silence.   As their anthem ceased,
Before them stood the palace clustered round
By many a stalwart form.   Midway the gate
On the first step, like angel newly lit,
Queen Bertha stood.   Back from her forehead meek,
The meeker for its crown, a veil descended,
While streamed the red robe to the foot snow-white
Sandalled in gold.   The morn was on her face,
The star of morn within those eyes upraised
That flashed all dewy with the grateful light
Of many a granted prayer.   O'er that sweet shape
Augustine signed the Venerable Sign ;
The lovely vision sinking, hand to breast,

Received it; while, by sympathy surprised,
Or taught of God, the monarch and his thanes
Knelt as she knelt, and bent like her their heads,
Sharing her blessing.   Like a palm the Faith
Thenceforth o'er England rose, those saintly men
Preaching by life severe, not words alone,
The doctrine of the Cross.   Some Power divine,
Stronger than patriot love, more sweet than Spring,
Made way from heart to heart, and daily God
Joined to His Church the souls that should be saved,
Thousands, where Medway mingles with the Thames,
Rushing to Baptism.   In his palace cell
High-nested on that Vaticanian Hill
Which o'er the Martyr-gardens kens the world,
Gregory, that news receiving, or from men,
Or haply from that God with whom he walked,
The Spirit's whisper ever in his ear,
Rejoiced that hour, and cried aloud, ' Rejoice,
Thou Earth ! that North which from its cloud but flung
The wild beasts' cry of anger or of pain,
Redeemed from wrath, its Hallelujahs sings;
Its waves by Roman galleys feared, this day
Kiss the bare feet of Christ's Evangelists;
That race whose oak-clubs brake our Roman swords
Glories now first in bonds—the bond of Truth :
At last it fears ;—but fears alone to sin,
Striving through faith for Virtue's heavenly crown.

THE CONSECRATION OF WESTMINSTER ABBEY.

Sebert, King of the East Saxons, having built the great church
of Saint Peter at Westminster, Mellitus the Bishop prepares to
consecrate it, but is warned in a vision that it has already been consecrated by one greater than he.

As morning brake, Sebert, East Saxon king,
Stood on the winding shores of Thames alone,
And fixed a sparkling eye upon Saint Paul's :
The sun new-risen had touched its roofs that laughed
Their answer back.   Beyond it London spread ;
But all between the river and that church
Was slope of grass and blossoming orchard copse
Glittering with dews dawn-reddened.   Bertha here,
That church begun, had thus besought her Lord,.
'Spare me this bank which God has made so fair !
Here let the little birds have leave to sing,
The bud to blossom!   Here, the vespers o'er,

Lovers shall sit; and here, in later days,
Children shall question, "Who was he—Saint Paul?
What taught, what wrought he that his name should
    shine
Thus like the stars in heaven?"'   .
                    As Sebert stood,
The sweetness of the morning more and more
Made way into his heart. The pale blue smoke,
Rising from hearths by woodland branches fed,
Dimmed not the crystal matin air; not yet
From clammy couch had risen the mist sun-warmed:
All things distinctly showed; the rushing tide,
The barge, the trees, the long bridge many-arched,
And countless huddled gables, far away,
Lessening, yet still descried.
                A voice benign
Dispersed the Prince's trance: 'I marked, my King,
Your face in yonder church; you took, I saw,
A blessing thence; and Nature's here you find:
The same God sends them both.' The man who spake,
Though silver-tressed, was countenanced like a child;
Smooth-browed, clear-eyed.   That still and luminous
    mien
Predicted realms where Time shall be no more;
Where gladness, like some honey-dew divine,
Freshens an endless present. Mellitus,

D

From Rome late missioned and the Cœlian Hill,
Made thus his greeting.
                           Westward by the Thames
The King and Bishop paced, and held discourse
Of him whose name that huge Cathedral bore,
Israel's great son, the man of mighty heart,
The man for her redemption zealous more
Than for his proper crown.   Not task for her
God gave him : to the Gentiles still he preached,
And won them to the Cross. 'That Faith once spurned,'
Thus cried the Bishop with a kindling eye,
'Lo, how it raised him as on eagle's wings,
And past the starry gates !   The Spirit's Sword
He wielded well !   Save him who bears the Keys,
Save him who made confession, "Thou art Christ,"
Saint Paul had equal none !   Hail, Brethren crowned !
Hail, happy Rome, that guard'st their mingled dust ! '

Next spake the Roman of those churches twain
By Constantine beside the Tyber built
To glorify their names.   With sudden turn,
Sebert, the crimson mounting to his brow,
Made question, ' Is your Tyber of the South
Ampler than this, our Thames ? '   The old man smiled ;
'Tyber to Thames is as that willow-stock
To yonder oak.'   The Saxon cried with joy:

' How true thy judgment is ! how just thy tongue !
What hinders, O my Father, but that Thames,
Huge river from the forests rolled by God,
Should image, like that Tyber, churches twain,
Honouring those Princes of the Apostles' Band?
King Ethelbert, my uncle, built Saint Paul's;
Saint Peter's Church be mine ! '

                An hour's advance
Left them in thickets tangled.   Low the ground,
Well-nigh by waters clipt, a savage haunt
With briar and bramble thick, and ' Thorny Isle '
For that cause named.   Sebert around him gazed,
A maiden blush upon him thus he spake :
'I know this spot ; I stood here once, a boy :
'Twas winter then : the swoll'n and turbid flood
Rustled the sallows.   Far I fled from men :
A youth had done me wrong, and vengeful thoughts
Burned in my heart : I warred with them in vain :
I prayed against them ; yet they still returned :
O'erspent at last, I cast me on my knees
And cried, " Just God, if Thou despise my prayer,
Faithless, thence weak, not less remember well
How many a man in this East Saxon land
Stands up this hour, in wood, or field, or farm,
Like me sore tempted, but with loftier heart :
To these be helpful—yea, to one of these ! "

And lo, the wrathful thoughts, like routed fiends,
Left me, and came no more !'
       Discoursing thus,
The friends a moment halted in a space
Where stood a flowering thorn. Adown it trailed
In zigzag curves erratic here and there
Long lines of milky bloom, like rills of foam
Furrowing the green back of some huge sea wave
Refluent from cliffs. Ecstatic minstrelsy
Swelled from its branches. Birds as thick as leaves
Thronged them ; and whether joy was theirs that hour
Because the May had come, or joy of love,
Or tenderer gladness for their young new-fledged,
So piercing was that harmony, the place
Eden to Sebert looked, while brake and bower
Shone like the Tree of Life. 'What minster choir,'
The Bishop cried, ' could better chant God's praise?
Here shall your church ascend :—its altar rise
Where yonder thorn tree stands !' The old man spake;
Yet in him lived a thought unbreathed : ' How oft
Have trophies risen to blazon deeds accursed !
Angels this church o'er-winging, age on age
Shall see that boy at prayer !'
       In peace, in war,
Daily the work advanced. The youthful King
Kneeling, himself had raised the earliest sod,

Made firm the corner stone.   Whate'er of gold
Sun-ripened harvests of the royal lands
Yielded from Thames to Stour, or tax and toll
From quays mast-thronged to loud-resounding sea,
Save what his realm required by famine vexed
At times, or ravage of the Mercian sword,
Went to the work.   His Queen her jewels brought,
Smiling, huge gift in slenderest hands up-piled ;
His thanes their store ; the poor their labour free.
Some clave the quarry's ledges : from its depths
Some haled the blocks ; from distant forests some
Dragged home the oak-beam on the creaking wain :
Alas, that arms in noble tasks so strong
Should e'er have sunk in dust !   Ere ten years passed
Saint Peter's towers above the high-roofed streets
Smiled on Saint Paul's.   That earlier church had risen
Where stood, in Roman days, Apollo's fane :
Upon a site to Dian dedicate
Now rose its sister.   Erring Faith had reached
In those twin Powers that ruled the Day and Night,
To Wisdom witnessing and Chastity,
Her loftiest height, and perished.   Phœnix-like,
From ashes of dead rites and truths abused
Now soared unstained Religion.
                              What remained ?
The Consecration.   On its eve, the King

Held revel in its honour, solemn feast,
And wisely-woven dance, where beauty and youth,
Through loveliest measures moving, music-winged,
And winged not less by gladness, interwreathed
Brightness with brightness, glance turned back on
    glance,
And smile on smile—a courtseying graciousness
Of stateliest forms that, winding, sank or rose
As if on heaving seas.   In groups apart
Old warriors clustered.   Eadbald discussed
And Snorr, that truce with Wessex signed, and said,
' Fear nought: it cannot last ! '   A shadow sat
That joyous night upon one brow alone,
Redwald's, East Anglia's King.   In generous youth
He, guest that time with royal Ethelbert,
Had gladly bowed to Christ.   From shallowest soil
Faith springs apace, but springs to die.   Returned
To plains of Ely, all that sweetness past
Seemed but a dream while scornful spake his wife,
Upon whose brow beauty from love divorced
Made beauty's self unbeauteous : ' Lose—why not ?—
Thwarting your liegeful subjects, lose at will
Your Kingdom ; you that might have reigned ere now
Bretwalda of the Seven ! '   In hour accursed
The weak man with his Faith equivocated:
Fraudful, beneath the self-same roofs he raised

Altars to Christ and idols. By degrees
That Truth he mocked forsook him. Year by year
His face grew dark, and barbed his tongue though smooth,
Manner and mind like grass-fields after thaw,
Silk-soft above, yet iron-hard below :
Spleenful that night at Sebert's blithe discourse
He answered thus, with seeming-careless eye
Wandering from wall to roof :

                         ' I like your Church :
Would it had rested upon firmer ground,
Adorned some airier height : its towers are good,
Though dark the stone : three quarries white have I ;
You might have used them gratis had you willed :
At Ely, Elmham, and beside the Cam
Where Felix rears even now his cloistral Schools,
I trust to build three churches soon: my Queen,
That seconds still my wishes, says, " Beware
Lest overhaste, your people still averse,
Frustrate your high intent." A woman's wit—
Yet here my wife is wiser than her wont.
I miss your Bishop : grandly countenanced he,
Save for that mole. He shuns our revel :—ay !
Monastic virtue never feels secure
Save when it skulks in corners !' As he spake,
Despite that varnish on his brow clear-cut,
Stung by remembrance, from the tutored eye

Forth flashed the fire barbaric : race and heart
A moment stood confessed.

Old Mellitus,
That night how fared he ?   In a fragile tent
Facing that church expectant, low he knelt
On the damp ground.   More late, like youthful knight
In chapel small watching his arms untried,
He kept his consecration vigil still,
With hoary hands screening a hoary head,
And thus made prayer: 'Thou God to Whom all worlds
Form one vast temple : Thou Who with Thyself,
Ritual eterne, dost consecrate *that* Church,
For aye creating, hallowing it forever ;
Thou Who in narrowest heart of man or child
Makest not less Thy dwelling, turn Thine eyes
To-morrow on our rite.   The work we work
Work it Thyself!   Thy storm shall try it well;
Consummate first its strength in righteousness;
So shall beginning just, whate'er befall,
Or guard it, or restore.'

So prayed the man,
Nor ever raised his head—saw nought—heard nought—
Nor knew that on the night had come a change,
Ill Spirits, belike, whose empire is the air,
Grudging its glories to that pile new raised,
And, while they might, assailing.   Through the clouds

A panic-stricken moon stumbled and fled,
And wildly on the waters blast on blast
Ridged their dark floor.   A spring-tide from the sea
Breasted the flood descending.   Woods of Shene
And Hampton's groves had heard that flood all day,
No more a whisperer soft ; and meadow banks,
Not yet o'er-gazed by Windsor's crested steep
Or Reading's tower, had yielded to its wave
Blossom and bud.   More high, near Oxenford,
Isis and Cherwell with precipitate stream
Had swelled the current.   Gathering thus its strength
Far off and near, allies and tributaries,
That night by London onward rolled the Thames
Beauteous and threatening both.

                        Its southern bank
Fronting the church had borne a hamlet long
Where fishers dwelt.   Upon its verge that night
Perplexed the eldest stood : his hand was laid
Upon the gunwale of a stranded boat ;
His knee was crooked against it.   Shrinking still
And sad, his eye pursued that racing flood,
Here black like night, dazzled with eddies there,
Eddies by moonshine glazed.   In doubt he mused :
Sudden a Stranger by him stood and spake :
' Launch forth, and have no fear.'   The fisher gazed
Once on his face ; and launched.   Beside the helm

That Stranger sat.　Then lo ! a watery lane
Before them opening, through the billows curved,
Level, like meadow-path.　As when a weed
Drifts with the tide, so softly o'er that lane
Oarless the boat advanced, and instant reached
The northern shore, dark with that minster's shade :—
Before them close it frowned.

　　　　　　　　　　　　' Where now thou stand'st
Abide thou : ' thus the Stranger spake : anon
Before the church's southern gate he stood :—
Then lo ! a marvel.　Inward as he passed,
Its threshold crossed, a splendour as of God
Forth from the bosom of that dusky pile
Through all its kindling windows streamed, and blazed
From wave to wave, and spanned that downward tide
With many a fiery bridge.　The moon was quenched ;
But all the edges of the headlong clouds
Caught up the splendour till the midnight vault
Shone like the noon.　The fisher knew, that hour,
That with vast concourse of the Sons of God
That church was thronged ; for in it many a head
Sun-bright, and hands lifted like hands in prayer,
High up he saw : meantime harmonic strain,
As though whatever moves in earth or skies,
Winds, waters, stars, had joined in one their song,
Above him floated like a breeze from God

And heaven-born · incense.   Louder swelled that
  strain ;
And still the Bride of God, that church late dark,
Glad of her saintly spousals, laughed and shone
In radiance ever freshening.   By degrees
That vision waned.   At last the fisher turned :
The matin star shook on the umbered wave ;
Along the East there lay a pallid streak,
That streak which preludes dawn.

                        Beside the man
Once more that Stranger stood :—' Seest thou yon tent ?
My Brother kneels within it.   Thither speed
And bid him know I sent thee, speaking thus,
" He whom the Christians name ' the Rock ' am I :
My Master heard thy prayer : I sought thy church,
And sang myself her Consecration rite :
Close thou that service with thanksgiving psalm." '

Thus spake the Stranger, and was seen no more :
But whether o'er the waters, as of old
Footing that Galilean Sea, with faith
Not now infirm he reached the southern shore,
Or passed from sight as one whom crowds conceal,
The fisher knew not.   At the tent arrived,
Before its little door he bent, and lo !
Within, there knelt a venerable man

With hoary hands screening a hoary head,
Who prayed, and prayed.   His tale the fisher told :
With countenance unamazed, yet well content,
That kneeler answered, 'Son, thy speech is true !
Hence, and announce thy tidings to the King,   ·
Who leaves his couch but now.'

'How beautiful'—
That old man sang, as down the Thames at morn
In multitudinous pomp the barges dropped,
Following those twain that side by side advanced,
One royal, one pontific, bearing each
The Cross in silver blazoned or in gold—
'How beautiful, O Sion, are thy courts !
Lo, on thy brow thy Maker's name is writ :
Fair is this place and awful ; porch of heaven :
Behold, God's Church is founded on a rock :
It stands, and shall not fall: the gates of Hell
Shall not prevail against it.'   ·

From the barge
Of Sebert and his Queen, antiphonal
Rapturous response was wafted : 'I beheld
Jerusalem, the City sage and blest ;
From heaven I saw it to the earth descending
In sanctity gold-vested, as a Bride
Decked for her Lord.   I heard a voice which sang,
Behold the House where God will dwell with men :

And God shall wipe the tears from off their face ;
And death shall be no more.'
                    Old Thames that day
Brightened with banners of a thousand boats
Winnowed by winds flower-scented.   Countless hands
Tossed on the brimming river chaplets wov'n
On mead or hill, or branches lopped in woods
With fruit-bloom red, or white with clustering cone,
Changing clear stream to garden.   Mile on mile
Now song was heard, now bugle horn that died
Gradual 'mid sedge and reed.   Alone the swan
High on the western waters kept aloof;
Remote she eyed the scene with neck thrown back,
Her ancient calm preferring, and her haunt
Crystalline still.   Alone the Julian Tower
Far down the eastern stream, though tap'stries waved
From every window, every roof o'er-swarmed
With anthem-echoing throngs, maintained, unmoved,
Roman and Stoic, her Cæsarean pride:
On Saxon feasts she fixed a cold, grey gaze ;
'Mid Christian hymns heard but the old acclaim—
' Consul Romanus.'
                When the sun had reached
Its noonday height, a people and its king
Around their minster pressed.   With measured tread
And Introit chanted, up the pillared nave

Reverent they moved : then knelt.   Between their
  ranks
Their Bishop last advanced with mitred brow
And in his hand the Cross, at every step
Signing the benediction of his Lord.
The altar steps he mounted.   Turning then
Westward his face to that innumerous host,
Thus spake he unastonished : ' Sirs, ere now
This church's Consecration rite was sung :—
Be ours to sing thanksgiving to our God,
" Ter-Sanctus," and " Te Deum." '

THE PENANCE OF SAINT LAURENCE.

Eadbald, King of Kent, persecuting the Church, Laurence the Bishop deems himself the chief of sinners because he has consented, like the neighbouring bishops, to depart ; but, being consoled by a wonderful reprimand, faces the King, and offers himself up to death. The King reproves them that gave him evil counsel.

THE day was dying on the Kentish downs
And in the oakwoods by the Stour was dead,
While sadly shone o'er snowy plains of March
Her comfortless, cold star.   The daffodil
That year was past its time.   The leaden stream
Had waited long that lamp of river-beds
Which, when the lights of Candlemas are quenched,
Looks forth through February mists.   A film
Of ice lay brittle on the shallows : dark
And swift the central current rushed : the wind
Sighed through the tawny sedge.
                                        'So fleets our life—
Like yonder gloomy stream ; so sighs our age—

Like yonder sapless sedge !'   Thus Laurence mused
Standing on that sad margin all alone,
His twenty years of gladsome English toil
Ending at last abortive.   ' Stream well-loved,
Here on thy margin standing saw I first,
My head by chance uplifting from my book,
King Ethelbert's strong countenance ; he is dead ;
And, next him, riding through the April gleams,
Bertha, his Queen, with face so lit by love
Its lustre smote the beggar as she passed
And changed his sigh to song.   She too is dead ;
And half their thanes that chased the stag that day,
Like echoes of their own glad bugle-horn,
Have passed and are not.   Why must I abide ?
And why must age, querulous and coward both,
Past days lamenting, fear not less that stroke
Which makes an end of grief?   Base life of man !
How sinks thy slow infection through our bones ;
Then when you fawned upon us, high-souled youth
Heroic in its gladness, spurned your gifts,
Yearning for noble death.   In age, in age
We kiss the hand that nothing holds but dust,
Murmuring, "Not yet ! " '

A tear, ere long ice-glazed,
Hung on the old man's cheek.   ' What now remains ? '
Some minutes passed ; then, lifting high his head,

He answered, 'God remains.' His faith, his heart,
Were unsubverted. 'Twas the weight of grief,
The exhausted nerve, the warmthless blood of age,
That pressed him down like sin, where sin was none—
Not sin, but weakness only. Long he mused,
Then slowly walked, and feebly, through the woods
Towards his house monastic. Vast it loomed
Through ground-fog seen ; and vaster, close beside,
That convent's church by great Augustine reared
Where once old woodlands clasped a temple old,
Vaunt of false Gods. To Peter and to Paul
That church was dedicate, albeit so long
High o'er the cloudy rack of fleeting years
It bore, and bears, its founder's name, not theirs.
Therein that holy founder slept in Christ,
And Ethelbert, and Bertha. All was changed :
King Eadbald, new-crowned and bad of life,
Who still, whate'er was named of great or good,
Made answer, 'Dreams ! I say the flesh rules all !'
Hated the Cross. His Queen, that portent crowned,
She that with name of wife was yet no wife,
Abhorred that Cross and feared. A Baptist new
In that Herodian court had Laurence stood,
Commanding, 'Put the evil thing away !'
Since then the woman's to the monarch's hate
Had added strength—the serpent's poison-bag

E

Venoming the serpent's fang.   'Depart the realm !'
With voice scarce human thus the tyrant cried,
'Depart or die ;' and gave the Church's goods
To clown and boor.

                    Upon the bank of Thames
Settled like ruin.   Holy Sebert dead,
In that East Saxon kingdom monarch long,
Three sons unrighteous now their riot held.
Frowning into the Christian Church they strode,
Full-armed, and each, with far-stretched foot firm set
Watching the Christian rite.   'Give us,' they cried,
While knelt God's children at their Paschal Feast,
'Give us those circlets of your sacred bread :
Ye feed therewith your beggars ; kings are we !'
The Bishop answered, 'Be, like them, baptized,
Sons of God's Church, His Sacrament with man,
For that cause Mother of Christ's Sacraments,
So shall ye share her Feast.'   With lightning speed
Their swords leaped forth ; contemptuous next they
        cried,
'For once we spare to sweep a witless head
From worthless shoulders.   Ere to-morrow's dawn
Hence, nor return ! '   He sped to Rochester :
Her bishop, like himself, was under ban :
The twain to Canterbury passed, and there   ˙
Resolved to let the tempest waste its wrath,
And crossed the seas.   By urgency outworn,

'Gainst that high judgment of his holier will
Laurence to theirs deferred, but tarried yet
For one day more to cast a last regard
On regions loved so long.

　　　　　　　As compline ceased
He reached the abbey gates, and entered in :
Sadly the brethren looked him in the face,
Yet no one said, ' Take comfort ! '　Sad and sole
He passed to the Scriptorium : round he gazed,
And thought of happy days, when Gregory,
One time their Abbot, next their Pope, would send
Some precious volume to his exiled sons,
While they in reverence knelt, and kissed its edge,
And, kissing, heard once more, as if in dream,
Gregorian chants through Roman palm trees borne
With echoes from the Coliseum's wall
Adown that Cœlian Hill ; and saw God's poor
At feast around that humble board which graced
That palace senatorial once.　He stood :
He raised a casket from an open chest,
And from that casket drew a blazoned scroll,
And placed it on the window-sill up-sloped
Breast-high, and faintly warmed by sinking sun ;
Then o'er it bent a space.

　　　　　　　With sudden hands
The old man raised that scroll ; aloud he read :

' I, Ethelbert the King, and all my Thanes,
· Honouring the Apostle Peter, cede to God
This Abbey and its lands.   If heir of mine
Cancel that gift, when Christ with angels girt
Makes way to judge the Nations of this world,
His name be cancelled from the Book of Life.'
The old man paused ; then read the signatures,
' I, Ethelbert, of Kent the King.'   Who next ?
' I, Eadbald, his son ;' to these succeeding,
' I, Hennigisil, Duke ;' ' I, Hocca, Earl.'—
' Can such things be ? ' Around the old man's brow
The veins swelled out; dilated nostril, mouth
Working as mouth of him that tasteth death,
With what beside is wiselier unrevealed,
Witnessed that agony which spake no more ;
He dashed the charter on the pavement down ;
Then on it gazed a space.
                              Remembering soon
Whose name stood first on that dishonoured list,
Contrite he raised that charter to his breast,
And pressed it there in silence.   Hours went by ;
Then dark was all that room, and dark around
The windy corridors and courts stone-paved ;
And bitter blew the blast: his unlooped cloak
Fell loose : the cold he noted not.   At last
A brother passed the door with lamp in hand :

Dazzled, he started first: then meekly spake,
' Beseech the brethren that they strew my bed
Within the church.   Until the second watch
There must I fast, and pray.'

                                 The brethren heard,
And strewed his couch within the vast, void nave,
A mat and deer-skin, and, more high, that stone
The old head's nightly pillow.   Echoes faint
Ere long of their receding footsteps died
While from the dark fringe of a rainy cloud
An ice-cold moon, ascending, streaked the church
With gleam and gloom alternate.   On his knees
Meantime that aged priest was creeping slow
From stone to stone, as when on battle-plain,
The battle lost, some warrior wounded sore,
By all forsaken, or some war-horse maimed,
Drags a blind bulk along the field in search
Of thirst-assuaging spring.   Glittered serene
That light before the Sacrament of Love:
Thither he bent his way, and long time prayed :
Thence onward crept to where King Ethelbert
Slept, marble-shrined—his ashes, not the King,
Yet ashes kingly since God's temple once,
And waiting God's great day.   Before that tomb,
Himself as rigid, with lean arms outspread,
Thus made the man his moan :

'King Ethelbert !
Hear'st thou in glory?   Ofttimes on thy knees
Thou mad'st confession of thine earthly sins
To me, a wounded worm this day on earth :
Now comforted art thou, and I brought low :
Yet, though I see no more that beaming front,
And haply for my sins may see it never,
Yet inwardly I gladden, knowing this
That thou art glad.   Perchance thou hear'st me not,
For thou wert still a heedless man of mirth,
Though sage as strong at need.   If this were so,
Not less thy God would hear my prayer to thee,
And grant it in thy reverence.   Ethelbert !
Thou hadst thy trial time, since, many a year
All shepherdless thy well-loved people strayed
What time thyself, their shepherd, knew'st not Christ,
Sole shepherd of man's race.   King Ethelbert !
Rememberest thou that day in Thanet Isle?
That day the Bride of God on English shores
Set her pure foot; and thou didst kneel to kiss it :
Thou gav'st her meat and drink in kingly wise ;   ·
Gav'st her thy palace for her bridal bower ;
This Abbey build'dst—her fortress !   O those days
Crowned with such glories, with such sweetness winged !
Thou saw'st thy realm made one with Christ's : thou
      saw'st

Thy race like angels ranging courts of Heaven:
This day, behold, thou seest the things thou seest!
If there be any hope, King Ethelbert,
Help us this day with God!'

                        Upon his knees
Then crept that exile old to Bertha's tomb,
And there made moan: 'Thou tenderest Queen and
    sweetest,
Whom no man ever gazed on save with joy,
Or spake of, dead, save weeping!   Well I know
That on thee in thy cradle Mary flung
A lily whiter from her hand, a rose
Warm from her breath and breast, for all thy life
Was made of Chastities and Charities—
This hour thine eyes are on that Vision bent
Whereof the radiance, ere by thee beheld,
Gave thee thine earthly brightness.   Mirrored there,
Seest thou, like moat in sunbeam well-nigh lost,
Our world of temporal anguish?   See it not!
For He alone, the essential Peace Eterne,
Could see it unperturbed.   In Him rejoice!
Yet, 'mid thy heavenly triumph, plead, O plead
For hearts that break below!'

                        Upon the ground
Awhile that man sore tried his forehead bowed;
Then raised it till the frore and foggy beam

Mixed with his wintry hair.   Once more he crept
Upon his knees through shadow; reached at length
His toilsome travel's last and dearest bourn,
The grave of Saint Augustine.   O'er it lay
The Patriarch's statued semblance as in sleep:
He knew it well, and found it, though to him
In darkness lost and veil beside of tears,
With level hands grazing those upward feet
Oft kissed, yet ne'er as now.

        ' Farewell forever !
Farewell, my Master, and farewell, my friend !
Since ever thou in heaven abid'st—and I——
Gregory the Pontiff from that Roman Hill
Sent thee to work a man's work far away,
And manlike didst thou work it.   Prince, yet child,
Men saw thee, and obeyed thee.   O'er the earth
Thy step was regal, meekness of thy Christ
Weighted with weight of conquerors and of kings :
Men saw a man who toiled not for himself,
Yet never ceased from toil; who warred on Sin ;
Had peace with all beside.   In happy hour
God laid His holy hand upon thine eyes :
I knelt beside thy bed : I leaned mine ear
Down to thy lips to catch their last ; in vain :
Yet thou perchance wert murmuring in thy heart:
" I leave my staff within no hireling's hand ;

Therefore my work shall last." Ah me! Ah me!
There was a Laurence once on Afric's shore :
He with his Cyprian died. I too, methinks,
Had shared—how gladly shared—my Bishop's doom.
Father, with Gregory pray this night! That God
Who promised, " for my servant David's sake,"
Even yet may hear thy prayer.'

                     Thus wept the man,
Till o'er him fell half slumber. Soon he woke,
And, from between that statue's marble feet
Lifting a marble face, in silence crept
To where far off his bed was strewn, and drew
The deer-skin covering o'er him. With its warmth
Deep sleep, that solace of lamenting hearts
Which makes the waking bitterer, o'er him sank,
Nor wholly left him, though in sleep he moaned
When from the neighbouring farm, an hour ere dawn,
The second time rang out that clarion voice
Which bids the Christian watch.

                     As thus he lay
T'wards him there moved in visions of the Lord
A Venerable Shape, compact of light,
And loftier than our mortal. Near arrived,
That mild, compassionate Splendour shrank his beam,
Or healed with strengthening touch the gazer's eyes
Made worthier of such grace; and Laurence saw

Princedom not less than his, the Apostles' Chief,
To whom the Saviour answered, ' Rock art thou,'
And later—crowning Love, not less than Faith—
'Feed thou My Sheep, My Lambs !' He knew that
    shape,
For oft, a child 'mid catacombs of Rome,
And winding ways girt by the martyred dead,
His eyes had seen it.   Pictured on those vaults
Stood Peter, Moses of the Christián Law,
Figured in one that by the Burning Bush
Unsandalled knelt, or drew with lifted hand
The torrent from the rock, yet wore not less
In aureole round his head the Apostle's name
' Petros,' and in his hand sustained the Keys—
Such shape once more he saw.

                     ' And comest thou then
Long-waited, or with sceptre-wielding hand
Earthward to smite the unworthiest head on earth,
Or with the darker of those Keys thou bearest
Him from the synod·of the Saints to shut
Who fled as flies the hireling?   Let it be !
Not less in that bright City by whose gate
Warder thou sitt'st, my Master thou shalt see
Pacing the diamond terraces of God
And bastions jacinth-veined, my great Augustine,
When all who wrought the ill have passed to doom,

And all who missed the good.   Nor walks he sole :
By him forever and forever pace
My Ethelbert, my Bertha !   Who can tell
But in the on-sweeping centuries thrice or twice
These three may name my name ?'   He spake and wept.
　　　To whom the Apostolic Splendour thus :
' Live, and be strong : for those thou lovest in Christ
Not only in far years shall name thy name ;
This day be sure that name they name in Christ :　　　·
Else wherefore am I here?   Not thou alone,
Much more in grief's bewilderment than fear,
Hast from the right way swerved.   Was I not strong ?
I, from the first Elect, and named anew ?
I who received, at first, divine command
The Brother-band to strengthen ; last to rule ?
I who to Hebrew and to Gentile both
Flung wide the portals of the heavenly realm ?
Was I not strong?   Behold, thou know'st my fall !
A second fall was near.   At Rome the sword
Against me raged.   Forth by the Appian Way
I fled ; and, past the gateway, face to face,
Him met, Who up the steep of Calvary, bare
For　man's　behoof　the　Cross.　"Where　goest　thou,
　　Lord?"
I spake ; then He : "I go to Rome, once more
To die for him who fears for me to die."

To Rome returned I ; and my end was peace.
Return thou too.   Thy brethren have not sinned :
They fled, consentient with the Will Supreme :
Their names are written in the Book of Life :
Enough that He Who gives to each his part
Hath sealed thy sons and thee to loftier fates ;
Therefore more sternly tries.   Be strong ; be glad :
For strength from joyance comes.'

       The Vision passed :
The old man, seated on his narrow bed,
Rolled thrice his eyes around the vast, dim church,
Desiring to retain it.   Vain the quest !
Yet still within his heart that Radiance lived :
The sweetness of that countenance fresh from God
Would not be dispossessed, but kindled there
Memorial dawn of brightness, more and more
Growing to perfect day : inviolate peace,
Such peace as heavenly visitants bequeath,
O'er-spread his spirit, gradual, like a sea :
Forth from the bosom of that peace upsoared
Hope, starry-crowned, and winged, that liberates oft
Faith, unextinct, though bound by Powers accursed
That o'er her plant the foot, and hold the chain—
Terror and Sloth.   To noble spirits set free
Delight means gratitude.   Thus Laurence joyed :
But soon, remembering that unworthy past,

Remorse succeeded, sorrow born of love,
Consoled by love alone. 'Ah I slave,' he cried,
That, serving such a God, could'st dream of flight :
How many a babe, too weak to lift his head,
Is strong enough to die ! ' While thus he mused
The day-dawn reaching to his pallet showed
That Discipline, wire-woven, in ancient days
Guest of monastic bed. He snatched it thence :
Around his bending neck and shoulders lean
In dire revenge he hurled it. Spent at last,
Though late, those bleeding hands down dropped : the
    cheek
Sank on the stony pillow. Little birds,
Low-chirping ere their songs began, attuned
Slumber unbroken. In a single hour
He slept a long night's sleep.
                    The rising sun
Woke him : but in his heart another sun,
New-risen serene with healing on its wings,
Outshone that sun in brightness. 'Mid the choir
His voice was loudest while they chanted lauds :
Brother to brother whispered, issuing forth,
' He walks in stature higher by a head
Than in the month gone by ! '
                  That day at noon
King Eadwald, intent to whiten theft

And sacrilege with sanctitudes of law,
Girt by his warriors and his Witena,
Enthronèd sat.   ' What boots it ? ' laughed a thane ;
' Laurence has fled ! we battle with dead men ! '
' Ay, ay,' the King replied, ' I told you oft
Sages can brag ; your dreamer weaves his dream :
But honest flesh rules all ! '   While thus they spake
Confusion filled the hall : through guarded gates
A priest advanced with mitre and with Cross,
A monk that seemed not monk, but prince disguised :
It was Saint Laurence.   As he neared the throne
The fashion of the tyrant's face was changed :
' Dar'st thou ? ' he cried, ' I deemed thee fled the realm—
What seek'st thou here ? '   The Saint made answer,
        ' Death.'
Calmly he told his tale ; then ended thus :
' To me that sinful past is sin of one
Buried in years gone by.   All else is dream
Save that last look the Apostle on me bent
Ere from my sight he ceased.   I saw therein
The reflex of that wondrous last Regard
Cast by the sentenced Saviour of mankind
On one who had denied Him, standing cold
Beside the High Priest's gate.   Like him, I wept ;
His countenance wrought my penance, not his hand :
I scarcely felt the scourge.'

King Eadbald
Drave back the sword half drawn, and round him stared ;
Then sat as one amazed.   He rose ; he cried,
' Ulf ! Kathnar !   Strip his shoulders bare !   If true
His tale, the brand remains ! '

                 Two chiefs stepped forth :
They dragged with trembling hand, and many a pause,
The external garb pontific first removed,
Dark, blood-stained garment from the bleeding flesh,
The old man kneeling.   Once, and only once,
The monarch gazed on that disastrous sight,
Muttering, ' and yet he lives ! '   A time it was
Of swift transitions.   Hearts, how proud soe'er,
Made not that boast—consistency in sin,
Though dark and rough accessible to Grace
As earth to vernal showers.   With hands hard-clenched
The King upstarted : thus his voice rang out :
' Beware, who gave ill counsel to their King !
The royal countenance is against them set,
Ill merchants trafficking with his lesser moods !
Does any say the King wrought well of late,
Warring on Christ, and chasing hence his priests ?
The man that lies shall die !   This day, once more
I ratify my Father's oath, and mine,
To keep the Church in peace : and though I sware
To push God's monks from yonder monastery

And lodge therein the horses of the Queen,
Those horses, and the ill-persuading Queen,
Shall flee my kingdom, and the monks abide !
Brave work ye worked, my loose-kneed Witena,
This day, Christ's portion yielding to my wrath !
See how I prize your labours ! ' With his sword
He clave the red seal from their statute scroll
And stamped it under foot.   Once more he spake,
Gazing with lion gaze from man to man :
' The man that, since my Father, Ethelbert,
Though monarch, stooped to common doom of men,
Hath filched from Holy Church fee-farm, or grange,
Sepulchral brass, gold chalice, bell or book,
See he restore it ere the sun goes down ;
If not, he dies !   Not always winter reigns ;
May-breeze returns, and bud-releasing breath,
When hoped the least :—'tis thus with royal minds ! '
He spake : from that day forth in Canterbury
Till reigned the Norman, crowned on Hastings' field,
God's Church had rest.   In many a Saxon realm
Convulsion rocked her cradle : altars raised
By earlier kings by later were o'erthrown :
One half the mighty Roman work, and more,
Fell to the ground : Columba's Irish monks
The ruin raised.   From Canterbury's towers,
' Rome of the North ' long named, from them alone

Above sea-surge still shone that vestal fire
By tempest fanned, not quenched ; and at her
    breast
For centuries six were nursed that Cœlian race,
The Benedictine Primates of the Land.

KING SIGEBERT OF EAST ANGLIA, AND HEIDA THE PROPHETESS.

Sigebert, King of East Anglia, moved by what he has heard from a Christian priest, consults the Prophetess Heida. In the doctrine he reports Heida recognises certain sacred traditions from the East, originally included in the Northern religion, and affirms that the new Faith is the fulfilment of the great Voluspà prophecy, the earliest record of that religion, which foretold the destruction both of the Odin-Gods and the Giant race, the restoration of all things, and the reign of Love.

LONG time upon the late-closed door the King
Kept his eyes fixed.   The wondrous guest was gone ;
Yet, seeing that his words were great and sage,
Compassionate for the sorrowful state of man,
Yet sparing not man's sin, their echoes lived
Thrilling large chambers in the monarch's breast
Silent for many a year.   Exiled in France
The mystery of the Faith had reached his ear
In word but not in power.   The westering sun

Lengthened upon the palace floor its beam,
Yet the strong hand which propped that thoughtful head
Sank not, nor moved.   Sudden, King Sigebert
Arose and spake : 'I go to Heida's Tower :
Await ye my return.'

       The woods ere long
Around him closed.   Upon the wintry boughs
An iron shadow pressed ; and as the wind
Increased beneath their roofs, an iron sound
Clangoured funereal.   Down their gloomiest aisle,
With snow flakes white, the monarch strode, till now
Before him, and not distant, Heida's Tower,
The Prophetess by all men feared yet loved,
Smit by a cold beam from the yellowing west,
Shone like a tower of brass.   Her ravens twain
Crested the turrets of its frowning gate,
Unwatched by warder.   Sigebert passed in :
Beneath the stony vault the queenly Seer
Sat on her ebon throne.

       With pallid lips
The King rehearsed his tale ; how one with brow
Lordlier than man's, and visionary eyes
Which, wander where they might, saw Spirits still,
Had told him many marvels of some God
Mightier than Odin thrice.   He paused awhile :
A warning shadow came to Heida's brow :

Nathless she nothing spake.　The King resumed :
' He spake—that stranger—of the things he saw :
For he, his body tranced, it may be dead,
In spirit oft hath walked the Spirit-Land :
Thence, downward gazing, once he saw our earth,
A little vale obscure, and, o'er it hung,
Those four great Fires that desolate mankind :
The Fire of Falsehood first ; the Fire of Lust, ·
· Ravening for weeds and scum ; the Fire of Hate,
Hurling, on war-fields, brother-man 'gainst man ;
The Fire of tyrannous Pride.　While yet he gazed,
Behold, those Fires, widening, commixed, then soared
Threatening the skies.　A Spirit near him cried,
" Fear nought ; for breeze-like pass the flames o'er him
In whom they won no mastery there below :
But woe to those who, charioted therein,
Rode forth triumphant o'er the necks of men,　　　　～
And had their day on earth.　Proportioned flames
Of other edge shall try their work and them ! "
Thus spake my guest : the frost wind smote his brows,
While on that moonlit crag we sat, ice-cold,
Yet down them, like the reaper's sweat at noon,
The drops of anguish streamed.　Till then, methinks,
That thing Sin is I knew not.
　　　　　　　　　　　　Calm of voice
Again he spake.　He told me of his God :

That God, like Odin, is a God of War :
Who serve Him wear His armour day and night :
The maiden, nay, the child, must wield the sword ;
Yet none may hate his neighbour.   Thus he spake,
That Prophet from far regions : " Wherefore wreck
Thy brother man ? upon his innocent babes
Drag down the ruinous roof?   Seek manlier tasks !
The death in battle is the easiest death :
Be yours the daily dying ; lifelong death ;
Death of the body that the soul may live :—
War on the Spirits unnumbered and accurst
Which, rulers of the darkness of this world,
Drive, hour by hour, their lances through man's soul
That wits not of the wounding ! " '

                               Heida turned
A keen eye on the King : ' Whence came your guest ?
Not from those sun-bright southern shores, I ween ? '
He answered, ' Nay, from western isle remote
That Prophet came.'   Then Heida's countenance fell :
' The West ! the West ! it should have been the East !
Conclude your tale : what saith your guest of God ? '
The King replied : ' His God so loved mankind
That, God remaining, he became a man ;
So hated sin that, sin to slay, He died.
One tear of His had paid the dreadful debt :—
Not so He willed it : thus He willed, to wake

In man, His lost one, quenchless hate of sin,
Proportioned to the death-pang of a God ;
Nor chose He lonely majesty of death :
'Twixt sinners paired He died.'

                   In Heida's eye
Trembled a tear.   ' A dream was mine in youth,
When first the rose of girlhood warmed my cheek,
A dream of some great Sacrifice that claimed
Not praise—not praise—it only yearned to die
Helping the Loved.   A maid alone, I thought,
Such sacrifice could offer.'   As she spake,
She pressed upon the pale cheek, warmed once more,
Her cold, thin hand a moment.

                     ' Maiden-born
Was He, my guest revealed,' the King replied :
' Then from that Angel's " Hail," and her response,
" So be it unto me," when sinless doubt
Vanished in world-renewing, free consent,
He told the tale ;—the Infant in the crib ;
The shepherds o'er him bowed ; ' (with widening eyes
Heida, bent forward, saw like them that Child)
' The Star that led the Magians from the East——'
' The East, the East !   It should have been the East ! '
Once more she cried ; ' our race is from the East :
The Persian worshipped t'ward the rising sun :   .
You said, but now, the West.'   The King resumed :

'God's priest was from the West; but in the East'
The great Deliverer sprang.'   Next, step by step,
Like herald panting forth in leaguered town
Tidings unhoped for of deliverance strange
Through victory on some battle field remote,
The King rehearsed his theme, from that first Word,
'The Woman's Seed shall bruise the Serpent's head,'
Prime Gospel, ne'er forgotten in the East,
To Calvary's Cross, the Resurrection morn,
Lastly the great Ascension into heaven :
And ever as he spake on Heida's cheek
The red spot, deepening, spread ; within her eyes
An unastonished gladness waxed more large:
Back to the marble woman came her youth :
Once more within her heaving breast it lived,
Once more upon her forehead shone, as when
The after-glow returns to Alpine snows
Left death-like by dead day.   Question at times
She made, yet seemed the answer to foreknow.
That tale complete, low-toned at last she spake :
'Unhappy they to whom these things are hard !'
Then silent sat, and by degrees became
Once more that dreaded prophet, stern and cold.
The silence deeper grew : the sun, not set,
Had sunk beneath the forest's western ridge ;
And jagged shadows tinged that stony floor

Whereon the monarch knelt. Slowly therefrom
He raised his head ; then slowly made demand:
' Is he apostate who discards old Faith ? '

Long time in musings Heida sat, then spake :
' Yea, if that Faith discarded be the Truth :
Not so, if it be falsehood.   God is Truth;
God-taught, true hearts discern that Truth, and guard:
Whom God forsakes forsake it.   O thou North,
That beat'st thy brand so loud against thy shield,
Hearing nought else, what Truth one day was thine !
Behold within corruption's charnel vaults
It sleeps this day.   What God shall lift its head?
We came from regions of the rising sun :
Scorning the temples built by mortal hand,
We worshipp'd God—one God—the Immense, All-Just:
That worship was the worship of great hearts :
Duty was worship then: that God received it :
I know not if benignly He received ;
If God be Love I know not.   This I know,
God loves not priest that under roofs of gold
Lifts, in his right hand held, the Sacrifice;
The left, behind him, fingering for the dole.
King of East Anglia's realm, the primal Truths
Are vanished from our Faith: the ensanguined rite,
The insane carouse survive ! '

          Thus Heida spake,
Heida, the strong one by the strong ones feared;
Heida, the sad one by the mourners loved;
Heida, the brooder on the sacred Past,
The nursling of a Prophet House, the child
Of old traditions sage !
          She paused, and then
Milder, resumed : ' What moved thee to believe ? '
And Sigebert made answer thus : ' The Sword :
For as a sword that Truth the stranger preached
Ran down into my heart.'   Heida to him,
' Well   saidst   thou   " as   a   Sword:"   a   Sword   is
  Truth ;—
As sharp a sword is Love : and many a time
In youth, but not the earliest, happiest youth,
When first I found that grief was in the world,
Had learned how deep its root, an infant's wail
Went through me like a sword.   Man's cry it seemed,
The blindfold, crownèd creature's cry for Truth,
His spirit's sole deliverer.'
          Once again
She mused, and then continued, ' Truth and Love
Are gifts too great to give themselves for nought ;
Exacting Gods.   Within man's bleeding heart,
If e'er to man conceded, both shall lie
Crossed, like two swords—

Behold thine image, crowned Humanity !
Better such dower than life exempt from woe :
Our Fathers knew to suffer ; joyed in pain ;
They knew not this—how deep its root ! '

Once more
The Prophetess was mute : again she spake :
' How named thy guest his God ? '   The King replied :
' The Warrior God, Who comes to judge the world ;
The Lord of Love ; the God Who wars on Sin,
And ceases not to war.'   ' Ay, militant,'
Heida rejoined, with eyes that shone like stars :
' The Persian knew Him.   Ormuzd was His name :
Unpitying Light against the darkness warred ;
Against the Light the Darkness.   Could the Light
Remit, one moment's length, to pierce that gloom,
Himself in gloom were swallowed.'

Yet again
In silence Heida sat ; then cried aloud,
' Odin, and all his radiant Æsir Gods
Forth thronging daily from the golden gates
Of Asgard City, their supernal house,
War on that giant brood of Jotünheim,
Lodged 'mid their mountains of eternal ice
Which circles still that sea surrounding earth,
Man's narrow home.   I know that mystery now !
That warfare means the war of Good on Ill :

We shared that warfare once ! This day, depraved,
Warring, we war alone for rage and hate ;
Men fight as fight the lion and the pard :
For them the sanctity of war is lost,
Lost like the kindred sanctity of Love,
Our household boast of old. The Father-God
Vowed us to battle but as Virtue's proof,
High test of softness scorned. His warrior knew
'Twas Odin o'er the battle field who sent
Pure-handed maiden Goddesses, the Norns,
Not vulture-like, but dove-like, mild as dawn,
To seal the foreheads of his sons elect,
Seal them to death, the bravest with a kiss :
His warrior, arming, cried aloud, " This day
I speed five Heroes to Valhalla's Hall:
To-morrow night in love I share their Feast ! "
He honoured whom he slew.'

      To her the King :
'That Stranger with severer speech than thine,
Sharp flail and stigma, charged the world with sin,
The vast, wide world, and not one race alone :
Each nation, he proclaimed, from Man's great stem
Issuing, had with it borne one Word divine
Rapt from God's starry volume in the skies,
Each word a separate Truth, that, angel-like,
Before them winging, on their faces flung

Splendour of destined morn, and led man's race
Triumphant long on virtue's road.   Themselves
Had changed that True to False.   The Judge had come;
That Power Who both beginning is and end
Had stooped to earth to judge the earth with fire;
A fire of Love, He came to cleanse the just;
A fire of Vengeance, to consume the impure :
His fan is in His hand : the chaff shall burn;
The grain be garnered.   " Fall, high palace roofs,"
He cried, " for ye have sheltered dens of sin:
Fall, he that, impious, scorned the First and Last ;
Fall, he that bowed not to the hoary head ;
Fall, he that loosed by fraud the maiden zone;
Fall, he that lusted for the poor man's field ;
Fall, rebel Peoples ; fall, disloyal Kings ;
And fall "—dread Mother, is the word offence ?—
" False Gods, long served ; for God Himself is nigh." '

The monarch ceased : on Heida's face that hour
He feared to look ; but when she spake, her voice
Betrayed no passion of a soul perturbed:
Austere it was ; not wrathful ; these her words :
' Son, as I hearkened to thy tale this day,
Memory returned to me of visions three
That lighted three great junctures of my life :
And thrice thy words were echoes strange of words

That shook my tender childhood, slumbering half,
Half-waked by matin beams—" The Gods must die."
Three times that awful sound was in mine ear :
Later I learned that voice was nothing new.
My Son, the earliest record of our Faith,
So sacred that on Runic stave or stone
None dared to grave it, lore from age to age
Transmitted by white lips of trembling seers,
Spared not to wing, like arrow sped from God,
That word to man, " Valhalla's Gods must die ! "
The Gods and Giant Race that strove so long,
Met in their last and mightiest battle field,
Must die, and die one death.   That prophet-voice
The Gods have heard.   Therefore they daily swell
Valhalla's Hall with heroes rapt from earth
To aid them in that fight.'
                              On Heida's face
At last the King, his head uplifting, gazed :—
There where the inviolate calm had dwelt alone
A million thoughts, each following each, on swept,
That calm beneath them still, as when some grove,
O'er-run by sudden gust of summer storm,
With inly-working panic thrills at first,
Then springs to meet the gale, while o'er it rush
Shadows with splendours mixed.   Upon her breast
Came down the fire divine.   With lifted hands

She stood: she sang a death-song centuries old,
The dirge prophetic both of Gods and men :

    ' The iron age shall make an iron end :
The men who lived in hate, or impious love,
Shall meet in one red battle field.   That day
The forests of the earth, blackening, shall die ;
The stars down-fall ; the Wingèd Hound of Heaven,
That chased the Sun from age to age, shall close
O'er it at last ; the Ash Tree, Ygdrasil,
Whose boughs o'er-roof the skies, whose roots descend
To Hell, whose leaves are lives of men, whose boughs
The destined empires that o'er-awe the world,
Shall drop its fruit unripe.   The Midgard Snake,
Circling that sea which girds the orb of earth,
Shall wake, and turn, and ocean in one wave
O'er-sweep all lands.   Thereon shall Naglfar ride,
The skeleton ship all ribbed with bones of men,
Whose sails are woven of night, and by whose helm
Stand the Three Fates.   When heaves that ship in sight,
Then know the end draws nigh.'

                           She ceased; then spake :
' If any doubt, the Voluspà tells all,
The song the mystic maiden, Vola, sang ;
Our first of prophets she, as I the last :
She sang that song no Prophet dared to write.'

But Sigebert made answer where he knelt,
Old Faith back rushing blindly on his heart :
' Though man's last nation lay a wreath of dust,
Though earth were sea, not less in heaven the Gods
Would hold their revels still; Valhalla's Halls
Resound the heroes' triumph ! '

                              Once again
Heida arose: once more her pallid face
Shone lightning-like, wan cheeks and flashing eyes ;
Once more she sang : ' The Warder of the Gods,
Soundeth the Gjallar Trumpet, never heard
Before by Gods or mortals : from their feast
The everlasting synod of the Gods
Rush forth, gold-armed, with chariot and with horse :
First rides the Father of the flock divine,
Odin, our King, and, at his right hand, Thor
Whose thunder hammer splits the mountain crags
And level lays the summits of the world ;
Heimdall and Bragi, Uller, Njord, and Tyr,
Behind them throng; with these the concourse huge
Of lesser Gods, and Heroes snatched from earth,
Since man's first battle, part to bear with Gods
In this their greatest.   From their halls of ice
To meet them stride the mighty Giant-Brood,
The moving mountains of old Jötunheim,
Strong with all strengths of Nature, flood or fire,

Glacier, or stream volcanic from red hills
Cutting through grass-green billows;—on they throng
Topping the clouds, and, leagues before them, flinging
Huge shade, like shade of mountains cast o'er wastes
When sets the sun.'   A little time she ceased ;
Then fiercelier sang : ' Flanking that Giant-Brood
I see two Portents, terrible as Sin :—
The Midgard Snake primeval at the right,
With demon-crest as haughtily upheaved
As though all ocean curled into one wave :—
A million rainbows braid that glooming arch ;
And Death therein is mirrored.   At the left,
On moves that brother Terror, wolf in shape,
Which, bound till now by craft of prescient Gods,
Weltered in Hell's abyss.   Till came the hour
A single hair inwoven by heavenly hand
Sufficed to chain that monster to his rock;—
His fast is over now; his dusky jaws
At last the Eternal Hunger lifts distent
As far as heaven from earth.'

                                        The Prophetess
One moment pressed her palms upon her eyes,
Then flung them wide.   ' The Father of the Gods,
Our Odin, at that Portent hurls his lance ;
And Thor, though bleeding fast, with hammer raised
Deals with that Serpent's scales.'

       ' The Gods shall win,
Shouted the King, forgetting at that hour
All save the strife, while on his brow there burned
Hue of the battle at the battle's height
When no man staunches wound. With voice serene
(The storm had left her) Heida made reply :
' If any doubt, the Voluspà tells all.
Ere yet Valhalla's lower heaven was shaped
Muspell, the great Third Heaven immeasurable,
Above it towered, throne of that God Supreme,
Who knew beginning none, and knows no end :
High on its southern cliff that dread One sits,
Nor ever from the South withdraws His gaze,
Nor ever drops that bright, sky-pointing Sword
Whose splendour dims the noontide sun. That God—
He, and the Spirit-Host that wing His light,
When shines the Judgment Sign, shall stand on earth,
And judge the earth with fire. Nor men nor Gods
Shall face that fire and live.'
       As Heida spake
The broad full moon above the forest soared,
And changed her form to light. With hands out-stretched
She sang her last of songs : ' The Hour is come :
Bifrost, the rainbow-bridge 'twixt heaven and earth
Shatters ; the crystal walls of heaven roll in:
Above the ruins ride the Sons of Light.

      G

That dread One first—
Forth from His helm the intolerable beam
Strikes to the battle-field; the Giant-Brood
Die in that flame; and Odin, and his Gods :
Valhalla falls, and with it Jötunheim,
Its ice-piled mountains melting into waves:
In fire are all things lost !'
                                    Then wept the King :
' Alas for Odin and his brethren Gods
That in their great hands stayed the northern land !
Alas for man !' But Heida, with fixed face
Whereon there sat its ancient calm, replied :   .
' Nothing that lived but shall again have life,
Such life as virtue claims.   Ill-working men
With Loki and with Hela, evil Gods,
Shall dwell far down in Náströnd's death-black pile
Compact of serpent scales, whose thousand gates
Face to the North, blinded by endless storm:
But from the sea shall rise a happier earth,
Holier and happier.   There the good and true
Secure shall gladden, and the fiery flame
Harm them no more.   Another Asgard there
Where stood that earlier, ere our fathers left
Their native East, shall lift sublimer towers
Dawn-lighted by a loftier Ararat :
Just men and pure shall pace its palmy steeps
With him of race divine yet human heart,

Baldur, upon whose beaming front the Gods
Gazing, exulted; from whose lips mankind
Shall gather counsel. Hand in hand with him
Shall stand the blind God, Hödur, now not blind,
That, witless, slew him with the mistletoe,
Yet loved him well. Others, both men and Gods,
That dread Third Heaven attained, shall make abode
With Him Who ever is, and ever was,
Enthroned like Him upon its southern cliff,
Drinking the light immortal. From beneath,
Like winds from flowery wildernesses borne,
The breath of all good deeds and virtuous thoughts,
Their own, or others', since the worlds were made,
All generous sufferings, o'er their hearts shall hang,
Fragrance perpetual; and, where'er they gaze,
The Vision of their God shall on them shine.'

Thus Heida spake, and ceased ; then added, 'Son,
Our Faith shall never suffer wreck : fear nought!
Fulfilment, not Destruction, is its end.
But thou return, and bid thy herald guest
Who sought thee, wandering from his westward Isle,
Approach my gates at dawn, and in mine ear
Divulge his message to this land. Farewell!'

Then from his knees the monarch rose, and took
Through the huge moonlit woods his homeward way.

KING SIGEBERT OF ESSEX, OR A
FRIEND AT NEED.

Sigebert, King of Essex, labours with Cedd the Bishop for the conversion of his people ; but he feasts with a certain impious kinsman ;
and it is foretold to him that for that sin, though pardoned, he shall
die by that kinsman's hand. This prophecy having been accomplished, Cedd betakes himself to Lastingham, there to pray with his
three brothers for the king's soul. His prayer is heard, and in a few
days he dies. Thirty of Cedd's monks, issuing from Essex to pray
at his grave, die also, and are buried in a circle round it.

'AT last resolve, my brother, and my friend!
Fling from you, as I fling this cloak, your Gods,
And cleave to Him, the Eternal, One and Sole,
The All-Wise, All-Righteous and Illimitable,
Who made us, and will judge.' Thus Oswy spake
To Sigebert, his friend, of Essex King,
Essex once Christian. Royal Sebert dead,
The Church of God had sorrow by the Thames :
Three Pagan brothers in his place held sway :
They warred upon God's people ; for which cause

God warred on them, and by the Wessex sword
In one day hewed them down.   King Sigebert,
Throned in their place, to Oswy thus replied :
'O friend, I saw the Truth, yet saw it not !
'Twas like the light forth flashed from distant oar,
Now vivid, vanished now.   Not less, methinks, ·
Thy Christ ere now had won me save for this ;
I feared that in my bosom love for thee,
Not Truth alone, prevailed.   I left thy court ;
I counselled with my wisest ; by degrees,
Though grieving thus to outrage loyal hearts,
Reached my resolve : henceforth I serve thy God :
My kingdom may renounce me if it will.'
Then came the Bishop old, and nigh that Wall
Which spans the northern land from sea to sea.
Baptized him to the God Triune.   At night
The King addressed him thus : ' My task is hard ;
Yield me four priests of thine from Holy Isle
To shape my courses.'   Finan gazed around
And made election—Cedd and others three ;
He consecrated Cedd with staff and ring ;
And by the morning's sunrise Sigebert
Rode with them, face to south.
                              The Spring, long checked,
Fell, like God's Grace, or fire, or flood, at once
O'er all the land : it swathed the hills in green ;

It fringed with violets cleft and rock ; illumed
The stream with primrose tufts : but mightier far
That Spring which triumphed in the monarch's breast,
All doubt dispelled.   That smile which knew not cause
Looked like his angel's mirrored on his face :
At times he seemed with utter gladness dazed ;
At times he laughed aloud.   ' Father,' he cried,
' That darkness from my spirit is raised at last :
Ah fool ! ah fool ! to wait for proof so long !
Unseal thine eyes, and all things speak of God :
The snows on yonder thorn His pureness show ;
You golden iris bank His love.   But now
I marked a child that by its father ran :
Some mystery they seemed of love in heaven
Imaged in earthly love.'   With sad, sweet smile
The old man answered : ' Pain there is on earth—
Bereavement, sickness, death.'   The King replied :
' It was by suffering, not by deed, or word,
God's Son redeemed mankind.'   Then answered Cedd :
'God hath thee in His net ; and well art thou !
That Truth thou seest this day, and feelest, live !
So shall it live within thee.   If, more late,
Rebuke should come, or age, remember then
This day-spring of thy strength, and answer thus,
" With me God feasted in my day of youth :
So feast He now with others ! " '

Years went by,
And Cedd in work and word was mighty still,
And throve with God.   The strong East Saxon race
Grew gentle in his presence : they were brave,
And faith is courage in the things divine,
Courage with meekness blent.   The heroic heart
Beats to the spiritual cognate, paltering not
Fraudulent with truth once known.   Like winds from
    God
God's message on them fell.   Old bonds of sin,
Snapt by the vastness of the growing soul,
Burst of themselves ; and in the heart late bound
Virtue had room to breathe.   As when that Voice
Primeval o'er the formless chaos rolled,
And, straight, confusions ceased, the greater orb
Ruling the day, the lesser, night ; even so,
Born of that Bethlehem Mystery, order lived :
Divine commandments fixed a firmament
Betwixt man's lower instincts and his mind :
From unsuspected summits of his spirit
The morning shone.   The nation with the man
Partook the joy : from duty freedom flowed ;
And there where tribes had roved a people lived.
A pathos of strange beauty hung thenceforth
O'er humblest hamlet : he who passed it prayed
' May never sword come here ! '   Bishop and King

Together laboured : well that Bishop's love
Repaid that royal zeal.   If random speech
Censured the King, though justly, sudden red
Circling the old man's silver-tressèd brow
Showed, though he spake not, that in saintly breast
The human heart lived on.

                    In Ithancester
He dwelt, and toiled : not less to Lindisfarne,
His ancient home, in spirit oft he yearned,
Longing for converse with his God alone ;
And made retreat there often, not to shun
Labour allotted, but to draw from heaven
Strength for his task.   One year, returning thence,
Dëira's King addressed him as they rode :
' My father, choose the richest of my lands
And build thereon a holy monastery ;
So shall my realm be blessed, and I, and mine.'
He answered : ' Son, no wealthy lands for us !
Spake not the prophet : "There where dragons roamed,
In later days the grass shall grow—the reed " ?
I choose those rocky hills that, on our left,
Drag down the skiey waters to the woods :
Such loved I from my youth : to me they said,
" Bandits this hour usurp our heights, and beasts
Cumber our caves : expel the seed accurst,
And yield us back to God ! " '

The King gave ear ;
And Cedd within those mountains passed his Lent,
Driving with prayer and fast the spirits accurst
With ignominy forth.   Foundations next
He laid with sacred pomp.   Fair rose the walls :
All day the March sea blew its thunder blasts
Through wide-mouthed trumpets of ravine or rift
On winding far to where in wooden cell
The old man prayed, while o'er him rushed the cloud
Storm-borne from crag to crag.   Serener breeze,
With alternation soft in Nature's course,
Following ere long, great Easter's harbinger,
Thus spake he : ' I must keep the Feast at home ;
My children there expect me.'   Parting thence,
He left his brothers three to consummate
His work begun, Celin, and Cynabil,
And Chad, at Lichfield Bishop ere he died.
Thus Lastingham had birth.

                  Beside the Thames
Meantime dark deeds were done. There dwelt two thanes,
The kinsmen of the King, his friends in youth,
Of meanest friend unworthy.   Far and wide
They ravined, and the laws of God and man
Despised alike.   Three times, in days gone by,
A warning hand their Bishop o'er them raised ;
The fourth like bolt from heaven on them it fell,

And clave them from God's Church.   They heeded not ;
And now the elder kept his birthday feast,
Summoning his friends around him, first the King.
Doubtful and sad, the o'er-gentle monarch mused :
' To feast with sinners is to sanction sin,
A deed abhorred ; the alternative is hard :
Must then their sovereign shame with open scorn
Kinsman and friend ?   I think they mourn the past,
And, were our Bishop here, would pardon sue.'
Boding, yet self-deceived, he joined that feast :
Thereat he saw scant sign of penitence :
Ere long he bade farewell.

                      That self-same hour
Cedd from his northern pilgrimage returned ;
The monarch met him at the offenders' gate,
And, instant when he saw that reverend face,
His sin before him stood.   Down from his horse
Leaping, he told him all, and penance prayed.
Long time the old man on that royal front
Fixed a sad eye.   ' Thy sin was great, my son,
Shaming thy God to spare a sinner's shame :
That sin thy God forgives, and I remit :
But those whom God forgives He chastens oft :
My son, I see a sign upon thy brow !
Ere yonder lessening moon completes her wane
Behold, the blood-stained hand late clasped in thine

Shall drag thee to thy death.' The King replied :
' A Sigebert there lived, East Anglia's King,
Whose death was glorious to his realm. May mine,
Dark and inglorious, strengthen hearts infirm,
And profit thus my land.'
                    A time it was
When Christian mercy, judged by Pagan hearts,
Not virtue seemed but sin. That sin's reproach
The King had long sustained. Ere long it chanced
That, near the stronghold of that impious feast,
A vanquished rebel, long in forests hid,
Drew near, and knelt to Sigebert for grace,
And won his suit. The monarch's kinsmen twain,
Those men of blood, forth-gazing from a tower,
Saw all ; heard all. Upon them fury fell,
As when through cloudless skies there comes a blast
From site unknown, that, instant, finds its prey, .
Circling some white-sailed bark, or towering tree,
And, with a touch, down-wrenching ; all things else
Unharmed, though near. They snatched their daggers up,
And rushed upon their prey, and, shouting thus,
' White-livered slave, that mak'st thy throne a jest,
And mock'st great Odin's self, and us, thy kin,
To please thy shaveling,' struck him through the heart ;
Then, spurring through the woodlands to the sea,
Were never heard of more.

Throughout the land
Lament was made ; lament in every house,
As though in each its eldest-born lay dead ;
Lament far off and near. The others wept :
Cedd, in long vigils of the lonely night,
Not wept alone, but lifted strength of prayer
And, morn by morn, that Sacrifice Eterne,
Mightier tenfold in impetrative power
Than prayers of all man's race, from Adam's first
To his who latest on the Judgment Day
Shall raise his hands to God. Four years went by :
That mourner's wound they staunched not. Oft in
    sleep
He murmured low, 'Would I had died for thee !'
And once, half-waked by rush of morning rains,
'Why saw I on his brow that fatal sign ?—
He might have lived till now !' Within his heart
At last there rose a cry, 'To Lastingham !
Pray with thy brothers three, for saints are they :
So shall thy friend, who resteth in the Lord
With perfect will submiss, the waiting passed,
Gaze on God's Vision with an eye unscaled,
In glory everlasting.' At that thought
Peace on the old man settled. Staff in hand
Forth on his way he fared. Nor horse he rode
Nor sandals wore. He walked with feet that bled,

Pâying, well pleased, that penance for his King ;
And murmured ofttimes, 'Not my blood alone !—
Nay, but my life, my life !'

                  Yet penance pain,
Like pain of suffering Souls at peace with God,
Quelled not that gladness which, from secret source
Rising, o'erflowed his heart.   Old times returned ;
Once more beside him rode his King in youth
Southward to where his realm—his duty—lay,
Exulting captive of the Saviour Lord,
With face love-lit.   As then, the vernal prime
Hourly with ampler respiration drew
Delight of purer green from balmier airs :
As then the sunshine glittered.   By their path
Now hung the woodbine ; now the hare-bell waved;
Rivulets new-swoll'n by melted snows, and birds
'Mid echoing boughs with rival rapture sang :
At times the monks forgat their Christian hymns,
By humbler anthems charmed.   They gladdened more
Beholding oft in cottage doors cross-crowned
Angelic faces, or in lonely ways ;
Once as they passed there stood a little maid,
Some ten years old, alone 'mid lonely pines,
With violets crowned and primrose.   Who were those,
The forest's white-robed guests, she nothing knew ;
Not less she knelt.   With hand uplifted Cedd

Signed her his blessing.   Hand she kissed in turn ; *
Then waved, yet ceased not from her song, ' Alone
' Two lovers sat at sunset.'
                              Every eve
Some village gave the wanderers food and rest,
Or half-built convent with its church·thick-walled
And polished shafts, great names in after times,
Ely, and Croyland, Southwell, Medeshamstede,
Adding to sylvan sweetness holier grace,
Or rising lonely o'er morass and mere
With bowery thickets isled, where dogwood brake
Retained, though late, its red.   To Boston near,
Where Ouse, and Aire, and Derwent join with Trent,
And salt sea waters mingle with the fresh,
They met a band of youths that o'er the sands
Advanced with psalm, cross-led.   The monks rejoiced,
Save one from Ireland—Dicul.   He, quick-eared,
Had caught that morn a war-cry on the wind,
And, sideway glancing from his Office-book,
Descried the cause.   From Mercia's realm a host
Had crossed Northumbria's bound.   His thin, worn face
O'er-flamed with sudden anger, thus he cried :
' In this, your land, men say, " Who worketh prays ; "
In mine we say, " Well prays who fighteth well : "
A Pagan race treads down your homesteads !   Slaves,
That close not with their throats ! '

Advancing thus,
On the tenth eve they came to Lastingham :
Forth rushed the brethren, watching long far off,
To meet them, first the brothers three of Cedd,
Who kissed him, cheek and mouth.   Gladly that night
Those foot-worn travellers laid them down, and slept,
Save one alone.   Old Cedd his vigil made,
And, kneeling by the tabernacle's lamp,
Prayed for the man he mourned for, ending thus :
'Thou Lord of Souls, to Thee the Souls are dear !
Thou yearn'st toward them as they yearn to Thee ;
Behold, not prayer alone for him I raise :
I offer Thee my life.'   When morning's light
In that great church commingled with its gloom,
The monks, slow-pacing, by that kneeler knelt,
And prayed for Sigebert, beloved of God ;
And lastly offered Mass : and it befell
That when, the Offering offered, and the Dead
Rightly remembered, he who sang that Mass
Had reached the ' Nobis quoque famulis,'
There came to Cedd an answer from the Lord
Heard in his heart ; and he beheld his King
Throned 'mid the Saints Elect of God who keep
Perpetual triumph, and behold that Face
Which to its likeness hourly more compels
Those faces t'ward It turned.   That function o'er,

Thus spake the Bishop: 'Brethren, sing " Te Deum ; "'
They sang it ; while within him he replied,
' Lord, let Thy servant now depart in peace.'

A week went by with gladness winged and prayer.
In wonder Cedd beheld those structures new
From small beginnings reared, though many a gift,
Sent for that work's behoof, had fed the poor
In famine time laid low.   Moorlands he saw
By cornfields vanquished ; marked the all-beauteous
      siege
Of pasture yearly threatening loftier crags
Loud with the bleat of lambs.   Their shepherd once
Had roved a bandit ; next had toiled a slave ;
Now with both hands he poured his weekly wage
Down on his young wife's lap, his pretty babes
Gambolling around for joy.   A hospital
Stood by the convent's gate.   With moistened eye,
Musing on Him Who suffers in His sick,
The Bishop paced it.   There he found his death :
That year a plague had wasted all the land :
It reached him.   Late that night he said, ''Tis well !'
In three days more he lay with hands death-cold
Crossed on a peaceful breast.
                            Like winter cloud
Borne through dark air, that portent feared of man,

Ill tidings, making way with mystic speed,
Shadowed ere long the troubled bank of Thames,
And spread a wailing round its Minsters twain,
Saint Peter's and Saint Paul's. Saint Alban's caught
That cry, and northward echoed. Southward soon
Forlorn it rang 'mid towers of Rochester ;
Then seaward died. But in that convent pile,
Wherein so long the Saint had made abode,
A different grief there lived, a deeper grief,
That grief which part hath none in sobs or tears—
Which needs must act. There thirty monks arose,
And, taking each his staff, made vow thenceforth
To serve God's altar where their father died,
Or share his grave. Through Ithancestor's gate
As forth they paced between two kneeling crowds,
A little homeless boy, who heard their dirge
(Late orphaned, at its grief he marvelled not),
So loved them that he followed, shorter steps
Doubling 'gainst theirs. At first the orphan wept :
That mood relaxed : before them now he ran
To pluck a flower ; as oft he lagged behind,
The wild bird's song so aptly imitating
That, by his music drawn, or by his looks,
That bird at times forgat her fears, and perched
Pleased on his arm. As flower and bird to him
Such to those monks the child. Better each day

H

He loved them ; yet, revering, still he mocked,
And though he mocked, he kissed.   The westering sun
On the eighth eve from towers of Lastingham
Welcomed those strangers.   In another hour,
Well-nigh arrived, they saw that grave they sought
Sole on the church's northern slope.   As when,
Some father, absent long, returns at last,
His children rush loud-voiced from field to house,
And cling about his knees ; and they that mark—
Old reaper, bent no more, with hook in hand,
Or ploughman, leaning 'gainst the old blind horse—
Beholding wonder not ; so to that grave   .
Rushed they ; so clung.   Around that grave ere long
Their own were ranged.   That plague which smote
     the sire
Spared not his sons.   With ministering hand
From pallet still to pallet passed the boy,
Now from the dark spring wafting colder draught,
Now moistening fevered lips, or on the brow
Spreading the new-bathed cincture.   Him alone
The infection reached not.   When the last was gone
He felt as though the earth, man's race—yea, God
Himself—were dead.   Around he gazed, and spake,
' Why then do I remain ? '
                              From hill to hill
(The monks on reverend offices intent)

All solitary oft that boy repaired,
From each in turn forth gazing, fain to learn
If friend were t'wards him nighing. Many a hearth
More late, bereavement's earlier anguish healed,
Welcomed the creature : many a mother held
The milk-bowl to his mouth, in both hands stayed,
With smile the deeper for the draught prolonged,
And lodged, as he departed, in his hand
Her latest crust. With children of his age
Seldom he played. That convent gave him rest ;
Nor lost he aught, surviving thus his friends,
Since childhood's sacred innocence he kept,
While life remained, unspotted. When mature
Five years he lived there monk, and reverence drew
To that high convent through his saintly ways ;
Then died. Within that cirque of thirty graves
They laid him, close to Cedd. In later years,
Because they ne'er could learn his name or race,
Nor yet forget his gentle looks, the name
Of Deodatus graved they on his tomb.

KING OSWALD OF NORTHUMBRIA, OR THE BRITON'S REVENGE.

Northumbria having been subdued by Pagan Mercia, Oswald raises there again the Christian standard. Penda wages war against him, in alliance with Cadwallon, a Cambrian prince who hates the Saxon conquerors the more bitterly when become Christians. Encouraged by St. Columba in a vision, Oswald with a small force vanquishes the hosts of Cadwallon, who is slain. He sends to Iona for monks of St. Columba's order, converts his country to the Faith, and dies for her. The earlier British race expiates its evil revenge.

THE agony was over which but late
Had shook to death Northumbria's realm new-raised
By Edwin, dear to God. The agony
At last was over ; but the tear flowed on :
The Faith of Christ had fallen once more to dust,
That Faith which spoused with golden marriage ring
The land to God, when Coiffi, horsed and mailed,
Chief Priest himself, hurled at the Temple's wall
His lance, and quivering left it lodged therein.

The agony had ceased ; yet Rachael's cry
Still pierced the childless region.   Penda's sword
Had swept it, Mercia's Christian-hating King ;
Fiercelier Cadwallon's, Cambria's Christian Prince,
Christian in vain.   The British wrong like fire
Burned in his heart.   Well-nigh two hundred years
That British race, they only of the tribes
By Rome subdued, sustained unceasing war
'Gainst those barbaric·hordes that, nursed long since
'Mid Teuton woods, when Rome her death-wound felt,
And ' *Habet* ' shrilled from every trampled realm,
Rushed forth in ruin o'er her old domain :—
That race against the Saxon still made head ;
Large remnant yet survived.   The Western coast
Was theirs ; old sea-beat Cornwall's granite cliffs,
And purple hills of Cambria ; northward thence
Strathclyde, from towered Carnegia's winding Dee
To Morecombe's shining sands, and those fair vales,
Since loved by every muse, where silver meres
Slept in the embrace of yew-clad mountain walls ;
With tracts of midland Britain and the East.
Remained the memory of the greatness lost ;
The Druid circles of the olden age ;
The ash-strewn cities radiant late with arts
Extinct this day ; bath, circus, theatre
Mosaic·paved ; the Roman halls defaced ;

The Christian altars crushed.   That last of wrongs
The vanquished punished with malign revenge :
Never had British priest to Saxon preached ;
And when that cry was heard, 'The Saxon King
Edwin hath bowed to Christ,' on Cambrian hills
Nor man nor woman smiled.

They had not lacked
The timely warning.   From his Kentish shores
Augustine stretched to them paternal hands :
Later, he sought them out in synod met,
Their custom, under open roof of heaven.
'The Mother of the Churches,' thus he spake,
'Commands—implores you !   Seek from her, and win
The Sacrament of Unity Divine !
Thus strengthened, be her strength !   With her con-
        joined,
Subdue your foe to Christ !'   He sued in vain.
The British bishops hurled defiance stern
Against his head, while Cambrian peaks far off
Darkened, and thunder muttered.   From his seat,
Slowly and sadly as the sun declined
At last, though late, that Roman rose and stretched
A lean hand t'ward that circle, speaking thus :
'Hear then the sentence of your God on sin !
Because ye willed not peace, behold the sword !
Because ye grudged your foe the Faith of Christ,

Nor holp to lead him on the ways of life,
For that cause from you by the Saxon hand
Your country shall be taken ! '

        Edwin slain,
Far off in exile dwelt his nephews long,
Oswald and Oswy. Alba gave them rest,
Alba, not yet called Scotland. Ireland's sons,
Then Scoti named, had warred on Alba's Picts :
Columba's Gospel vanquished either race ;
Won both to God. It won not less those youths,
In boyhood Oswald, Oswy still a child.
That child was wild and hot, and had his moods,
Despotic now, now mirthful. Mild as Spring
Was Oswald's soul, majestic and benign ;
Thoughtful his azure eyes, serene his front ;
He of his ravished sceptre little recked ;
The shepherds were his friends ; the mountain deer
Would pluck the ivy fearless from his hand:
In gladness walked he till Northumbria's cry
Smote on his heart. 'Why rest I here in peace,'
Thus mused he, ' while my brethren groan afar ? '
By night he fled with twelve companion youths,
Christians like him, and reached his native land.
Too fallen it seemed to aid him. On he passed ;
The ways were desolate, yet evermore ·
A slender band around his footsteps drew,

Less seeking victory than an honest death.
Oft gazed their King upon them ; murmured oft,
'Few hands—true hearts !' Sudden aloud he cried,
'Plant here the royal Standard, friends, and hence
Let sound the royal trumpet.'

                        Stern response
Reached him ere long : not Mercia's realm alone ;
Cambria that heard the challenge joined the war :
Cambria, upon whose heart the ancestral woe,
For ever with the years, like letters graved
On growing pines, grew larger and more large ;—
To Penda forth she stretched a hand blood-red ;
Christian with Pagan joined, an unblest bond,
A league accursed. The indomitable hate
Compelled that league. Still from his cave the Seer
Admonished, 'Set the foe against the foe ;
Slay last the conqueror !' and from rock and hill
The Bard cried, 'Vengeance !' In the bardic clan
That hatred of their country's ancient bane
Lived like a faith. One night it chanced a tarn,
Secreted high 'mid cold and moonless hills,
Bursting its bank down burst. That valley's Bard
Clomb to the church-roof from his buried house :
Thence rang his song,—'twas ' Vengeance !—Vengeance
    still !
That torrent reached the roof : he clomb the tower :

The torrent mounted : on the bleak hill-side
All night the dalesmen, wailing o'er their drowned,
Amid the roar of winds and downward rocks,
Still heard that war-song, 'Vengeance ! Blood for blood !'
At last the tower fell flat, and winter morn
Shone on the waters only.
                              Three short weeks
Dinned with alarums passed ; in Mercia still
Lay Penda, sickness-struck, when, face to face,
The Cambrian host and Oswald's little band
Exulting met at sunset near a height
Then ' Heaven-Field ' named, but later ' Oswald's Field,'
Backed by that Wall the Roman built of old
His fence from sea to sea.   There Oswald stood :
There raised with hands outstretched a mighty Cross,
Strong-based, and deep in earth : his comrades twelve
Around it heaped the soil, while priests white-stoled
Chanted 'Vexilla Regis.'   Work and rite
Complete, the King knelt down and made his prayer :
'True God Eternal, look upon this Cross,
The sole now standing on Northumbria's breast,
And help Thine own, though few, who trust in Thee !'

That night before his tent the wanderer sate
Listening the circling sentinel, or bay
Of wakeful hound remote, or downward course

Of streams from moorland hills.   Before his view
His whole life rose : his father's angry brow ;
The eyes all-wondrous, and all-tender hand
Of her, his mother, striving evermore
To keep betwixt her husband and her sire
Unbroken bond : his exiled days returned,
The kind that pitied them, the rude that jeered ;
Lastly, that monk whose boast was evermore
Columba of Iona, Columkille ;
That monk who made him Christian. 'Come what may,'
Thus Oswald mused, " I have not lived in vain :
Lose I or win, a kingdom there remains ;
Though not on earth ! '   A tear the vision dimmed
As thus he closed, ' My mother will be there ! '
Then sank his lids in slumber.

                         On his sleep—
Was this indeed but dream ?—a glory brake :
Columba, dear to Oswald from his youth,
Columba, clad in glory as the sun,
Beside him stood, and spake : ' Be strong !   On earth
There lives not who can guess the might of prayer :
What then is prayer on high ? '   The saintly Shape
Heavenward his hands upraised, while rose to heaven
His stature, towering ever high and higher,
Warlike and priestly both.   As morning cloud
Blown by a mighty wind his robe ran forth,

Then stood, a golden wall that severance made
'Twixt Oswald's band and that unnumbered host.
Again he spake, ' Put on thee heart of man
And fight : though few, thy warriors shall not die
In darkness of an unbelieving land,
But live, and live to God.'   The vision passed :
By Oswald's seat his warriors stood and cried,
' The Bull-horn !   Hark ! '   The monarch told them all :
They answered, ' Let thy God sustain thy throne :—
Thenceforth our God is He.'
                              The sun uprose :
Ere long the battle joined.   Three dreadful hours
Doubtful the issue hung.   Fierce Cambria's sons
With chief and clan, with harper and with harp,
Though terrible yet mirthful in their mood,
Rushed to their sport.   Who mocked their hope that day ?
Did Angels help the just ?   Their falling blood,
Say, leaped it up once more, each drop a man
Their phalanx to replenish ?   Backward driven,
Again that multitudinous foe returned
With clangour dire ; futile, again fell back
Down dashed, like hailstone showers from palace halls
Where princes feast secure.   Astonishment
Smote them at last.   Through all those serried ranks,
Compact so late, sudden confusions ran
Like lines divergent through a film of ice

Stamped on by armèd heel, or rifts on plains
Prescient of earthquake underground.   Their chiefs
Sounded the charge ;—in vain : Distrust, Dismay,
Ill Gods, the darkness lorded of that hour :
Panic to madness turned.   Cadwallon sole
From squadron on to squadron speeding still
As on a wingèd steed—his snow-white hair
Behind him blown—a mace in either hand—
Stayed while he might the inevitable rout ;
Then sought his death, and found.   Some fated Power
Mightier than man's that hour dragged back his hosts
Against their will and his ; as when the moon,
Shrouded herself, drags back the great sea-tides
That needs must follow her receding wheels
Though wind and wave gainsay them, breakers wan
Thundering indignant down nocturnal shores,
And city-brimming floods against their will
Down drawn to river-mouths.

                 In after days
Who scaped made oath that in the midmost fight
The green earth sickened with a brazen glare
While darkness held the skies.   They saw besides
On Heaven-Field height a Cross, and, at its foot,
A sworded warrior vested like a priest,
Who still in stature high and higher towered
As raged the battle.   Higher far that Cross

Above him rose, barring with black the stars
That bickered through the eclipse's noonday night,
And ever from its bleeding arms sent forth
Thick-volleyed lightnings, azure fork and flame,
Through all that headlong host.

                        At eventide,
Where thickest fight had mingled, Oswald stood
With raiment red as his who treads alone
The wine-vat when the grapes are all pressed out,
Yet scathless and untouched.   His mother's smile
Was radiant on his pure and youthful face,
Joyous, but not exulting.   At his foot
Cadwallon lay, with four-score winters white,
A threatening corse : not death itself could shake
The mace from either rigid hand close-clenched,
Or smooth his brow.   Above him Oswald bent,
Then spake : 'He also loved his native land :
Bear him with honour hence to hills of Wales,
And lay him with his Fathers.'

                        Thus was raised
In righteousness King Oswald's throne.   But he,
Mindful in victory of Columba's word,
Thus mused, 'The Master is as he that serves :
How shall I serve this people?'   O'er the waves
Then sent he of his Twelve the eldest three :
They to Iona sailed, and standing there

In full assembly of Iona's saints
Addressed them : ' To Columba Oswald thus :
Let him that propped the King on Heaven-Field's height,
That held the battle-balance high that day,
Unite my realm to Christ !'   The monks replied,
' Such mission should be Aidan's.'   Aidan went.
With gladness Oswald met him, and with gifts :
But Aidan said, ' Entreat me not to dwell
There where Paulinus dwelt, the man of God,
In thy chief city, York.   Thy race is fierce ;
And meekness only can subdue the proud :
Thy people first I want ;—through them the great.
Grant me some island 'mid the raging main,
Humble and low, not cheered by smiling meads,
Where with my brethren I may watch with God,
Henceforth my only aid.'   Oswald replied,
' Let Lindisfarne be thine.   That rock-based keep
Built by my grandsire Ida o'er it peers :
I shall be near thee though I see thee not.'

Then Aidan on the Isle of Lindisfarne
Upreared that monastery which ruled in Christ
So long the Northern realm.   A plain rock-girt
Level it lies and low : nor flower nor fruit
Gladdens its margin : thin its sod, and bleak :
Twice, day by day, the salt sea hems it round :

And twice a day the melancholy sands,
O'er-wailed by sea-bird, and with sea-weed strewn,
Replace the lonely ocean. Sacred Isles
That westward, eastward, guard the imperial realm,
Iona ! Lindisfarne ! With you compared
How poor that lilied Delos of old Greece,
For all its laurel bowers and nightingales ! ,
England's great hands were ye to God forth stretched
Through adverse climes, beneath the Boreal star,
That took His Stigmata. In sanctity
Were her foundations laid. Her later crowns
Of Freedom first, of Science, and of Song
She owes them all to you !

                    In Lindisfarne
Aidan, and his, rejoicing dwelt with God :
Amid the winter storm their anthems rose ;
And from their sanctuary lamp the gleam
Far shone from wave to wave. On starless nights
From Bamborough's turret Oswald watched it long,
Before his casement kneeling—first alone,
Companioned later. Kineburga there
Beside him knelt ere long, his tender bride,
Young, beauteous, modest, noble. ' Not for them,'
Thus spake the newly wedded, ' not for them,
For man's sake severed from the world of men,
In ceaseless vigil warring upon sin,

Ah, not for them the flower of life, the harp,
High feast, or bridal torch!' Purer perchance
Their bridal torch burned on because from far
That sacred lamp had met its earliest beam!

There Aidan lived, and wafted, issuing thence,
O'er wilds Bernician and fierce battle-fields
The strength majestic of his still retreat,
The puissance of a soul whose home was God.
'What man is this,' the warriors asked, 'that moves
Unarmed among us; lifts his crucifix,
And says, "Ye swords, lie prone"?' The revelling crew
Rose from their cups: ' He preaches abstinence:
Behold, the man is mortified himself:
The moonlight of his watchings and his fasts
He carries on his face.' When Princes forced
Largess upon him, he replied, ' I want
Not yours but you ;' and with their gifts redeemed
The orphan slave. The poor were as his children:
He to the beggar stinted not his hand
Nor, giving, said ' Be brief.' Such seed bare fruit:—
God in the dark, primeval woods had reared
A race whose fierceness had its touch of ruth;
Brave, cordial, chaste, and simple. Reverence
That race preserved: Reverence advanced to Love:
The ties of life it honoured: lit from heaven

They wore, a meaning new.   The Faith of Christ
Banished the bestial from the heart of man ;
Restored the Hope divine.

     In all his toils
Oswald with Aidan walked.   Impartial law,
Not licence, not despotic favour, stands
To Truth auxiliar true.   Such laws were his :
Yet not through such alone he worked for Truth ;
Function he claimed more high.   When Aidan preached ;
In forest depths when thousands girt him round ;
When countless eyes, a clinging weight, were bent
Upon his lips—all knew they spake from God,—
The King, with monks from Ireland knit of old,
Beside the Bishop stood ; each word he spake
Changed to the Saxon tongue.

     Earth were not earth,
If reign like Oswald's lasted.   Penda lived ;
Nor e'er from Oswald turned for eight long years
An eye like some swart planet feared of man,
Omen of wars or plague.   Cadwallon's fate,
Ally ill-starred, that fought without his aid,
O'er-flushed old hatred with a fiery shame :
Cadwallon nightly frowned above his dreams.
The tyrant watched his time.   At Maserfield
The armies met.   There on Northumbria's day
Settled what seemed, yet was not, endless night

I

There Faith and Virtue, deathless, seemed to die :
There holy Oswald fell.   For God he fought,
Fought for his country.   Walled with lances round,
A sheaf of arrows quivering in his breast,
One moment yet he stood.   'Preserve,' he cried,
' My country, God !' then added, gazing round,
' And these my soldiers : make their spirits thine !'
  Thus perished good King Oswald, King and Saint ;
Saint by acclaim of nations canonised
Ere yet the Church had spoken.   Year by year
The Hexham monks to Heaven-Field, where of old
Had stood that ' Cross which conquered,' made repair,
With chanted psalm ; and pilgrims daily prayed
Where died the just and true.   Not vain their vows :
In righteousness foundations had been laid :
The earthquake reached them not. The Dane passed by
High up the Norman glittered : but beneath,
On Faith profounder based, and gentler Law
The Saxon realm lived on.
       But never more
From Heaven-Field's wreck the Briton raised his head
Britain thenceforth was England.   His the right ;
The land was his of old ; and in God's House
His of the island races stood first-born :
Not less he sinned through hate, esteeming more
Memories of wrong than forward-looking hopes

And triumphs of the Truth. For that cause God
His face in blessing to the younger turned,
More honouring Pagans who in ignorance erred,
Than those who, taught of God, concealed their gift,
Divorcing Faith from Love. Natheless they clung,
That remnant spared, to rocky hills of Wales
With eagle clutch, whoe'er in England ruled,
From Horsa's day to Edward's. Centuries eight
In gorge or vale sea-lulled they held their own,
By native monarchs swayed, while native harps
Rang out from native cliffs defiant song
Wild as their singing pines. Heroic Land !
Freedom was thine; the torrent's plunge ; the peak ;
The pale mist past it borne ! Heroic Race !
Caractacus was thine, and Galgacus,
And Boadicea, greater by her wrongs
Than by her lineage. Battle-axe of thine
Rang loud and long on Roman helms ere yet
Hengist had trod the island. Thine that King
World-famed, who led to fifty war-fields forth
'Gainst Saxon hosts his sinewy, long-haired race
Unmailed, yet victory-crowned; that King who left
Tintagel, Camelot, and Lyonnesse,
Immortal names, though wild as elfin notes
From phantom rocks echoed in fairy land—
Great Arthur ! Year by year his deeds were sung,

While he in Glastonbury's cloister slept,
First by the race he died for, next by those
Their children, exiles in Armoric Gaul,
By Europe's minstrels then, from age to age ;
But ne'er by ampler voice, or richlier toned
Than England lists to-day.   Race once of Saints !
Thine were they, Ninian thine and Kentigern,
Iltud and Beino, yea and David's self,
Thy crown of Saints, and Winifred, their flower,
Who fills her well with healing virtue still.
Cadoc was thine, who to his Cambrian throne
Preferred that western convent at Lismore,
Yet taught the British Princes thus to sing :
' None loveth Song that loves not Light and Truth:
None loveth Light and Truth that loves not Justice :
None loveth Justice if he loves not God :
None loveth God that lives not blest and great.'

CEADMON THE COWHERD, THE FIRST ENGLISH POET.

Ceadmon, a cowherd, being at a feast, declares when the harp reaches him, that he cannot sing. As he sleeps, a divine Voice commands him to sing. He obeys, and the gift of song is imparted to him. Hilda, Abbess of Whitby, enrolls him among her monks ; and in later years he sings the revolt of the Fallen Angels, and many Christian mysteries, thus becoming the first English poet.

ALONE upon the pleasant bank of Esk
Ceadmon the Cowherd stood.   The sinking sun
Reddened the bay, and fired the river-bank,
And flamed upon the ruddy herds that strayed
Along the marge, clear-imaged.   None was nigh :
For that cause spake the Cowherd, ' Praise to God !
'He made the worlds ; and now, by Hilda's hand
Planteth a crown on Whitby's holy crest:
Daily her convent towers more high aspire :
Daily ascend her Vespers.   Hark that strain !

He stood and listened. Soon the flame-touched
   herds
Sent forth their lowings, and the cliffs replied,
And Ceadmon thus resumed : ' The music note
Rings through their lowings dull, though heard by
   few !
Poor kine, ye do your best !   Ye know not God,
Yet man, his likeness, unto you is God,
And him ye worship with obedience sage,
A grateful, sober, much-enduring race
That o'er the vernal clover sigh for joy,
With winter snows contend not.   Patient kine,
What thought is yours, deep-musing?   Haply this,
" God's help ! how narrow are our thoughts, and few!
Not so the thoughts of that slight human child
Who daily drives us with her blossomed rod
From lowland valleys to the pails long-ranged !"
Take comfort, kine!   God also made your race !
If praise from man surceased, from your broad chests
That God would perfect praise, and, when ye died,
Resound it from yon rocks that gird the bay :
God knoweth all things.   Let that thought suffice ! '

Thus spake the ruler of the deep-mouthed kine :
They were not his; the man and they alike
A neighbour's wealth.   He was contented thus:

Humble he was in station, meek of soul,
Unlettered, yet heart-wise.   His face was pale;
Stately his frame, though slightly bent by age :
Slow were his eyes, and slow his speech, and slow
His musing step; and slow his hand to wrath ;
A massive hand, but soft, that many a time
Had succoured man and woman, child and beast,
And yet could fiercely grasp the sword.   At times
As mightily it clutched his ashen goad
When like an eagle on him swooped some thought :
Then stood he as in dream, his pallid front
Brightening like eastern sea-cliffs when a moon
Unrisen is near its rising.

                    Round the bay
Meantime, as twilight deepened, many a fire
Up-sprang, and horns were heard.   Around the steep
With bannered pomp and many a tossing plume
Advancing slow a cavalcade made way.
Oswy, Northumbria's king, the foremost rode,
Oswy triumphant o'er the Mercian host,
Invoking favour on his sceptre new ;
With him an Anglian prince, student long time
In Bangor of the Irish, and a monk
Of Frankish race far wandering from the Marne :
They came to look on Hilda, hear her words
Of far-famed wisdom on the Interior Life ;

For Hilda thus discoursed: 'True life of man
Is life within: inward immeasurably
The being winds of all who walk the earth ;
But he whom sense hath blinded nothing knows
Of that wide greatness : like a boy is he,
A boy that clambers round some castle's wall
In search of nests, the outward wall of seven,
Yet nothing knows of those great courts within,
The hall where princes banquet, or the bower
Where royal maids discourse with lyre and lute,
Much less its central church, and sacred shrine
Wherein God dwells alone.'   Thus Hilda spake ;
And they that gazed upon her widening eyes
Low whispered, each to each, 'She speaks of things
Which she hath seen and known.'

       On Whitby's height
The royal feast was holden: far below,
A noisier revel dinned the shore; therein
The humbler guests made banquet.   Many a tent
Gleamed on the yellow sands by ripples kissed ;
And many a savoury dish sent up its steam ;
The farmer from the field had brought his calf ;
Fishers that increase scaled which green-gulfed seas
From womb crystalline, teeming, yield to man ;
And Jock, the woodsman, from his oaken glades
The tall stag, arrow-pierced.   In gay attire

Now green, now crimson, matron sat and maid :
Each had her due: the elder, reverence most,
The lovelier that and love. Beside the board
The beggar lacked not place.

                When hunger's rage,
Sharpened by fresh sea-air, was quelled, the jest
Succeeded, and the tale of foreign lands ;
Yet, boast who might of distant chief renowned,
His battle-axe, or fist that felled an ox,
The Anglian's answer was ' our Hilda ' still :
' Is not her prayer trenchant as sworded hosts ?
Her insight more than wisdom of the seers ?
What birth like hers illustrious ? Edwin's self,
Dëira's exile, next Northumbria's king,
Her kinsman was. Together bowed they not
When he of holy hand, missioned from Rome,
Paulinus, o'er them poured the absolving wave
And joined to Christ ? Kingliest was she, that maid
Who spurned earth-crowns !' More late the miller
    rose—
He ruled the feast, the miller old, yet blithe—
And cried, 'A song !' So song succeeded song,
For each man knew that time to chant his stave,
But ɲo man yet sang nobly. Last the harp
Made way to Ceadmon, lowest at the board :
He pushed it back, answering, 'I cannot sing: '

The rest around him flocked with clamour, ' Sing ! '
And one·among them, voluble and small,
Shot out a splenetic speech: ' This lord of kine,
Our herdsman, grows to ox !   Behold, his eyes
Move slow, like eyes of oxen !'

                              Slowly rose
Ceadmon, and spake: ' I note full oft young men
Quick-eyed, but small-eyed, darting glances round
Now here, now there, like glance of some poor bird,
That light on all things and can rest on none :
As ready are they with their tongues as eyes ;
But all their songs are chirpings backward blown
On winds that sing God's song, by them unheard :
My oxen wait my service : I depart.'
Then strode he to his cow-house in the mead,
Displeased though meek, and muttered, ' Slow of eye !
My kine are slow : if rapid I, my hand
Might tend them worse.'   Hearing his step, the kine
Turned round their hornèd fronts; and angry thoughts
Went from him as a vapour.   Straw he brought,
And strewed their beds; and they, contented well,
Laid down ere long their great bulks, breathing deep
Amid the glimmering moonlight.   He, with head
Propped on a favourite heifer's snowy flank,
Rested, his deer-skin o'er him drawn.   Hard days
Bring slumber soon.   His latest thought was this :

' Though witless things we are, my kine and I,
Yet God it was who made us.'

As he slept,
Beside him stood a Man Divine, and spake :
' Ceadmon, arise, and sing.'   Ceadmon replied,
' My Lord, I cannot sing, and for that cause
Forth from the revel came I.   Once, in youth,
I willed to sing the bright face of a maid,
And failed, and once a gold-faced harvest-field,
And failed, and once the flame-eyed face of war,
And failed again.'   To him the Man Divine,
' Those themes were earthly.   Sing ! '   And Ceadmon
     said,
' What shall I sing, my Lord ? '   Then answer came,
' Ceadmon, stand up, and sing thy song of God.'

At once obedient, Ceadmon rose, and sang;
And help was with him from great thoughts of old
Yearly within his silent nature stored,
That swelled, collecting like a flood which bursts
In spring its icy bar.   The Lord of all
He sang ; that God beneath whose hand eterne,
Then when He willed forth-stretched athwart the
     abyss,
Creation like a fiery chariot ran,
Forth-borne on wheels of ever-living stars :

Him first he sang. The builder, here below,
From fair foundations rears at last the roof;
But Song, a child of heaven, begins with heaven,
The archetype divine, and end of all;
More late descends to earth. He sang that hymn,
'Let there be light, and there was light;' and lo!
On the void deep came down the seal of God
And stamped immortal form. Clear laughed the
    skies;
From circumambient deeps the strong earth brake,
Both continent and isle; while downward rolled
The sea-surge summoned to his home remote.
Then came a second vision to the man
There standing 'mid his oxen. Darkness sweet,
He sang, of pleasant frondage clothed the vales,
And purple glooms ambrosial cast from hills
Now by the sun deserted, which the moon,
A glory new-created in her place,
Silvered with virgin beam, while sang the bird
Her first of love-songs on the branch first-flower'd—
Not yet the lion stalked. And Ceadmon sang
O'er-awed, the Father of all humankind
Standing in garden planted by God's hand,
And girt by murmurs of the rivers four,
Between the trees of Knowledge and of Life,
With eastward face. In worship mute of God,

Eden's Contemplative he stood that hour,
Not her Ascetic, since, where sin is none,
No need for spirit severe.

                     And Ceadmon sang
God's Daughter, Adam's Sister, Child, and Bride,
Our Mother Eve. Lit by the matin star,
That nearer drew to earth and brighter flashed
To meet her gaze, that snowy Innocence
Stood up with queenly port : she turned ; she saw
Earth's King, mankind's great Father : taught by
    God,
Immaculate, unastonished, undismayed,
In love and reverence to her Lord she drew,
And, kneeling, kissed his hand : and Adam laid
That hand, made holier, on that kneeler's head,
And spake ; ' For this shall man his parents leave,
And to his wife cleave fast.'

                    When Ceadmon ceased,
Thus spake the Man Divine : ' At break of day
Seek out some prudent man, and say that God
Hath loosed thy tongue ; nor hide henceforth thy gift.'
Then Ceadmon turned, and slept among his kine
Dreamless. Ere dawn he stood upon the shore
In doubt : but when at last o'er eastern seas
The sun, long wished for, like a god upsprang,
Once more he found God's song upon his mouth

Murmuring high joy ; and sought an ancient friend,
And told him all the vision.   At the word
He to the Abbess with the tidings sped,
And she made answer, ' Bring me Ceadmon here.'

Then clomb the pair that sea-beat mount of God
Fanned by sea-gale, nor trod, as others used,
The curving way, but faced the abrupt ascent,
And halted not, so worked in both her will,
Till now between the unfinished towers they stood
Panting and spent.   The portals open stood :
Ceadmon passed in alone.   Nor ivory decked,
Nor gold, the walls.   That convent was a keep
Strong 'gainst invading storm or demon hosts,
And naked as the rock whereon it stood,
Yet, as a church, august.   Dark, high-arched roofs
Slowly let go the distant hymn.   Each cell
Cinctured its statued saint, the peace of God
On every stony face.   Like caverned grot
Far off the western window frowned : beyond,
Close by, there shook an autumn-blazoned tree :
No need for gems beside of storied glass.

He entered last that hall where Hilda sat
Begirt with a great company, the chiefs
Far ranged from end to end.   Three stalls, cross-crowned,

Stood side by side, the midmost hers.   The years
Had laid upon her brows a hand serene ;
There left alone a blessing.   Levelled eyes
Sable, and keen, with meditative might
Conjoined the instinct and the claim to rule :
Firm were her lips and rigid.   At her right
Sat Finan, Aidan's successor, with head
Snow-white, and beard that rolled adown a breast
Never by mortal passion heaved in storm,
A cloister of majestic thoughts that walked,
Humbly with God. ' High in the left-hand stall
Oswy was throned, a man in prime, with brow
Less youthful than his years.   Exile long past,
Or deepening thought of one disastrous deed,
Had left a shadow in his eyes.   The strength
Of passion held in check looked lordly forth
From head and hand : tawny his beard ; his hair
Thick-curled and dense.   Alert the monarch sat
Half turned, like one on horseback set that hears,
And he alone, the advancing trump of war.
Down the long gallery strangers thronged in mass,
Dane or Norwegian, huge of arm through weight
Of billows oar-subdued, with stormy looks
Wild as their waves and crags ; Southerns keen-browed ;
Pure Saxon youths, fair-fronted, with mild eyes,
These less than others strove for nobler place,

And Pilgrim travel-worn.   Behind the rest,
And higher-ranged in marble-arched arcade,
Sat Hilda's sisterhood.   Clustering they shone,
White-veiled, and pale of face, and still and meek,
An inly-bending curve, like some young moon
Whose crescent glitters o'er a dusky strait.
In front were monks dark-stoled : for Hilda ruled,
Though feminine, two houses, one of men :
Upon two chasm-divided rocks they stood,
To various service vowed, though single Faith :—
Not ever, save at rarest festival,
Their holy inmates met.

        ' Is this the man
Favoured, though late, with gift of song?' thus spake
Hilda with gracious smile.   Severer then
She added : 'Son, the commonest gifts of God
He counts His best, and oft temptation blends
With ampler boon.   Yet sing !   That God who lifts
The violet from the grass could draw not less
Song from the stone hard by.   That strain thou
   sang'st,
Once more rehearse it.'

       Ceadmon from his knees
Arose and stood.   With princely instinct first
The strong man to the Abbess bowed, and next
To that great twain, the bishop and the king,

Last to that stately concourse each side ranged
Down the long hall ; then, dubious, answered thus :
'Great Mother, if that God who sent the song
Vouchsafe me to recall it, I will sing ;
But I misdoubt it lost.' Slowly his face
Down-drooped, and all his body forward bent
While brooding memory, step by step, retraced
Its backward way. Vainly long time it sought
The starting-point. Then Ceadmon's large, soft hands
Opening and closing worked ; for wont were they,
In musings when he stood, to clasp his goad,
And plant its point far from him, thereupon
Propping his stalwart weight. Customed support
Now finding not, unwittingly those hands
Reached forth, and on Saint Finan's crosier-staff
Settling, withdrew it from the old bishop's grasp ;
And Ceadmon leant thereon, while passed a smile
From chief to chief to see earth's meekest man
The spiritual sceptre claim of Lindisfarne.
They smiled ; he triumphed : soon the Cowherd found
That first fair corner-stone of all his song ;
Thence rose the fabric heavenward. Lifting hands,
Once more his lordly music he rehearsed,
The void abyss at God's command forth-flinging
Creation like a Thought : where night had reigned,
The universe of God.

K

The singing stars
Which with the Angels sang when earth was made
Sang in his song.   From highest shrill of lark
To ocean's moaning under cliffs low-browed,
And roar of pine-woods on the storm-swept hills,
No tone was wanting ; while to them that heard
Strange images looked forth of worlds new-born,
Fair, phantom mountains, and, with forests plumed
Heaven-topping headlands, for the first time glassed
In waters ever calm.   O'er sapphire seas
Green islands laughed.   Fairer, the wide earth's flower,
Eden, on airs unshaken yet by sighs
From bosom still inviolate forth poured
Immortal sweets that sense to spirit turned.
In part those noble listeners *made* that song !
Their flashing eyes, their hands, their heaving breasts,
Tumult self-stilled, and mute, expectant trance,
'Twas these that gave their bard his twofold might—
That might denied to poets later born
Who, singing to soft brains and hearts ice-hard,
Applauded or contemned, alike roll round
A vainly-seeking eye, and, famished, drop
A hand clay-cold upon the unechoing shell,
Missing their inspiration's human half.

Thus Ceadmon sang, and ceased.   Silent awhile

The concourse stood, for all had risen, as though
Waiting from heaven its echo.   Each on each
Gazed hard and caught his hands.   Fiercely ere long
Their gratulating shout aloft had leaped
But Hilda laid her finger on her lip,
Or provident lest praise might stain the pure,
Or deeming song a gift too high for praise.
She spake : ' Through help of God thy song is sound :
Now hear His Holy Word, and shape therefrom
A second hymn, and worthier than the first.'

    She spake, and Finan standing bent his head
Above the sacred tome in reverence stayed
Upon his kneeling deacon's hands and brow,
And sweetly sang five verses, thus beginning,
' *Cum esset desponsata,*' and was still ;
And next rehearsed them in the Anglian tongue :
Then Ceadmon took God's Word into his heart,
And ruminating stood, as when the kine,
Their flowery pasture ended, ruminate ;
And was a man in thought.   At last the light
Shone from his dubious countenance, and he spake :
' Great Mother, lo ! I saw a second Song !
T'wards me it sailed ; but with averted face,
And borne on shifting winds.   A man am I
Sluggish and slow, that needs must muse and brood ;

Therefore those verses till the sun goes down
Will I revolve.   If song from God be mine
Expect me here at morn.'
                              The morrow morn
In that high presence Ceadmon stood and sang
A second song, and worthier than his first ;
And Hilda said, ' From God it came, not man ;
Thou therefore live a monk among my monks,
And sing to God.'   Doubtful he stood—' From youth
My place hath been with kine ; their ways I know,
And how to cure their griefs.'   Smiling she spake,
' Our convent hath its meads, and kine ; with these
Consort each morn : at noon to us return.'
Then Ceadmon knelt, and bowed, and said, ' So be it : '
And aged Finan, and Northumbria's king
Oswy, approved ; and all that host had joy.

    Thus in that convent Ceadmon lived, a monk,
Humblest of all the monks, save him that knelt
In cell close by, who once had been a prince.
Seven times a day he sang God's praises, first
When earliest dawn drew back night's sable veil
With trembling hand, revisiting the earth
Like some pale maid that through the curtain peers
Round her sick mother's bed, misdoubting half
If sleep lie there, or death ; latest when eve

Through nave and chancel stole from arch to arch,
And laid upon the snowy altar-step
At last a brow of gold.   In later years,
By ancient yearnings driven, through wood and vale
He tracked Dëirean or Bernician glades
To holy Ripon, or late-sceptred York,
Not yet great Wilfred's seat, or Beverley :
The children gathered round him, crying, ' Sing ! '
They gave him inspiration with their eyes,
And with his conquering music he returned it.
Oftener he roamed that strenuous eastern coast
To Jarrow and to Wearmouth, sacred sites
The well-beloved of Bede, or northward more
To Bamborough, Oswald's keep.   At Coldingham
His feet had rest ; there where St. Ebba's Cape
That ends the lonely range of Lammermoor,
Sustained for centuries o'er the wild sea-surge
In region of dim mist and flying bird,
Fronting the Forth, those convent piles far-kenned,
The worn-out sailor's hope.

                            Fair English shores,
Despite those blinding storms of north and east,
Despite rough ages blind with stormier strife,
Or froz'n by doubt, or sad with worldly care,
A fragrance as of Carmel haunts you still
Bequeathed by feet of that forgotten Saint

Who trod you once, sowing the seed divine !
Fierce tribes that kenned him distant round him flocked;
On sobbing sands the fisher left his net,
His lamb the shepherd on the hills of March,
Suing for song.   With wrinkled face all smiles,
Like that blind Scian circling Grecian coasts,
If God the song accorded, Ceadmon sang ;
If God denied it, after musings deep
He answered, ' I am of the kine and dumb ; '—
The man revered his art, and fraudful song
Esteemed as fraudful coin.

                    Music denied,
He solaced them with tales wherein, so seemed it,
Nature and Grace, inwoven, like children played,
Or like two sisters o'er one sampler bent,
Braided one text.   Ever the sorrowful chance
Ending in joy, the human craving still,
Like creeper circling up the Tree of Life,
Lifted by hand unseen, witnessed that He,
Man's Maker, is the Healer too of man,
And life His school parental.   Parables
He shewed in all things.   ' Mark,' one day he cried,
' Yon silver-breasted swan that stems the lake
Taking nor chill nor moisture !   Such the soul
That floats o'er waters of a world corrupt,
Itself immaculate still.'

Better than tale
They loved their minstrel's harp.   The songs he sang
Were songs to brighten gentle hearts ; to fire
Strong hearts with holier courage ; hope to breathe
Through spirits despondent, o'er the childless floor
Or widowed bed, flashing from highest heaven
A beam half faith, half vision.   Many a tear,
His own, and tears of those that listened, fell
Oft as he sang that hand, lovely as light,
Forth stretched, and gathering from forbidden boughs
That fruit fatal to man.   He sang the Flood,
Sin's doom that quelled the impure, yet raised to height
Else inaccessible, the just.   He sang
That patriarch facing at divine command
The illimitable waste—then, harder proof,
Lifting his knife o'er him, the seed foretold :
He sang of Israel loosed, the ten black seals
Down pressed on Egypt's testament of woe,
Covenant of pride with penance ; sang the face
Of Moses glittering from red Sinai's rocks,
The Tables twain, and Mandements of God.
On Christian nights he sang that jubilant star
Which led the Magians to the Bethlehem crib
By Joseph watched, and Mary.   Pale, in Lent,
Tremulous and pale, he told of Calvary,
Nor added word, but, as in trance, rehearsed

That Passion fourfold of the Evangelists,
Which, terrible and swift—not like a tale—
With speed of things which must be done, not said,
A river of bale, from guilty age to age
Along the astonied shores of common life
Annual makes way, the history of the world,
Not of one day, one People.   To its fount
That stream he tracked, that primal mystery sang
Which, chanted later by a thousand years,
Music celestial, though with note that jarred,
Some wandering orb troubling its starry chime,
Amazed the nations, ' There was war in heaven :
Michael and they, his angels, warfare waged
With Satan and his angels.'   Brief that war,
That ruin total.   Brief was Ceadmon's song :
Therein the Eternal Face was undivulged :
Therein the Apostate's form no grandeur wore :
The grandeur was elsewhere.   Who hate their God
Change not alone to vanquished but to vile.
On Easter morns he sang the Saviour Risen,
Eden Regained.   Since then on England's shores
Though many sang, yet no man sang like him.

O holy House of Whitby ! on thy steep
Rejoice, howe'er the tempest, night or day,
Afflict thee, or the hand of Time to earth

Drag down thine airy arches long suspense ;
Rejoice, for Ceadmon in thy cloisters knelt,
And singing paced beside thy sounding sea !
Long years he lived ; and with the whitening hair
 More youthful grew in spirit, and more meek ;
Yea, those that saw him said he sang within
Then when the golden mouth but seldom breathed
Sonorous strain, and when—that fulgent eye
No longer bright—still on his forehead shone
Not flame but purer light, like that last beam
Which, when the sunset woods no longer burn,
Maintains high place on Alpine throne remote,
Or utmost beak of promontoried cloud,
And heavenward dies in smiles.   Esteem of men
Daily he less esteemed, through single heart
More knit with God.   To please a sickly child
He sang his latest song, and, ending, said,
'Song is but body, though 'tis body winged :
The soul of song is love : the body dead,
The soul should thrive the more.'   That Patmian Sage
Whose head had lain upon the Saviour's breast,
Who in high vision saw the First and Last,
Who heard the harpings of the Elders crowned,
Who o'er the ruins of the Imperial House
And ashes of the twelve great Cæsars dead
Witnessed the endless triumph of the Just,

To humbler life restored, and, weak through age,
But seldom spake, and gave but one command,
The great ' *Mandatum Novum* ' of his Lord,
' My children, love each other ! '   Like to his
Was Ceadmon's age.   Weakness with happy stealth
Increased upon him : he was cheerful still :
He still could pace, though slowly, in the sun,
Still gladsomely converse with friends who wept,
Still lay a broad hand on his well-loved kine.

The legend of the last of Ceadmon's days :—
That hospital wherein the old monks died
Stood but a stone's throw from the monastery :
' Make there my couch to-night,' he said, and smiled :
They marvelled, yet obeyed.   There, hour by hour,
The man, low-seated on his pallet-bed,
In silence watched the courses of the stars,
Or casual spake at times of common things,
And three times played with childhood's days, and twice
His father named.   At last, like one that, long
Compassed with good, is smit by sudden thought
Of greater good, thus spake he : ' Have ye, sons,
Here in this house the Blessed Sacrament ? '
They answered, wrathful, ' Father, thou art strong ;
Shake not thy children !   Thou hast many days ! '
' Yet bring me here the Blessed Sacrament,'

Once more he said.   The brethren issued forth
Save four that silent sat waiting the close.
Ere long in grave procession they returned,
Two deacons first, gold-vested ; after these
That priest who bare the Blessed Sacrament,
And acolytes behind him, lifting lights.
Then from his pallet Ceadmon slowly rose
And worshipped Christ, his God, and reaching forth
His right hand, cradled in his left, behold !
Therein was laid God's Mystery.   He spake :
'Stand ye in flawless charity of God
T'ward me, my sons ; or lives there in your hearts
Memory the least of wrong?'   The monks replied :
'Father, within us lives nor wrong, nor wrath,
But love, and love alone.'   And he : ' Not less
Am I in charity with you, my sons,
And all my sins of pride, and other sins,
Humbly I mourn.'   Then, bending the old head
O'er the old hand, Ceadmon received his Lord
To be his soul's viaticum, in might
Leading from life that seems to life that is ;
And long, unpropped by any, kneeling hung
And made thanksgiving prayer.   Thanksgiving made,
He sat upon his bed, and spake : ' How long
Ere yet the monks begin their matin psalms?'
'That hour is nigh,' they answered ; he replied,

' Then let us wait that hour,' and laid him down
With those kine-tending and harp-mastering hands
Crossed on his breast, and slept.

                           Meanwhile the monks,
The lights removed in reverence of his sleep,
Sat mute nor stirred such time as in the Mass
Between ' *Orate Fratres* ' glides away,
And ' *Hoc est Corpus Meum.* '   Northward far
The great deep, seldom heard so distant, roared.
Round those wild rocks half way to Bamborough
     Head ;
For now the mightiest spring-tide of the year,
Following the magic of a maiden moon,
Approached its height.   Nearer, that sea which sobbed
In many a cave by Whitby's winding coast,
Or died in peace on many a sandy bar
From river-mouth to river-mouth outspread,
They heard, and mused upon eternity
That circles human life.   Gradual arose
A softer strain and sweeter, making way
O'er that sea-murmur hoarse ; and they were ware
That in the black far-shadowing church whose bulk
Up-towered between them and the moon, the monks
Their matins had begun.   A little sigh
That moment reached them from the central gloom
Guarding the sleeper's bed ; a second sigh

Succeeded : neither seemed the sigh of pain :
And some one said, ' He wakens.' Large and bright
Over the church-roof sudden rushed the moon,
And smote the cross above that sleeper's couch,
And smote that sleeper's face. The smile thereon
Was calmer than the smile of life. Thus died
Ceadmon, the earliest bard of English song.

KING OSWY OF NORTHUMBRIA, OR
THE WIFE'S VICTORY.

Oswy, King of Bernicia, being at war with his kinsman Oswin, slays him unarmed. He refuses to repent of this sin; yet at last, subdued by the penitence, humility, and charity of Eanfleda, his wife, repents likewise, and builds a monastery over the grave of Oswin. Afterwards he becomes a great warrior and dies a saint.

YOUNG, beauteous, brave—the bravest of the brave—
Who loved not Oswin ? All that saw him loved :
Aidan loved most, monk of Iona's Isle,
Northumbria's bishop next, from Lindisfarne
Ruling in things divine. One morn it chanced
That Oswin, noting how with staff in hand
Old Aidan roamed his spiritual realm, footbare,
Wading deep stream, and piercing thorny brake,
Sent him a horse—his best. The Saint was pleased ;
But, onward while he rode, and, musing, smiled
To think of these his honours in old age,
A beggar claimed his alms. ' Gold have I none,'

Aïdan replied ; 'this horse be thine ! ' The King,
Hearing the tale, was grieved. 'Keep I, my lord,
No meaner horses fit for beggar's use
That thus my best should seem a thing of naught?'
The Saint made answer : 'Beggar's use, my King !
What was that horse ? The foal of some poor mare !
The least of men—the sinner—is God's child !'
Then dropped the King on both his knees, and cried :
'Father, forgive me !' As they sat at meat
Oswin was mirthful, and at jest and tale
His hungry thanes laughed loud. But great, slow
    tears
In silence trickled down old Aidan's face :
These all men marked ; yet no man question made.
At last to one beside him Aidan spake
In Irish tongue, unknown to all save them,
'God will not leave such meekness long on earth.'

Who loved not Oswin ? Not alone his realm,
Dëira, loved him, but Bernician lords
Whose monarch, Oswy, was a man of storms,
Fierce King albeit in youth baptized to Christ ;
At heart half pagan. Swift as northern cloud
Through summer skies, he swept with all his host
Down on the rival kingdom. Face to face
The armies stood. But Oswin, when he marked

His own a little flock 'mid countless wolves,
Addressed them thus : ' Why perish, friends, for me ?
From exile came I : for my people's sake
To exile I return, or gladlier die :
Depart in peace.'   He rode to Gilling Tower ;
And waited there his fate.   Thither next day
King Oswy marched, and slew him.

                                Twelve days passed ;
Then Aidan, while through green Northumbria's woods.
Pensive he paced, steadying his doubtful steps,
Felt death approaching.   Giving thanks to God,
The old man laid him by a church half raised
Amid great oaks and yews, and, leaning there
His head against the buttress, passed to God.
They made their bishop's grave at Lindisfarne ;
But Oswin rested at the mouth of Tyne
Within a wave-girt, granite promontory
Where sea and river meet.   For many an age
The pilgrim from far countries came in faith
To that still shrine—they called it ' Oswin's Peace,'—
Thither the outcast fled for sanctuary :
The sick man there found health.   Thus Oswin lived,
Though dead, a benediction in the land.

    What gentlest form kneels on the rain-washed
        ground

From Gilling's keep a stone's-throw? Whose those hands
Now pressed in anguish on a bursting heart,
Now o'er a tearful countenance spread in shame?
What purest mouth, but roseless for great woe,
With zeal to youthful lovers never known
Presses a new-made grave, and through the blades
Of grass wind-shaken breathes her piteous prayer?
Save from remorse came ever grief like hers?
Yet how could ever sin, or sin's remorse,
Find such fair mansion? Oswin's grave it is;
And she that o'er it kneels is Eanfleda,
Kinswoman of the noble dead, and wife
To Oswin's murderer—Oswy.

                  Saddest one
And sweetest! Lo, that cloud which overhung
Her cradle swathes once more in deeper gloom
Her throne late won, and new-decked bridal bed.
This was King Edwin's babe, whose natal star
Shone on her father's pathway doubtful long,
Shone there a line of light, from pagan snares
Leading to Christian baptism. Penda heard—
Penda, that drew his stock from Odin's loins,
Penda, that drank his wine from skulls of foes,
Penda, fierce Mercia's king. He heard, and fell
In ruin on the region. Edwin dead,

Paulinus led the widow and her babe
Back to that Kentish shore whereon had reigned
Its grandsire Ethelbert.

　　　　　　The infant's feet
Pattered above the pavement of that church
In Canterbury by Augustine raised ;
The child grew paler when Gregorian chants
Shook the dim roofs.　Gladly the growing girl
Hearkened to stories of her ancestress
Clotilda, boast of France, but weeping turned
From legends whispered by her Saxon nurse
Of Loke, the Spirit accursèd that slanders gods,
And Sinna, Queen of Hell.　The years went by ;
The last had brought King Oswy's embassage
With suit obsequious, ' Let the princess share
With me her father's crown.'　To simple hearts
Changes come gently.　Soon, all trust, she stood
Before God's altar with her destined lord :
Adown her finger while the bride-ring ran
So slid into her heart a true wife's love :
Rooted in faith, it ripened day by day—
And now the end was this !

　　　　　　There as she knelt
A strong foot clanged behind her.　' Weeping still !
Up, wife of mine !　If Oswin had not died
His gracious ways had filched from me my realm,

The base so loved his meekness !'   Turning not
She answered low : 'He died an unarmed man :'
And Oswy : 'Fool that fought not when he might ;
At least his slaughtered troop had decked his grave !
I scorned him for his grief that men should die ;
And, scorning him, I hated ; yea, for that
His blood is on my sword !'
                              The priests of God
Had faced the monarch and denounced his crime :
They might as well have preached to ocean waves :
He felt no anger : he but deemed them mad,
And smiling went his way.   Thus autumn passed :
The queen—he knew it—when alone wept on :
Near him the pale face smiled ; the voice was sweet ;
Loving the service ; the obedience full :
Neither by words, by silence, nor by looks
She chid him.   Like some penitent she walked
That mourns her own great sin.
                                    Yet Oswy's heart,
Remorseless thus, had moods of passionate love :
A warrior of his host, Tosti by name,
Lay low, plague-stricken : kith and kin had fled :
Whole days the king sustained upon his knees
The sufferer's head, and cheered his heart with songs
Of Odin, strangely blent with Christian hymns,
While ofttimes stormy bursts of tears descended

Upon that face upturned.   Ministering he sat
Till death the vigil closed.

>   One winter night
From distant chase belated he returned,
And passed by Oswin's grave.   The snow, new-fallen,
Whitened the precinct.   In the blast she knelt,
While coldly glared the broad and bitter moon
Upon those flying flakes that on her hair
Settled, or on her thin, light raiment clung.
She heard him not draw nigh.   She only beat
Her breast, and, praying, wept : 'Our sin, our sin !'
There as the monarch stood a change came o'er him :
Old, exiled days in Alba as a dream
Redawned upon his spirit, and that look
In Aidan's eyes when, binding first that cross
Long by his pupil craved, around his neck,
He whispered: 'He who serveth Christ, his Lord,
Must love his fellow-man.'   As when a stream,
The ice dissolved, grows audible once more,
So came to him those words.   They dragged him down :
He knelt beside his wife, and beat his breast,
And said, 'My sin, my sin !'   Till earliest morn
Glimmered through sleet that twain wept on, prayed
    on :—
Was it the rising sun that lit at last
The fair face upward lifted ;—kindled there

A lovelier dawn than o'er it blushed when first
Dropped on her bridegroom's breast?   Aloud she cried :
' Our prayer is heard : our penitence finds grace : '
Then added: ' Let it deepen till we die !
A monastery build we on this grave :.
So from this grave,.while fleet the years, that prayer
Shall rise both day and night, till Christ returns
To judge the world—a prayer for him who died ;
A prayer for one who sinned, but sins no more.'

  Where Gilling's long and lofty hill o'erlooks
For leagues the forest-girdled plain, ere long
A monastery stood.   That self-same day
In tears the penitential work began ;
In tears the sod was turned.   The rugged brows
Of March relaxed 'neath April's flying kiss :
Again the violet rose, the thrush was loud ;
Mayday had come.   Around that hallowed spot
Full many a warrior met ; some Christians vowed ;
Some muttering low of Odin.   Near to these
Stood one of lesser stature, keener eye,
More fiery gesture.   Splenetic, he marked,
Christian albeit himself, those Christian walls
By Saxon converts raised:—he was a Briton.
Invisibly that morn a dusky crape
O'erstretched the sky ; and slowly swayed the bough

Heavy with midnight rains.   Through mist the woods
Let out the witchery of their young fresh green
Backed by the dusk of ruddy oaks that still
Reserved at heart the old year's stubbornness,
Yet blent it with that purple distance glimpsed
Beyond the forest alleys.

                    In a tent
Finan sang Mass : his altar was that stone
Which told where Oswin died.   Before it knelt
The king, the queen : alone their angels know
Their thoughts that hour !   The sacred rite complete,
They raised their brows, and, hand-in-hand, made way
To where, beyond the portal, shone blue skies,
Nature's long-struggling smile at last divulged.
The throng—with passion it had prayed for each—
Divided as they passed.   In either face
They saw the light of that conceded prayer,
The peace of souls forgiven.

                        From that day forth
Hourly in Oswy's spirit soared more high
The one true greatness.   Flaming heats of soul,
Through faith subjected to a law divine,
Like fire, man's vassal, mastering iron ore,
Learned their true work.   The immeasurable strength
Had found at once its master and its end,
And, balanced thus while weighted, soared to God.

In all his ways he prospered, work and word
Yoked to one end.   Till then the Kingdoms Seven,
Opposed in interests as diverse in name,
Had looked on nothing like him.   Now, despite
Mercia that frowned, they named him king of kings,
Bretwalda ; and the standard of the Seven
In peace foreran his feet.   The Spirits of might
Before his vanguard winged their way in war,
Scattering the foe ; and in his peacefuller years
Upon the aerial hillside high and higher
The golden harvest clomb, waving delight
On eyes upraised from winding rivers clear
That shone with milky sails.   His feet stood firm,
For with his growing greatness ever grew
His penitence.   Still sang the cloistered choir,
Year after year pleading o'er Oswin's tomb,
' To him who perished grant thy Vision, Lord ;
To him the slayer, penitence and peace;
Let Oswin pray for Oswy : ' Oswin prayed.

    What answered Penda when the tidings came
Of Oswy glorying in the yoke of Christ,
Of Oswy's victories next?   Grinding his teeth,
He spake what no man heard.   Then rumour rose
Of demon-magic making Oswy's tongue
Fell as his sword.   ' Within the sorcerer's court,'

It babbled, 'stood the brave East Saxon king:
Upon his shoulder Oswy laid a hand
Accursed and whispered in his ear.   The king,
Down sank, perforce, a Christian !'   Lightning flashed
From under Penda's gray and shaggy brows ;—
'Forth to Northumbria, son,' he cried, 'and back;
And learn if this be true.'

                    That son obeyed,
Peada, to whose heart another's heart,
Alcfrid's, King Oswy's son, was knit long since
As David's unto Jonathan's.   One time
A tenderer heart had leaned, or seemed to lean,
Motioning that way, Alfleda's, Alcfrid's sister,
Younger than he six years.   'Twas so no more :
No longer on Peada's eyes her eyes
Rested well-pleased : not now the fearless hand
Tarried in his contented.   'Sir and king,'
Peada thus to Oswy spake, 'of old
Thy child—then child indeed—would mount my knee;
Now, when I seek her, like a swan she fleets
That arches back its neck 'twixt snowy wings,
And, swerving, sideway drifts.   My lord and king,
The child is maiden : give her me for wife !'
Oswy made answer : 'He that serves not Christ
Can wed no child of mine.'   Alfleda then
Dropping her broidery lifted on her sire

Gently the dewy light of childlike eyes
And spake, 'But he in time will worship Christ ! '
Then, without blush or tremor, to her work
Softly returned.   Silent her mother smiled.
That moment, warned of God, from Lindisfarne
Finan, unlooked for, entered.   Week by week
Reverend and mild he preached the Saviour-Lord:
Grave-eyed, with listening face and forehead bowed,
The prince gave ear, not like that trivial race
Who catch the sense ere spoken, smile assent,
And in a moment lose it.   On his brow
At times the apprehension dawned, at times
Faded.   Oft turned he to his Mercian lords :—
'How trow ye, friends?   He speaks of what he
      knows !
Good tidings these !   Each evening while I muse
Distinct they shine like yonder mountain range ;
Each morning, mists conceal them.'   Passed a month ;
Then suddenly, as one that wakes from dream,
Peada rose: ' Far rather would I serve
Thy Christ,' he said, ' and thus Alfleda lose,
Than win Alfleda, and reject thy Christ.'
He spake : old Finan first gave thanks to God,
Who grants the pure heart valour to believe,
Then took his hand and led him to that Cross
On Heaven-Field raised beneath the Roman Wall,

That cross King Oswald's standard in the fight,
That cross Cadwallon's sentence as he fell,
' That cross which conquered ; '—there to God baptized ;
Likewise his thanes and earls.

                         Meantime, far off
In Penda's palace-keep the revel raged,
High feast of rites impure.   At banquet sat
The monarch and his chiefs ; chant followed chant
Bleeding with wars foregone.   The day went by,
And, setting ere its time, a sanguine sun
Dipped into tumult vast of gathering storm
That soon incumbent leant from tower to tower
And shook them to their base.   As high within
The gladness mounted, meeting storm with storm,
Till cried that sacrificial priest whose knife
Had pierced the warrior victim's willing throat
That morn, ' Already with the gods we feast !
Hark ! round Valhalla swell the phantom wars ! '
Ere ceased the shout applausive, from his seat
Uprose the warrior Saxo, in his hand
The goblet, in the other Alp, his sword,
Pointing to heaven.   ' To Odin health ! ' he cried ;
' Would that this hour he rode into this hall !
He should not hence depart till blood of his
Had reddened Sleipner's flank, his snow-white steed :
This sword would shed that blood ! '   Warriors sixteen

Leaped up in wrath, and for a moment rage
Rocked the huge hall.   But Saxo waved his sword,
And, laughing, shouted, 'Odin's sons, be still !
Count it no sin to battle with high gods !
Great-hearted they !   They give the blow and take !
To Odin who was ever leal as I ?'
As sudden as it rose the tumult fell :
So ceased the storm without : but with it ceased
The rapture and the madness, and the shout :
The wine-cup still made circuit ; but the song
Froze in mid-air.   Strange shadow hung o'er all :
Neighbour to neighbour whispered : courtiers slid
Through doors scarce open.   Rumour had arrived,
If true or false none knew.

       The morrow morn
From Penda's court the bravest fled in fear,
Questioning with white lips, 'Will he slay his son ?'
Or skulked at distance.   Penda by the throat
Catching a white-cheeked courtier, cried : 'The truth !
What whisper they in corners ?'   On his knees
That courtier made confession.   Penda then,
'Live, since my son is yet a living man !
A Christian, say'st thou ?   Let him serve his Christ !
That man whom ever most I scorned is he
Who vows him to the service of some god,
Yet breaks his laws ; for that man walks, a lie.

My son shall live, and after me shall reign :
Northumbria's realm shall die ! '
                                   Thus Penda spake
And sent command from tower and town to blow
Instant the trumpet of his last of wars,
Fanning from Odin's hall with airs ice-cold
Of doom the foes of Odin.   ' Man nor child,'
He sware, ' henceforth shall tread Northumbrian soil,
Nor hart nor hind : I spare the creeping worm :
My scavenger is he.'   The Mercian realm
Rose at his call, innumerable mass
Of warriors iron-armed.   East Anglia sent
Her hosts in aid.   Apostate Ethelwald,
Though Oswy's nephew, joined the hostile league,
And thirty chiefs beside that ruled by right
Princedom or province.   Mightier far than these
Old Cambria, brooding o'er the ancestral wrong,
The Saxon's sin original, met his call,
And vowed her to the vengeance.
                                   Bravest hearts
Hate most the needless slaughter.   Oswy mused :
' Long since too much of blood is on this hand :
Shall I for pride or passion risk once more
Northumbria, my mother ;—rudely stain
Her pretty babes with blood?'   To Penda then,
Camped on the confines of the adverse realms,

He sent an embassage of reverend men,
Warriors and priests.   Before them, staff in hand,
Peaceful, with hoary brows and measured tread,
Twelve heralds paced.   Twelve caskets bare they heaped
With gems and gold, and thus addressed the King :
'Lord of the Mercian realm, renowned in arms !
Our lord, Northumbria's monarch, bids thee hail :
He never yet in little thing or great
Hath wronged thy kingdom ; yet thy peace he woos :
Accept the gifts he sends thee, and, thus crowned,
Depart content.'   Penda with backward hand
Waved them far from him, and vouchsafed no word.
In sadness they returned : but Oswy smiled
Hearing their tale, and said : ' My part is done :
Let God decide the event.'   He spake, and took
The caskets twelve, and placed them, side by side,
Before the altar of his chiefest church,
And vowed to raise to God twelve monasteries,
In honour of our Lord's Apostles Twelve,
On greenest upland, or in sylvan glade
Where purest stream kisses the richest mead.
His vow recorded, sudden through the church
Ran with fleet foot a lady mazed with joy,
Crying, 'A maiden babe ! and lo, the queen
Late dying lives and thrives ! '   That eve the king
Bestowed on God the new-born maiden babe,

Laying her cradled 'mid those caskets twelve,
Six at each side ; and said : ' For her nor throne
Nor marriage bower !   She in some holy house
Shall dwell the Bride of Christ.   But thou, just God,
This day avenge my people ! '

                           Windwaed field
Heard, distant still, that multitudinous foe
Trampling the darksome ways.   With pallid face
Morning beheld their standards, raven-black—
Penda had thus decreed, before him sending
Northumbria's sentence.   On a hill, thick-set
Stood Oswy's army, small, yet strong in faith,
A wedge-like phalanx, fenced by rocks and woods ;
A river in its front.   His standards white
Sustained the Mother-Maid and Babe Divine :
From many a crag his altars rose, choir-girt,
And crowned by incense wreath.

                         An hour ere noon,
That river passed, in thunder met the hosts ;
But Penda, straitened by that hilly tract,
Could wield not half his force.   Sequent as waves
On rushed they : Oswy's phalanx like a cliff
Successively down dashed them.   Day went by :
At last the clouds dispersed : the westering sun
Glared on the spent eyes of those Mercian ranks
Which in their blindness each the other smote,

Or, trapped by hidden pitfalls, fell on stakes,
And died blaspheming. Little help that day
Gat they from Cambria. She on Heaven-Field height
Had felt her death-wound, slow albeit to die.
The apostate Ethelwald in panic fled :
The East Anglians followed. Swollen by recent rains,
And choked with dead, the river burst its bound,
And raced along the devastated plain
Till cry of drowning horse and shriek of man
Rang far and farther o'er that sea of death,
A battle-field but late. This way and that
Briton or Mercian where he might escaped
'Through flood or forest. Penda scorned to fly :
Thrice with extended arms he met and cursed
The fugitives on rushing. As they passed
He flung his crownèd helm into the wave,
And bit his brazen shield, above its rim
Levelling a look that smote with chill like death
Their hearts that saw it. Yet one moment more
He sat like statue on some sculptured horse
With upraised hand, close-clenched, denouncing Heaven :
Then burst his mighty heart. As stone he fell
Dead on the plain. Not less in after times
Mercian to Mercian said, ' Without a wound
King Penda died, although on battle-field,
Therefore with Odin Penda shares not feast.'

Thus pagan died old Penda as he lived :
Yet Penda's sons were Christian, kindlier none ;
His daughters nuns ; and lamb-like Mercia's House,
Lion one while, made end.   King Oswy raised
His monasteries twelve : benigner life
Around them spread : wild waste, and robber bands
Vanished : the poor were housed, the hungry fed :
And Oswy sent his little new-born babe
Dewed with her mother's tear-drops, Eanfleda,
Like some young lamb with fillet decked and flower,
Yet dedicated not to death, but life,
To Hilda sent on Whitby's sea-washed hill,
Who made her Bride of Christ.   The years went by,
And Oswy, now an old king, glory-crowned,
His country from the Mercian thraldom loosed
And free from north to south, in heart resolved
A pilgrim, Romeward faring with bare feet,
To make his rest by Peter's tomb and Paul's.
God willed not thus : within his native realm
The sickness unto death clasped him with hold
Gentle but firm.   Long sleepless, t'ward the close
Amid his wanderings smiling, from the couch
He stretched a shrivelled hand, and pointing said,
' Who was it fabled she had died in age ?
In all her youthful beauty holy and pure,
Lo, where she kneels upon the wintry ground,

The snow-flakes circling round her, yet with face
Bright as a star !' so spake the king, and taking
Into his heart that vision, slept in peace.
His daughter, abbess then on Whitby's height,
Within her church interred her father's bones
Beside her grandsire's, Edwin.   Side by side
They rested, one Bernicia's king, and one
Dëira's—great Northumbria's sister realms ;
Long foes, yet blended by that mingling dust.

THE VENGEANCE OF THE MONKS OF
BARDENEY.

Osthryda, Queen of Mercia, translates the relics of her uncle, Oswald of Northumberland, to the Abbey of Bardeney. The monks refuse them admittance because King Oswald had conquered and kept for one year Lindsay, a province of Mercia. Though hourly expecting the destruction of their Abbey, they will yield neither to threats nor to supplications, nor even to celestial signs and wonders. At last, being convinced by the reasoning of a devout man, they repent of their anger.

SILENT, with gloomy brows in conclave sat
The monks of Bardeney, nigh the eastern sea ;—
Rumour, that still outruns the steps of ill,
Smote on their gates with news : ' Osthryda comes
To bury here her royal uncle's bones,
Northumbrian Oswald.' Oswald was a Saint ;
Had loosed from Pagan bonds that Christian land
His own by right. But Oswald had subdued
Lindsay, a Mercian province ; and the monks
Were sons of Mercia leal and true. Osthryda,

Northumbrian born, had wedded Mercia's King ;
Therefore the monks of Bardeney pondered thus :
' This Mercian Queen spurns her adopted country !
Must Mercia therefore build her conqueror's tomb ?
Though earth and hell cried " Ay," it should not be ! '
    Thus mused the brethren till the sun went down :
Then lo ! beyond a vista in the woods
Drew nigh a Bier, black-plumed, with funeral train :
Thereon the stern monks gazed, and gave command
To close the Abbey's gate.   Beside that gate
Tent-roofed that Bier remained.
                      Before them soon
Stood up the royal herald.   Thus he spake :
' Ye sacred monks of Bardeney's Abbey, hail !
Osthryda, wife of Ethelred our King,
Prays that God's peace may keep this House forever.
The Queen has hither brought, by help of God,
King Oswald's bones, and sues for them a grave
Within this hallowed precinct.'   Answer came :
' King Oswald, living, was Northumbria's King ;
King Oswald, by the pride of life seduced,
Wrested from Mercia's sceptre Lindsay's soil ;
Therefore in Lindsay's soil King Oswald, dead,
May never find repose.'
                      Before them next
Three earls advanced full-armed, and spake loud-voiced :

'Our Queen is consort of the Mercian King ;
Ye, monks, are Mercian subjects ! Sirs, beware !
Our King and Queen have loved you well till now,
And ranked your abbey highest in their realm :
But hearts ingrate can sour the mood of love ;
And Ethelred, though mild as summer skies
When mildly used, once angered '——Answer came :
' We know it, and await our doom, content :
If Mercia's King contemns his realm, more need
That Mercia's priests her confessors should die :
In Bardeney's church King Oswald ne'er shall rest :
Ye have your answer, Earls ! '

                        Through that dim hall
Ere long a gentler embassage made way,
Three priests ; arrived, they knelt, and, reverent, spake:
' Fathers and brethren, Oswald was a Saint !
He loosed his native land from pagan thrall :
Churches and convents everywhere he built :
His relics, year by year, grow glorious more
Through miracles and signs. Fathers revered,
Within this sanctuary beloved of God
Vouchsafe his dust interment ! ' They replied :
' We know that Oswald is a Saint with God :
We know he freed his realm from pagan thrall ;
We know that churches everywhere he built ;
We know that from his relics Grace proceeds

As light from sun and moon.   In heaven a crown
Rests on Saint Oswald's head : yet here on earth
King Oswald's foot profaned our Mercian bound :
Therefore in Mercian earth he finds not grave.'
    Silent those priests withdrew.   An hour well-nigh
Went by in silence.   Then with forehead crowned
And mourner's veil, and step of one that mourns,
The Queen advanced, a lady at each side,
And 'mid the circle stood, and thus implored :
' Not as your Sovereign come I, holy Sirs,
Since all are equal in the House of God ;
Nor stand I here a stranger.   Many a day
In this your church, I knelt, while yet a child ;
Then too, as now, within my breast there lived
The tenderest of its ardours and the best,
Zeal for my kinsman's fame.   That time how oft
I heard my Father, Oswy, cry aloud,
" O Brother, had I walked but in thy ways
My foot had never erred ! "   In maiden youth
I met with one who shared my loyal zeal,
Mercian himself : 'twas thus he won my heart :
My royal husband shared it ; shares this hour
My trust that 'mid the altars reared by us
To grace this chiefest Minster of our realm
May rest the relics of our household Saint—
To spurn them from your threshold were to shame.'

She spake : benign and soft the answering voice :
' Entreat us not, thou mourner true and kind,
Lest we, by pity from the straight path drawn,
Sin more than thou.   Thou know'st what thing love is,
Thus loving one who died before thy birth !
Up to the measure of high love and fit
Thou lov'st him for this cause, because thy heart
Hath never rested on base love and bad :
Lady, a sterner severance monks have made :
Not base and bad alone do they reject,
But lesser good for better and for best :
Therefore what yet remains they love indeed :
A single earthly love is theirs unblamed,
Their Country !   Lo, the wild-bird loves her nest,
Lions their caves :—to us God gave a Country.
What heart of man but loves that mother-land
Whose omnipresent arms are round him still
In vale and plain ; whose voice in every stream ;
Whose breath his forehead cools ; whose eyes with
       joy
Regard her offspring issuing forth each morn
On duteous tasks ; to rest each eve returning ?
And who that loves her but must hate her foes ?
Lady, accept God's Will, nor strive by prayer
To change it.   In our guest-house rest this night,
Thou, and thy train.'

Severe the Queen replied :
' Yea, in thy guest-house I will lodge this night,
Unvanquished, undiscouraged, not to cease
From prayer : of that be sure.   I make henceforth
My prayer to God, not man.   To Him I pray,
That Lord of all, Who changes at His will
The stony heart to flesh.'

She spake : then turned
On those old faces, keenlier than before,
Her large slow eyes ; and instant in her face
The sadness deepened : but the wrath was gone.
That sadness said, ' Love then as deep as mine,
And grief like mine, in other breasts may spring
From source how different ! '   Long she gazed, like child
That knows not she is seen to gaze, with looks
As though she took that hoary-headed band
Into her sorrowing heart.   Silent she sighed ;
Then passed into the guest-house with her train :
There prayed all night for him, that Saint in heaven
Ill-honoured upon earth.

Within their church
Meantime the monks the ' Dies Iræ ' sang,
The yellow tapers ranged as round a corse,
And Penitential Psalms in order due.
Their rite was for the living : ere the time

They sang the obsequies of sentenced men,
Foreboding wrath to come. Sad Fancy heard
The flames up-rushing o'er their convent home,
The ruin of their church late-built, the wreck
It might be of their Order. Fierce they knew
That Mercian royal House ! Against their King
They hurled no ban : venial they deemed his crime ɩ
' He moves within the limits of his right,
Though wrongly measuring right. He sees but this,
His subjects break his laws. Some sin of youth
It may be hides from him a right more high :'—
Thus spake they in their hearts.

                         While rival thus
The brethren and the Queen sent up their prayer,
And sacred night hung midway in her course,
Behold, there fell from God tempest and storm
Buffeting that abbey's walls. The woods around,
Devastated by stress of blast on blast,
Howled like the howling of wild beasts when fire
Invests their ambush, and their cubs late-born
Blaze in red flame. Trembling, the strong-built towers
Echoed the woodland moans. All night the Queen,
Propped by those two fair Seraphs, Faith and Love,
Prayed on in hope, or hearing not that storm,
Or mindful that where danger most abounds
There God is nearest still. Meantime the Tent

'Covering that royal Bier, unshaken stood
· Beside the unyielding abbey-gates close-barred,
Like something shielded by a heavenly charm:
When morning came, shattered all round it lay
Both trunk and bough ; but in the rising sun
The storm-drop shook not on that snowy shrine.

Things wondrous more that Legend old records :
An hour past sunrise from the meads and moors
Came wide-eyed herdsmen thronging, with demand,
'What means this marvel ?   All the long still night,
While heaven and earth were dark, and peaceful sleep
Closed in her arms the wearied race of men,
Keeping our herds on meads and moorlands chill,
We saw a glittering Tent beside your gates :
Above it, and not far, a pillar stood,
All light, and high as heaven !'   The abbot answered,
'Fair Sirs, ye dreamed a dream ; and sound your sleep
Untroubled by the terror of the storm
Whereof those woodland fragments witness still,
And many a forest patriarch prostrate laid :
There rose no pillar by our gates : yon Tent
Stood there, and stood alone.'   In two hours' space
Shepherds arrived, from hills remoter sped,
Making the same demand.   With eye ill pleased
Thus answered brief the prior : 'Friends, ye jest !'

And they in wrath departed.   Once again
Came foresters from Lindsay's utmost bound,
On horses blown, and spake : 'O'er yonder Tent,
Through all the courses of the long still night,
Behold, a shining pillar hovering stood :
It rained a glory on your convent walls :
It flung a trail of splendour o'er your woods :
We watched it hour by hour.   Like Oswald's Cross
On Heaven-Field planted in the days of old,
It waxed in height :—the stars were quenched.'   Replied
With reddening brows the youngest of those monks,
'Sirs, ye have had your bribe, and told your tale :
Depart !' and they departed great in scorn.

Long time the brethren sat; discoursed long time
Each with his neighbour.   'Craft of man would force
Dishonest deed on this our holy House,
By miracles suborned;' thus spake the first :
The second answered, 'Ay, confederates they !
The good Queen knew not of it :' then the third,
'Not so! these men are simple folks, I ween :
Nor time for fraud had they.   What sail is yon
So weather-worn that nears the headland?'   Soon
A pilot stood before them; at his side
A priest, long years an inmate of their House,
But late a pilgrim in the Holy Land.

Their greetings over, greetings warm and kind,
Thus spake the Pilgrim : 'Brothers mine, rejoice ;
Our God is with us !   For our House I prayed
Three times with forehead on the Tomb of Christ ;
Last night there came to me, in visible form,
An answer to that prayer.   All day our ship,
Before a great wind rushed t'ward Mercian shores :
To them I turned not: on the East I gazed :
" O happy East," I mused, " O Land, true home
Of every Christian heart !   The Saviour's feet
Thy streets, thy cornfields trod !   With these compared
Our country's self seems nothing ! "   In my heart
Imaged successive, rose once more those sites
Capernaum, Nain, Bethsaida, Bethlehem—
Where'er my feet had strayed.   At midnight, cries
Of wonder rang around me, and I turned :
I saw once more our convent on its hill :
I saw beside its gate a Tent snow-white ;
I saw a glittering pillar o'er that Tent
'Twixt heaven and earth suspense !   Serene it shone,
Such pillar as led forth the Chosen Race
By night from Egypt's coasts.   From wave to wave
Moon-like it paved a path !   I cried, "Thank God !
For who shall stay yon splendour till it reach
That Syrian shore ?   England," I said, " my country,
Shall lay, upon Christ's Tomb a hand all light,

Whatever tempest shakes the world of men,
Thenceforth His servant vowed ! " '
                              When ceased that voice
There fell upon the monks a crisis strange ;
And where that Pilgrim looked for joy, behold,
Doubt, wrath, and anguish !   Faces old long since
Grew older, stricken as by hectic spasm,
So fierce a pang had clutched them by the throat ;
While drops of sweat on many a wrinkled brow
Hung large like dewy beads condensed from mist
On cliffs by torrents shaken.   Mute they sat ;
Then sudden rose, uplifting helpless hands,
As when from distant rock sore-wounded men,
Who all day long have watched some dreadful fight,
Behold it lost, or else foresee it lost,
And with it lost their country's hearths and homes,
And yet can bring no succour.   Thus with them—
They knew themselves defeated ; deemed the stars
Of heaven had fought against them in their course ;
Yet still believed, and could not but believe
Their cause the cause of Justice, and its wreck
The wreck of priestly honour, patriot faith :
At last the youngest of the brethren spake :
'Come what come may, God's monks must guard the
          Right.'
     Death-like a silence on that conclave fell —

Then rose a monk white-headed, well-nigh blind,
Esteemed a Saint, who had not uttered speech
Since came the tidings of the Queen's resolve :
Low-voiced he spake, with eyes upon the ground
And inward smile that dimly reached his lips :
' Brethren, be wary lest ye strive with God
Through wrath, that blind incontinence of age,
For what He wills He works.   By passion warped
Ye deem this trial strange, this conflict new,
Yourselves doomed men that stand between two Fates,
On one side right, on one side miracles !
Brethren, the chief of miracles is this,
That knowing what ye know ye know no more :
Ye know long since that Oswald is a Saint :
Ye know the sins of Saints are sins forgiven :
What then ?   Shall man revenge where God forgives ?
Be wroth with those He loves ?   Ye, seeing much,
See not the sun at noontide ! God last night
Sent you in love a miracle of love
To quell in you a miracle of wrath :—
Discern its import true !

                   Sum up the past !
Thus much is sure : we heard those thunder peals
Unheard by hind or shepherd, near or far :
'Tis sure not less that light the shepherds saw
We saw not ; neither we nor yet the Queen

What then ?   Is God not potent to divulge
The thing He wills, or hide it ?   Brethren, God
Shrouding from us that beam far dwellers saw
Admonished us perchance that far is near ;
That ofttimes distance makes intelligible
What, nigh at hand, is veiled.   This too He taught,
That when Northumbrian foot our Mercia spurned
The men who saw that ruin saw not all :
The light of Christ drew near us in that hour ;
His pillar o'er us stood, and in our midst :
The pang, the shame, were transient.   See the whole ! '
        The old man paused a space, and then resumed :
' Brethren, that day our country suffered wrong :
One day she may inflict it.   Years may bring
The aggressor of past time a penitent grief ;
The wronged may meet her penitence with scorn
Guiltier through malice than her foe's worst rage :
Were it not well to leave that time unborn
Magnanimous ensample ?   Hard it were
To lay in Mercian earth the unforgiven :
Wholly to pardon—that I deem not hard.
My voice is this : forgive we Oswald's sin,
And lay his relics in our costliest shrine ! '
        Thus spake the aged man.   That self-same eve,
The western sun descending, while the church,
Grey shaft transfigured by the glow divine,

Grey wall in flame of light pacific washed,
Shone out all golden like that flower all gold
Which shoots through sunset airs an arrowy beam,
In charity perfected moved the monks,
No longer sad, a long procession forth,
With foreheads smoothed as by the kiss of death
And eyes like eyes of Saints from death new risen,
Bearing the relics of Northumbria's King,
Oswald, the man of God.   Behind them paced
Warriors and chiefs ; Osthryda last, the Queen,
With face whereon that great miraculous light,
By her all night unseen, appeared to rest,
And foot that might have trod the ocean waves
Unwetted save its palm.   A shrine gem-wrought
Received the royal relics.   O'er them drooped
Northumbria's standard, guest of Mercian airs
Through which it once had sailed, a portent dire :
And whosoe'er in after centuries knelt
On Oswald's grave, and, praying, wooed his prayer,
Departed, in his heart the peace of God,
Passions corrupt expelled, and demon snares,
Irreverent love, and anger past its bound.

HOW SAINT CUTHBERT KEPT HIS
PENTECOST AT CARLISLE.

Saint Cuthbert while a boy wanders among the woods of Northumbria, bringing solace to all. Later he lives alone in the island
of Farne. Being made bishop, many predict that he will be able
neither to teach his people nor to rule his diocese. His people flock
to him gladly, but require that he should teach them by parable and
tale. This he does, and likewise rules his diocese with might. He
discourses concerning common life. Keeping his Pentecost at
Carlisle, he preaches on that Feast and the Resurrection from the
Dead. Herbert, an eremite, beseeching him that the two may die
the same day, he prays accordingly, and they die the same hour.

SAINT CUTHBERT, yet a youth, for many a year
Walked up and down the green Northumbrian vales
Well loving God and man. The rockiest glens
And promontories shadowing loneliest seas,
Where lived the men least cared for, most forlorn,
He sought, and brought to each the words of peace.
Where'er he went he preached that God all Love ;

For, as the sun in heaven, so flamed in him
That love which later fired Assisi's Saint :
Yea, rumour ran that every mountain beast
Obeyed his loving call; that when all night
He knelt upon the frosty hills in prayer,
The hare would couch her by his naked feet
And warm them with her fur.   To manhood grown,
He dwelt in Lindisfarne; there, year by year,
Prospering yet more in vigil and in fast ;
And paced its shores by night, and blent his hymns
With din of waves.   Yet ofttimes o'er the strait
He passed, once more in search of suffering men,
Wafting them solace still.   Where'er he went,
Those loved as children first, again he loved
As youth and maid, and in them nursed that Faith
Through which pure youth passes o'er passion's waves,
Like Him Who trod that Galilean sea :
He clasped the grey-grown sinner in his arms,
And won from him repentance long delayed,
Then with him shared the penance he enjoined.
O heart both strong and tender ! offering Mass,
Awe-struck he stood as though on Calvary's height :
The men who marked him shook.

                            Twelve winters passed :
Then mandate fell upon the Saint from God,
Or breathed upon him from the heavenly height,

Or haply from within.   It drave him forth
A hermit into solitudes more stern.
' Farewell,' he said, ' my brethren and my friends !
No holier life than yours, pure Cœnobites
Pacing one cloister, sharing one spare meal,
Chanting to God one hymn ! yet I must forth—
Farewell, my friends, farewell ! '   On him they gazed,
And knew that God had spoken to his soul,
And silent stood, though sorrowing.

                                        Long that eve,
The brethren grieved, noting his vacant stall,
Yet thus excused their sadness : ' Well for him,
And high his place in heaven ; but woe to those
Henceforth of services like his amerced !
Here lived he in the world ; here many throng ;—
To him in time some lesser bishopric
Might well have fallen, behoof of countless souls !
Such dream is past forever ! '

                                        Forth he fared
To Farne, a little rocky islet nigh,
Where man till then had never dared to dwell,
By dreadful rumours scared.   In narrow cave
Worn from the rock, and roughly walled around,
The anchoret made abode, with lonely hands
Raising from one poor strip his daily food,
Barley thin-grown, and coarse.   He saw by day

The clouds on-sailing, and by night the stars ;
And heard the eternal waters. Thus recluse
The man lived on in vision still of God
Through contemplation known : and as the shades
Each other chase all day o'er steadfast hills,
Even so, athwart that Vision unremoved,
Forever rushed the tumults of this world,
Man's fleeting life, the rise and fall of states,
While changeless measured change ; the spirit of prayer
Fanning that wondrous picture oft to flame
Until the glory grew insufferable.
Long years thus lived he. As the Apostle Paul,
Though raised in raptures to the heaven of heavens,
Not therefore loved his brethren less, but longed
To give his life—his all—for Israel's sake,
So Cuthbert, loving God, loved man the more,
His wont of old. To him the mourners came,
And sinners bound by Satan. At his touch
Their chains fell from them light as summer dust :
Each word he spake was as a Sacrament
Clothed with God's grace ; beside his feet they sat,
And in their perfect mind ; thence through the world
Bare their deliverer's name.

                        So passed his life :
There old he grew, and older yet appeared,
By fasts outworn, though ever young at heart ;

When lo ! before that isle a barge there drew
Bearing the royal banner.   Egfrid there
With regal sceptre sat, and many an earl,
And many a mitred bishop at his side.
Northumbria's see was void : a council's voice
Joined with a monarch's called him to its throne :
In vain he wept, and knelt, and sued for grace :
Six months' reprieve alone he won ; then ruled
In Lindisfarne, chief Bishop of the North.
    But certain spake who deemed that they were wise,
Fools all beside : ' Shall Cuthbert crosier lift ?
A child, 'tis known he herded flocks for hire,
Housed in old Renspid's hut, his Irish nurse,
Who told him tales of Leinster Kings, his sires,
And how her hands, their palace wrecked in war,
Had snatched him from its embers.   Yet a boy
He rode to Melrose and its wondering monks,
A mimic warrior, in his hand a lance,
With shepherd youth for page, and spake: " 'Tis
    known
Christ's kingdom is a kingdom militant :
A son of Kings I come to guard His right
And battle 'gainst his foes ! "   For lance and sword
A book they gave him ; and they made him monk :
Savage since then he couches on a rock,
As fame reports, with birds' nests in his beard !

Can dreamers change to Bishops?   Vision-dazed,
Move where he may, that slowly wandering eye
Will see in man no more than kites or hawks ;
Men, if they note, will flee him.'   Thus they buzzed,
Self-praised, and knowing not that simpleness
Is sacred soil, and sown with royal seed,
The heroic seed and saintly.

                              Mitred once
Such gibes no more assailed him : one short month
Sufficed the petty cavil to confute ;
One month well chronicled in book which verse
Late born, alas, in vain would emulate.
At once he called to mind the days that were ;
His wanderings in Northumbrian glens ; the hearths
That welcomed him so joyously ; at once
Within his breast the heart parental yearned ;
He longed to see his children, scattered wide
From Humber's bank to Tweed, from sea to sea,
And cried to those around him : ' Let us forth,
And visit all my charge ; and since Carlisle
Remotest sits upon its western bound,
Keep there this year our Pentecost !'   Next day
He passed the sands, left hard by ebbing tide,
His cross-bearer and brethren six in front,
And trod the mainland.   Reverent, first he sought
His childhood's nurse, and 'neath her humble roof

Abode one night.   To Melrose next he fared
Honouring his master old.

                    Southward once more
Returning, scarce a bow-shot from the woods
There rode to him a mighty thane, one-eyed,
With warriors circled, on a jet-black horse,
Barbaric shape and huge, yet frank as fierce,
Who thus made boast : ' A Jute devout am I !
What raised that convent-pile on yonder rock ?
This hand !   I wrenched the hillside from a foe
By force, and gave it to thy Christian monks
To spite yet more those Angles !   Island Saint,
Unprofitable have I found thy Faith !
Behold, those priests, thy thralls, are savage men,
Unrighteous, ruthless !   For a sin of mine
They laid on me a hundred days of fast !
A man am I keen-witted : friend and liege
I summoned, shewed my wrong, and ended thus :
"Sirs, ye are ninety-nine, the hundredth I ;
I counsel that we share this fast among us !
To-morrow from the dawn to evening's star
No food as bulky as a spider's tongue
Shall pass our lips ; and thus in one day's time
My hundred days of fast shall stand fulfilled."
Wrathful they rose, and sware by Peter's keys
That fight they would, albeit 'gainst Peter's self ;

But fast they would not save for personal sins.
Signal I made: then backward rolled the gates,
And, captured thus, they fasted without thanks,
Cancelling my debt—a hundred days in one !
Beseech you, Father, chide your priests who breed
Contention thus 'mid friends !' The Saint replied,
' Penance is irksome, Thane: to 'scape its scourge
Ways are there various ; and the easiest this,
Keep far from mortal sin.'
                              Where'er he faced,
The people round him pressed—the sick, the blind,
Young mothers sad because a babe was pale ;
Likewise the wives of fishers, praying loud
Their husbands' safe return. Rejoiced he was
To see them, hear them, touch them ; wearied never :
Whate'er they said delighted still he heard :
The rise and fall of empires touched him less,
The book rich-blazoned, or the high-towered church :
' We have,' he said, ' God's children, and their God :
The rest is fancy's work.' Him too they loved ;
Loved him the more because, so great and wise,
He stumbled oft in trifles. Once he said,
' How well those pine-trees shield the lamb from wind !'
A smile ran round ; at last the boldest spake,
'Father, these are not pine-trees—these are oaks.'
And Cuthbert answered, ' Oaks, good sooth, they are !

In youth I knew the twain apart : the pine
Wears on his head the Cross.'   Instruction next
He gave them, how the Cross had vanquished sin :
Then first abstruse to some appeared his words.
'Father,' they answered, 'speak in parables !
For pleasant is the tale, and, onward passed,
Keeps in our hearts thy lesson.'

                    While they spake,
A youth rich-vested tossed his head and cried :
'Father, why thus converse with untaught hinds ?
Their life is but the life of gnats and flies :
They think but of the hour.   Behold yon church !
I reared it both for reverence of thy Christ,
And likewise that through ages yet to come
My name might live in honour !'   At that word
Cuthbert made answer : 'Hear the parable !
My people craved for such.

                    A monk there lived
Holiest of men reputed.   He was first
On winter mornings in the freezing stall ;
Meekest when chidden ; fervent most in prayer :
And, late in life, when heresies arose,
That book he wrote, like tempest winged from God,
Drave them to darkness back.   Grey-haired he died ;
With honour was interred.   The years went by ;
His grave they opened.   Peacefully he slept,

Unchanged, the smile of death upon his lips :
O'er the right hand alone, for so it seemed,
Had Death retained his power : five little lines,
White ashes, showed where once the fingers lay.
All saw it—simple, learned, rich and poor :
None might divine the cause.   That night, behold !
A Saintly Shape beside the abbot stood,
Bright like the sun except one lifted palm—
Thereon there lay a stain.   ' Behold that hand ! '
The Spirit spake, ' that, toiling twenty years,
Sent forth that book which pacified the world ;
For it the world would canonise me Saint !
See that ye do it not !   Inferior tasks
I wrought for God alone.   Building that book
Too oft I mused, " Far years will give thee praise."
I expiate that offence.'

Another day
A sweet-faced woman raised her voice, and cried,
' Father ! those sins denounced by God I flee ;
Yet tasks imposed by God too oft neglect :
Stands thus a soul imperilled ? '   Cuthbert spake :
' Ye sued for parables ; I speak in such,
Though ill, a language strange to me, and new.
There lived a man who shunned committed sin,
Yet daily by omission sinned and knew it :
In his own way, not God's, he served his God ;

And there was with him peace ; yet not God's peace.
So passed his youth.   In age he dreamed a dream :
He dreamed that, being dead, he raised his eyes,
And saw a mountain range of frozen snows,
And heard, " Committed sins innumerable
Though each one small—so small thou knew'st them
    not—
Uplifted, flake by flake as sin by sin,
Yon barrier 'twixt thy God and thee !   Arise,
Remembering that of sins despair is worst :
Be strong, and scale it ! "   Fifty years he scaled
Those hills ; so long it seemed.   A cavern next
Entering, with mole-like hands he scooped his way,
And reached at last the gates of morn.   Ah me !
A stone's cast from him rose the Tree of Life :
He heard its sighs ecstatic :   Full in view
The Beatific River rolled ; beyond
All-glorious shone the City of the Saints
Clothed with God's light !   And yet from him that realm
Was severed by a gulf !   Not wide that strait ;
It seemed a strong man's leap twice told—no more ;
But, as insuperably soared that cliff,
Unfathomably thus its sheer descent
Walled the abyss.   Again he heard that Voice :
" Henceforth no place remains for active toils,
Penance for acts perverse.   Inactive sloth

Through passive suffering meets its due.   On earth
That sloth a nothing seemed ; a nothing now
That chasm whose hollow bars thee from the Blest,
Poor slender film of insubstantial air.
Self-help is here denied thee ; for that cause
A twofold term thou need'st of pain love-taught
To expiate Love that lacked."   That term complete
An angel caught him o'er that severing gulf :—
Thenceforth he saw his God.'

                             With such discourse
Progress, though slow and interrupted oft,
The Saint of God, by no delay perturbed,
Made daily through his sacred charge.   One eve
He walked by pastures arched along the sea,
With many companied.   The on-flowing breeze
Glazed the green hill-tops, bending still one way
The glossy grasses : limitless below
The ocean mirror, clipped by cape or point
With low trees inland leaning, lay like lakes
Flooding rich lowlands.   Southward far, a rock
Touched by a rainy beam, emerged from mist,
And shone, half green, half gold.   That rock was Farne :
Though strangers, those that kenned it guessed its name :
' Doubtless 'twas there,' they said, ' our Saint abode !'
Then pressed around him, questioning : ' Rumour goes,
Father beloved, that in thine island home

Thou sat'st all day with hammer small in hand,
Shaping, from pebbles veined, miraculous beads
That save their wearers still from sword and lance :—
Are these things true?'　Smiling the Saint replied :
'True, and not true !　That isle in part is spread
With pebbles divers-fashioned, some like beads :
I gathered such, and gave to many a guest,
Adding, "Such beads shall count thy nightly prayers ;
Pray well ; then fear no peril ! "'

       Others came
And thus demanded : 'Rumour fills the world,
Father, that birds miraculous crowned thine isle,
And awe-struck let thee lift them in thy hand,
Though scared by all beside.'　Smiling once more
The Saint made answer, 'True, and yet not true !
Sea-birds elsewhere beheld not throng that isle ;
A breed so loving and so firm in trust
That, yet unharmed by man, they flee not man ;
Wondering they gaze ; who wills may close upon them !
I signed a league betwixt that race and man,
Pledging the mariners who sought my cell
To reverence still that trust.'　He ended thus :
'My friends, ye seek me still for parables ;
Seek them from Nature rather :—here are two !
Those pebble-beads are words from Nature's lips
Exhorting man to pray ; those fearless birds

Teach him that trust to innocence belongs
By right divine, and more avails than craft
To shield us from the aggressor.' Some were glad
Hearing that doctrine ; others cried, ' Not so !
Our Saint—all know it—makes miraculous beads ;
But, being humble, he conceals his might : '
And many an age, when slept that Saint in death,
Passing his isle by night the sailor heard
Saint Cuthbert's hammer clinking on the rock ;
And age by age men cried, ' Our Cuthbert's birds
Revere the Saint's command.'

                        While thus they spake
A horseman over moorlands near the Tweed
Made hasty way, and thus addressed the Saint :
' Father, Queen Ermenburga greets thee well,
And this her message :—" Queen am I forlorn,
Long buffeted by many a storm of state,
And worn at heart besides ; for in our house
Peace lived not inmate, but a summer guest ;
And now, my lord, the King is slain in fight ;
And changed the aspect now things wore of old ;
Thou therefore, man of God, approach my gates
With counsel sage. This further I require ;
Thy counsel must be worthy of a Queen,
Nor aught contain displeasing." ' Cuthbert spake :
' My charge requires my presence at Carlisle ;

Beseech the Queen to meet me near its wall
On this day fortnight.'

                  Thitherwards thenceforth
Swiftlier he passed, while daily from the woods
The woodmen flocked, and shepherds from the hills,
Concourse still widening. These among there moved
A hermit meek as childhood, calm as eld,
Long years Saint Cuthbert's friend. Recluse he lived
Within a woody isle of that fair lake
By Derwent lulled and Greta. Others thronged
Round Cuthbert's steps ; that hermit stood apart
With large dark eyes upon his countenance fixed,
And pale cheek dewed with tears. The name he bore
Was ' Herbert of the Lake.'

                    Two weeks went by,
And Cuthbert reached his journey's end. Next day
God sent once more His Feast of Pentecost
To gladden men ; and all His Church on earth
Shone out, irradiate as by silver gleams
Flashed from her whiter Sister in the skies ;
And every altar laughed, and every hearth ;
And many a simple hind in spirit heard
The wind which through that ' upper chamber ' swept
Careering through the universe of God,
New life through all things poured. Cuthbert that day,
Borne on by wingèd winds of rapturous thought,

Forth from Carlisle had fared alone, and reached
Ere long a mead tree-girded ;—in its midst
Swift-flowing Eden raced from fall to fall,
Showering at times her spray on flowers as fair
As graced that earlier Eden ; flowers so light
Each feeblest breath impalpable to man
Now shook them and now swayed. Delighted eye
The Saint upon them fixed. Ere long he gazed
As glad on crowds thronging the river's marge,
For now the high-walled city poured abroad
Her children rich and poor. At last he spake :
' Glory to Him Who made both flowers and souls !
He doeth all things well ! A few weeks past
Yon river rushed by wintry banks forlorn ;
What decks it thus to-day ? The voice of Spring !
She called those flowers from darkness forth : she
    flashed
Her life into the snowy breast of each :
'This day she sits enthroned on each and all :
The thrones are myriad ; but the Enthroned is One ! '
He paused ; then, kindling, added thus : ' O friends !
'Tis thus with human souls through faith re-born :
One Spirit calls them forth from darkness ; shapes ·
One Christ, in each conceived, its life of life ;
One God finds rest enthroned on all. Once more
The thrones are many ; but the Enthroned is One ! '

Again he paused, and mused : again he spake :
' Yea, and in heaven itself, a hierarchy
There is that glories in the name of " Thrones : "
The high cherubic knowledge is not theirs ;
Not theirs the fiery flight of Seraph's love,
But all their restful beings they dilate
To make a single, myriad throne for God—
Children, abide in unity and love !
So shall your lives be one long Pentecost,
Your hearts one throne for God ! '
                        As thus he spake
A breeze, wide-wandering through the woodlands near,
Illumed their golden roofs, while louder sang
The birds on every bough.   Then horns were heard
Resonant from stem to stem, from rock to rock,
While moved in sight a stately cavalcade
Flushing the river's crystal.   Of that host
Foremost and saddest Ermenburga rode,
A Queen sad-eyed, with large imperial front
By sorrow seamed : a lady rode close by ;
Behind her earls and priests.   Though proud to man
Her inborn greatness made her meek to God :
She signed the Saint to stay not his discourse,
And placed her at his feet.
                  His words were great :
He spake of Pentecost ; no transient grace,

No fugitive act, consummated, then gone,
But God's perpetual presence in that Church
O'er-shadowed still, like Mary, by His Spirit,
Fecundated in splendour by His Truth,
Made loving through His Love. The reign of Love
He showed, though perfected in Christ alone,
Not less co-eval with the race of man :
For what is man? Not mind : the beasts can think :
Not passions ; appetites : the beasts have these :
Nay, but Affections ruled by Laws Divine:
These make the life of man. Of these he spake ;
Proclaimed of these the glory. These to man
Are countless loves revealing Love Supreme :
These and the Virtues, warp and woof, enweave
A single robe—that sacrificial garb
Worn from the first by man, whose every act
Of love in spirit was self-sacrifice,
And prophesied the Sacrifice Eterne :
Through these the world becomes one household vast ;
Through these each hut swells to a universe
Traversed by stateliest energies wind-swift,
And planet-crowned, beneath their Maker's eye.
All hail, Affections, angels of the earth !
Woe to that man who boasts of love to God,
And yet his neighbour scorns ! While Cuthbert spake
A young man whispered to a priest, ' Is yon

That Anchoret of the rock? Where learned he then
This loving reverence for the hearth and home?
Mark too that glittering brow!' The priest replied:
'What! shall a bridegroom's face alone be bright?
He knows a better mystery! This he knows,
That, come what may, all o'er the earth forever
God keeps His blissful Bridal-feast with man:
Each true heart there is guest!'

                              Once more the Saint
Arose and spake: 'O loving friends, my children,
Christ's sons, His flock committed to my charge!
I spake to you but now of humbler ties,
Not highest, with intent that ye might know
How pierced are earthly bonds by heavenly beam;
Yet, speaking with lame tongue in parables,
I shewed you but similitudes of things—
Twilight, not day. Make question then who will;
So shall I mend my teaching.'

                              Prompt and bright
As children issuing forth to holyday,
Then flocked to Cuthbert's school full many a man
Successive: each with simpleness of heart
His doubt propounded; each his question asked,
Or, careless who might hear, confessed his sins,
And absolution won. Among the rest,
A little seven years' boy, with sweet, still face,

Yet strong not less, and sage, drew softly near,
His great calm eyes upon the patriarch fixed,
And silent stood.   From Wessex came that boy :
By chance Northumbria's guest.   Meantime a chief
Demanded thus : ' Of all the works of might,
What task is worthiest ? '   Cuthbert made reply :
' His who to land barbaric fearless fares,
And open flings God's palace gate to all,
And cries "Come in ! "'   That concourse thrilled for
     joy :
Alone that seven years' child retained the word :
The rest forgat it.   ' Winifrede ' that day
Men called him ; later centuries, ' Boniface,'
Because he shunned the ill, and wrought the good :
In time the Teuton warriors knew that brow—
Their great Apostle he : they knew that voice :
And happy Fulda venerates this day
Her martyr's gravestone.
                    Next, to Cuthbert drew
Three maidens hand in hand, lovely as Truth,
Trustful, though shy : their thoughts, when hidden most,
Wore but a semilucid veil, as when
Through gold-touched crystal of the lime new-leaved
On April morns the symmetry looks forth
Of branch and bough distinct.   Smiling, they put
At last their question : ' Tell us, man of God,

What life, of lives that women lead, is best ;
Then show us forth in parables that life ! '
    He answered : ' Three ; for each of these is best :
First comes the Maiden's : she who lives it well
Serves God in marble chapel white as snow,
His priestess—His alone. Cold flowers each morn
She culls ere sunrise by the stainless stream,
And lays them on that chapel's altar-stone,
And sings her matins there. Her feet are swift
All day in labours 'mid the vales below,
Cheering sad hearts : each evening she returns
To that high fane, and there her vespers sings ;
Then sleeps, and dreams of heaven.'
                            With witching smile
The youngest of that beauteous triad cried :
' That life is sweetest ! I would be that maid ! '
Cuthbert resumed : ' The Christian Wife comes next :
She drinks a deeper draught of life : round her
In ampler sweep its sympathies extend :
An infant's cry has knocked against her heart,
Evoking thence that human love wherein
Self-love hath least. Through infant eyes a spirit
Hath looked upon her, crying, " I am thine !
Creature from God—dependent yet on thee ! "
Thenceforth she knows how greatness blends with weak-
    ness ;

Reverence, thenceforth, with pity linked, reveals
To her the pathos of the life of man,
A thing divine, and yet at every pore
Bleeding from crownèd brows.   A heart thus large
Hath room for many sorrows.   What of that ?
Its sorrow is its dowry's noblest part.
She bears it not alone.   Such griefs, so shared—
Sickness, and fear, and vigils lone and long,
Waken her heart to love sublimer far
Than ecstasies of youth could comprehend ;
Lift her perchance to heights serene as those
The Ascetic treadeth.'
                              'I would be that wife !'
Thus cried the second of those maidens three :
Yet who that gazed upon her could have guessed
Creature so soft could bear a heart so brave ?
She seemed that goodness which was beauteous too ;
Virtue at once, and Virtue's bright reward ;
Delight that lifts, not lowers us ; made for heaven ;—
Made too to change to heaven some brave man's hearth.
She added thus : 'Of lives that women lead
Tell us the third !'
                              Gently the Saint replied :
'The third is Widowhood—a wintry sound ;
And yet, for her who widow is indeed,
That winter something keeps of autumn's gold,

Something regains of Spring's first flower snow-white,
Snow-cold, and colder for its rim of green.
She feels no more the warmly-greeting hand ;
The eyes she brightened rest on her no more ;
Her full-orbed being now is cleft in twain :
Her past is dead : daily from memory's self
Dear things depart ; yet still she is a wife,
A wife the more because of bridal bonds
Lives but their essence, waiting wings in heaven ;—
More wife ; and yet, in that great loneliness,
More maiden too than when first maidenhood
Lacked what it missed not.   Like that other maid
She too a lonely Priestess serves her God ;
Yea, though her chapel be a funeral vault,
Its altar black like Death ;—the flowers thereon,
Tinct with the Blood Divine.   Above that vault
She hears the anthems of the Spouse of Christ,
Widowed, like her, though Bride.'

                              'O fair, O sweet,
O beauteous lives all three ; fair lot of women ! '
Thus cried again the youngest of those Three,
Too young to know the touch of grief—or cause it—
A plant too lightly leaved to cast a shade.
The eldest with pale cheek, and lids tear-wet,
Made answer sad : ' I would not be a widow.'
    Then Cuthbert spake once more with smile benign :

'I said that each of these three lives is best :—
There are who live those three conjoined in one :
The nun thus lives ! What maid is maid like her
Who, free to choose, has vowed a maidenhood
Secure 'gainst chance or choice?   What bride like her
Whose Bridegroom is the spouse of vestal souls ?
What widow lives in such austere retreat,
Such hourly thought of him she ne'er can join
Save through the gate of death ?   If those three lives
In separation lived are fair and sweet,
How show they, blent in one ?'

                        Of those who heard
The most part gladdened ; those who knew how high
Virtue, renouncing all besides for God,
Hath leave to soar on earth.   Yet many sighed,
Jealous for happy homesteads.   Cuthbert marked
That shame-faced sadness, and continued thus :
'To praise the nun reproaches not, O friends,
But praises best that life of hearth and home
At Cana blessed by Him who shared it not.
The uncloistered life is holy too, and oft
Through changeful years in soft succession links
Those three fair types of woman ; holds, diffused,
That excellence severe which life detached
Sustains in concentration.'   Long he mused ;
Then added thus : 'When last I roved these vales

There lived, not distant far, a blessed one
Revered by all : her name was Ethelreda :
I knew her long, and much from her I learned.
Beneath her Pagan father's roof there sat
Ofttimes a Christian youth.   With him the child
Walked, calling him " her friend."   He loved the
      maid :
Still young, he drew her to the fold of Christ ;
Espoused her three years later ; died in war
Ere three months passed.   For her he never died !
Immortalised by faith that bond lived on ;
And now close by, and now 'mid Saints of heaven
She saw her husband walk.   She never wept ;
That fire which lit her eye and flushed her cheek
Dried up, it seemed, her tears : the neighbours round
Called her " the lady of the happy marriage."
She died long since, I doubt not.'   Forward stepped
A slight, pale maid, the daughter of a bard,
And answered thus : ' Two months ago she died.'
Then Cuthbert : ' Tell me, maiden, of her death ;
And see you be not chary of your words,
For well I loved that woman.'   Tears unfelt
Fast streaming down her pallid cheek, the maid
Replied—yet often paused : ' A sad, sweet end !
A long night's pain had left her living still :
I found her on the threshold of her door :—

Her cheek was white ; but, trembling round her lips,
And dimly o'er her countenance spread, there lay
Something that, held in check by feebleness,
Yet tended to a smile.   A cloak tight-drawn
From the cold March wind screened her, save one hand
Stretched on her knee, that reached to where a beam,
Thin slip of watery sunshine, sunset's last,
Slid through the branches.   On that beam, methought,
Rested her eyes half-closed.   It was not so :
For when I knelt, and kissed that hand ill-warmed,
Smiling she said : " The small, unwedded maid
Has missed her mark ! You should have kissed the
    ring !
Full forty years upon a widowed hand
It holds its own.   It takes its latest sunshine."
She lived through all that night, and died while dawned
Through snows Saint Joseph's morn.'
                         The Queen, with hand
Sudden and swift, brushed from her cheek a tear ;
And many a sob from that thick-crowding host
Confessed what tenderest love can live in hearts
Defamed by fools as barbarous.   Cuthbert sat
In silence long.   Before his eyes she passed,
The maid, the wife, the widow, all in one ;
With these,—through these—he saw once more the child,
Yea, saw the child's smile on the lips of death,

That magic, mystic smile !   O heart of man,
What strange capacities of grief and joy
Are thine ! · How vain, how ruthless such, if given
For transient things alone !   O life of man !
What wert thou but some laughing demon's scoff,
If prelude only to the eternal grave !
' Deep cries to deep '—ay, but the deepest deep
Crying to summits of the mount of God
Drags forth for echo, 'Immortality.'
It was the Death Divine that vanquished death !
Shorn of that Death Divine the Life Divine,
Albeit its feeblest tear had cleansed all worlds,
Cancelled all guilt, had failed to reach and sound
The deepest in man's nature, Love and Grief,
Profoundest each when joined in penitent woe ;
Failed thence to wake man's hope.   The loftiest light
Flashed from God's Face on Reason's orient verge
Answers that bird-cry from the *Heart* of man—
Poor Heart that, darkling, kept so long its watch—
The auspice of the dawn.

               Like one inspired
The Saint arose, and raised his hands to God ;
Then to his people turned with such discourse
As mocks the hand of scribe.   No more he spake
In parables ; adumbrated no more
' Dimly as in a glass ' his doctrine high,

But placed it face to face before men's eyes,
Essential Truth, God's image, meet for man,
Himself God's image. Worlds he showed them new,
Worlds countless as the stars that roof our night,
Fair fruitage of illimitable boughs,
Pushed from that Tree of Life from Calvary sprung
That over-tops and crowns the earth and man ;
Preached the Resurgent, the Ascended God
Dispensing 'gifts to men.' The tongue he spake
Seemed Pentecostal—grace of that high Feast—
For all who heard, the simple and the sage,
Heard still a single language sounding forth
To all one Promise. From that careworn Queen,
Who doffed her crown, and placed it on the rock,
Murmuring, ' Farewell forever, foolish gaud,'
To him the humblest hearer, all made vow
To live thenceforth for God. The form itself
Of each was changed to saintly and to sweet ;
Each countenance beamed as though with rays cast down
From fiery tongues, or angel choirs unseen.
    Thus like high gods on mountain-tops of joy
Those happy listeners sat. The body quelled—
With all that body's might usurped to cramp
Through ceaseless, yet unconscious, weight of sense
Conceptions spiritual, might more subtly skilled
Than lusts avowed, to sap the spirit's life—

In every soul its nobler Powers released
Stood up, no more a jarring crowd confused
Each trampling each and oft the worst supreme,
Not thus, but grade o'er grade, in order due,
And pomp hierarchical.　Yet hand in hand,
Not severed, stood those Powers.　To every Mind
That truth new learned was palpable and dear,
Not abstract nor remote, with cordial strength
Enclasped as by a heart ; through every Heart
Serene affections swam 'mid seas of light,
Reason's translucent empire without bound,
Fountained from God.　Silent those listeners sat
Parleying in wordless thought.　For them the world
Was lost—and won ; its sensuous aspects quenched ;
Its heavenly import grasped.　The erroneous Past
Lay like a shrivelled scroll before their feet ;
And sweet as some immeasurable rose,
Expanding leaf on leaf, varying yet one,
The Everlasting Present round them glowed.
Dead was desire, and dead not less was fear—
The fear of change—of death.
　　　　　　　　　　An hour went by ;
The sun declined : then rising from his seat,
Herbert, the anchoret of the lonely lake,
Made humble way to Cuthbert's feet with suit :
' O Father, and O friend, thou saw'st me not ;

Yet day by day thus far I tracked thy steps
At distance, for my betters leaving place,
The great and wise that round thee thronged ; the young
Who ne'er till then had seen thy face ; the old
Who saw it then, yet scarce again may see.
Father, a happier lot was mine, thou know'st,
Or had been save for sin of mine : each year
I sought thy cell, thy words of wisdom heard;
Yet still, alas ! lived on like sensual men
Who yield their hearts to creatures—fixing long
A foolish eye on gold-touched leaf, or flower—
Not Him, the great Creator.   Father and Friend,
The years run past.   I crave one latest boon :
Grant that we two may die the self-same day !'
Then Cuthbert knelt, and prayed.   At last he spake :
'Thy prayer is heard ; the self-same day and hour
We two shall die.'
                        That promise was fulfilled ;
For two years only on exterior tasks
God set His servant's hands—the man who 'sought.
In all things rest,' nor e'er had ceased from rest
Then when his task was heaviest.   Two brief years
He roamed on foot his spiritual realm :
The simple still he taught : the sad he cheered :
Where'er he went he founded churches still,
And convents ; yea, and, effort costlier far,

Spared not to scan defect with vigilant eye :
That eye the boldest called not 'vision-dazed';
That Saint he found no 'dreamer :' sloth or greed
'Scaped not his vengeance : scandals hid he not,
But dragged them into day, and smote them down :
Before his face he drave the hireling priest,
The bandit thane : unceasing cried, ' Ye kings,
Cease from your wars! Ye masters, loose your slaves ! '
Two years sufficed ; for all that earlier life
Had trained the Ascetic for those works of might
Beyond the attempt of all but boundless love,
And in him kept unspent the fire divine.
Never such Bishop walked till then the North,
Nor ever since, nor ever, centuries fled,
So lived in hearts of men.   Two years gone by,
His strength decayed.   He sought once more his cell
Sea-lulled ; and lived alone with God ; and saw
Once more, like lights that sweep the unmoving hills,
God's providences girdling all the world,
With glory following glory.   Tenderer-souled
Herbert meantime within his isle abode,
At midnight listening Derwent's gladsome voice
Mingling with deep-toned Greta's, ' Mourner ' named ; .
Pacing, each day, the shore ; now gazing glad
On gold-touched leaf, or bird that cut the mere,
Now grieved at wandering thoughts.   For men he prayed ;

And ever strove to raise his soul to God ;
And God, Who venerates still the pure intent,
Forgat not his ; and since his spirit and heart
Holy albeit, were in the Eyes Divine
Less ripe than Cuthbert's for the Vision Blest,
Least faults perforce swelling where gifts are vast,
That God vouchsafed His servant sickness-pains
Virtue to perfect in a little space,
That both might pass to heaven the self-same hour.
　　It came : that sun which flushed the spray up-hurled
In cloud round Cuthbert's eastern rock, while he
Within it dying chanted psalm on psalm,
Ere long enkindled Herbert's western lake :
The splendour waxed ; mountain to mountain laughed,
And, brightening, nearer drew, and, nearing, clasped
That ˙heaven-dropp'd beauty in more strict embrace :
The cliffs successive caught their crowns of fire ;
Blencathara last.   Slowly that splendour waned ;
And from the glooming gorge of Borrodale,
Her purple cowl shadowing her holy head
O'er the dim lake twilight with silent foot
Stepped like a spirit.   Herbert from his bed
Of shingles watched that sunset till it died ;
And at one moment from their distant isles
Those friends, by death united, passed to God.

SAINT FRIDESWIDA, OR THE FOUNDA-TIONS OF OXFORD.

Frideswida flies from the pursuit of a wicked king, invoking the Divine aid and the prayers of St. Catherine and St. Cecilia. She escapes ; and at the hour of her death those Saints reveal to her that in that place, near the Isis, where she has successively opened a blind man's eyes and healed a leper, God will one day raise up a seat of Learning, the light and the health of the realm.

'ONE love I ; One : within His bridal bower
My feet shall tread : One love I, One alone ;
His Mother is a Virgin, and His Sire
The unfathomed fount of pureness undefiled :
Him love I Whom to love is to be chaste :
Him love I touched by Whom my forehead shines :
Whom she that clasps grows spotless more and more :
Behold, to mine His spirit He hath joined :
And His the blood that mantles in my cheek :
His ring is on my finger.'

Thus she sang ;
Then walked and plucked a flower : she sang again :
'That which I longed for, lo, the same I see :
That which I hoped for, lo, my hand doth hold :
At last in heaven I walk with Him conjoined
Whom, yet on earth, I loved with heart entire.'
Thus carolled Frideswida all alone,
Treading the opens of a wood far spread
Around the upper waters of the Thames.
Christian almost by instinct, earth to her
Was shaped but to sustain the Cross of Christ.
Her mother lived a saint : she taught her child,
From reason's dawn, to note in all things fair
Their sacred undermeanings. 'Mark, my child,
In lamb and dove, not fleshly shapes,' she said,
'But heavenly types : upon the robin's breast
Revere that red which bathed her from the Cross
With slender bill striving to loose those Nails !'
Dying, that mother placed within her hand
A book of saintly legends. . Thus the maid
Grew up with mysteries clothed, with marvels fed,
A fearless creature swift as wind or fire :
But fires of hers were spirit-fires alone,
All else like winter moon. The Wessex King
Had gazed upon the glory of her face,
And deemed that face a spirit's. He had heard

P

Her voice ; it sounded like an angel's song ;
But wonder by degrees declined to love,
Such love as Pagans know.   The unworthy suit,
She scorned, from childhood spoused in heart to Christ :
She fled : upon the river lay a boat :
She rowed it on through forests many a mile ;
A month had passed since then.

> Midsummer blazed

On all things round : the vast, unmoving groves
Stretched silent forth their immemorial arms
Arching a sultry gloom.   Within it buzzed
Feebly the insect swarm : the dragon-fly
Stayed soon his flight : the streamlet scarce made way :
In shrunken pools, panting, the cattle stood,
Languidly browsing on the dried-up sprays :
No bird-song shook the bower.   Alone that maid
Glided light-limbed, as though some Eden breeze,
Hers only, charioted the songstress on,
Like those that serve the May.   Beneath a tree
Low-roofed at last she sank, with eyes up-raised
On boughs that, ivy-twined and creeper-trailed,
Darkened the shining splendour of the sky :—
Between their interspaces, here and there,
It flashed in purple stars.

> Enraptured long,

For admiration was to her as love,

The maiden raised at last her mother's book,
And lit upon her childhood's favourite tale,
Catherine in vision wed to Bethlehem's Babe
Who from His Virgin-Mother leaning, dropped
His ring adown her finger.   Princely pride,
And pride not less of soaring intellect,
At once in her were changed to pride of love :
In vain her country's princes sued her grace ;
Kingdoms of earth she spurned.   Around her seat
The far-famed Alexandrian Sages thronged,
Branding her Faith as novel.   Slight and tall,
'Mid them, keen-eyed the wingless creature stood
Like daughter of the sun on earth new-lit :—
That Faith she shewed of all things first and last ;
All lesser truths its prophets.   Swift as beams
Forth flashed such shafts of high intelligence
That straight their lore sophistic shrivelled up,
And Christians they arose.   The martyr's wheel
Was pictured in the margin, dyed with red,
And likewise, azure-tinct on golden ground,
Her queenly throne in heaven.   'Ah shining Saint !'
Half weeping, smiling half, the virgin cried ;
'Yet dear not less thy sister of the West ;
For never gaze I on that lifted face,
Or mark that sailing angel near her stayed,
But straight her solemn organs round me swell ;

All discords cease.'   Then with low voice she read
Of Rome's Cecilia, her who won to Christ,
(That earlier troth inviolably preserved)
Her Roman bridegroom, wondering at that crown
Invisible itself, that round her breathed
Rose-breath celestial ; her that to the Church
Gave her ancestral house ; and, happier gift,
Devotion's heavenliest instrument of praise ;
Her that, unfearing, dared that Roman sword ;
And when its work was done, for centuries lay
Like marble, 'mid the catacombs, unchanged,
In sleep-resembling death.

                      From earliest dawn
That maiden's eyes had watched : wearied at noon
Their silver curtains closed.   Huge mossy roots
Pillowed her head, that slender book wide-leaved
In stillness, like some brooding, white-winged dove,
Spread on her bosom : 'gainst its golden edge
Rested, gold-tinged, the dimpled ivory chin—
Loud thunders broke that sleep ; the tempest blast
Came up against the woods, while bolt on bolt
Ran through them sheer.   She started up : she saw
That Pagan prince and many a sworded serf
Rushing towards her.   Fleeter still she fled ;
But, as some mountain beast tender and slight,
That, pasturing spring-fed lilies of Cashmere,

Or slumbering where its rock-nursed torrents fall,
Sudden not distant hears the hunter's cry
And mocks pursuit at first, but slackens soon
Breathless and spent, so failed her limbs ere long ;
A horror of great faintness o'er her crept ;
More near she heard their shout.   She staggered on :
To threat'ning phantoms all things round were changed ;
About her towered in ruin hollow trunks
Of spiked and branchless trees, survivors sole
Of woods that, summer-scorched, then lightning-struck
A century past, for one short week had blazed
And blackened ever since.   She knelt : she raised
Her hands to God : she sued for holier prayer
Saint Catherine, Saint Cecilia.   At that word
Behind her close a cry of anguish rang :
Silence succeeded.   As by angels' help
She reached a river's bank : sun-hardened clay
Retained the hoof-prints of the drinking herd ;
And, shallower for long heats, the oxen's ford
Challenged her bleeding feet.   She crossed unharmed,
And soon in green-gold pastures girt by woods
Stood up secure.   Then forth she stretched her hands,
Like Agnes praising God amid the flame :
' Omnipotent, Eternal, Worshipful,
One God, Immense, and All-compassionate,
Thou from the sinner's snare hast snatched the feet

Of her that loved Thee. Glory to Thy name.'

Thenceforth secure she roamed those woods and meads ;
The dwellers in that region brought her bread,
Upon that countenance gazing, some with awe
But all with love. To her the maidens came :
'Tell us,' they said, 'what mystery hast thou learned
So sweet and good ;—thy Teacher, who was he ;
Grey-haired, or warrior young ?' To them in turn
Ceaseless she sang the praises of her Christ,
His Virgin Mother and His heavenly court,
Warriors on earth for justice. They for her
Renounced all else, the banquet and the dance,
And nuptial rites revered. A low-roofed house
Inwoven of branches 'mid the woods they raised ;
There dwelt, and sang her hymn, and prayed her prayer,
And loved her Saviour-Sovereign. Year by year
More high her bright feet scaled the heavenly mount
Of lore divine and knowledge of her God,
And with sublimer chant she hymned His praise ;
While oft some bishop, tracking those great woods
In progress to his charge, beneath their roof
Baptizing or confirming made abode,
And all which lacked supplied, nor discipline
Withheld, nor doctrine high. The outward world
To them a nothing, made of them its boast :
A Saint, it said, within that forest dwelt,

A Saint that helped their people.   Saint she was,
And therefore wrought for heaven her holy deeds ;
Immortal stand they on the heavenly roll ;
Yet fewest acts suffice for heavenly crown ;
And two of hers had consequence on earth,
Like water circles widening limitless,
For man still helpful.   Hourly acts of hers,
Intérior acts invisible to men,
Perchance were worthier.   Humblest faith and prayer
Are oft than miracle miraculous more :—
To us the exterior marks the interior might :
These two alone record we.
                              Years had passed :
One day when all the streams were dried by heat
And rainless fields had changed from green to brown,
T'wards her there drew, by others led, a man
Old, worn, and blind.   He knelt, and wept his prayer :
'Help, Saint of God !   That impious King am I,
That King abhorred, his people's curse and bane,
Who chased thee through these woods with fell resolve,
Worst vengeance seeking for insulted pride :—
Rememberest thou that, near thee as I closed,
Kneeling thou mad'st thy prayer?   Instant from God
Blindness fell on me.   Forward still I rushed,
Ere long amid those spiked and branded trunks
To lie as lie the dead.   If hope remains,

For me if any hope survives on earth,
It rests with thee ; thee only ! '   On her knees
She sank in prayer ; her fingers in the fount
She dipped ; then o'er him signed the Saviour's cross,
And thrice invoked that Saviour.   At her word
Behold, that sightless King arose, and saw,
And rendered thanks to God.

                              The legend saith
Saint Catherine by her stood that night, and spake :
'Once more I greet thee on thy dying day.'

   Again the years went by.   That sylvan lodge
Had changed to convent.   Beautiful it stood
Not far from Isis, though on loftier ground :
Sad outcasts knew it well : whate'er their need
There found they solace.   One day toward it moved,
Dread apparition and till then unknown,
Like one constrained, with self-abhorrent steps,
A leper, long in forest caverns hid.
Back to their cells the nuns had shrunk, o'erawed :
Remained but Frideswida.   Thus that wretch
With scarce organic voice, and aiding sign,
Wailed out the supplication of despair :
' Fly not, O saintly virgin !   Yet, ah me !
What   help   though   thou   remainest ?   Warned from
      heaven,

I know that not thy fountain's healing wave
Could heal my sorrow : not those spotless hands :
Not even thy prayer.   To me the one sole aid
Were aid impossible—a kiss of thine.'
A moment stood she : not in doubt she stood :
First slowly, swiftly then to where he knelt
She moved : with steadfast hand she raised that cloth
Which veiled what once had been a human face :
O'er it she signed in faith the cross of Christ :
She wept aloud, ' My brother ! '   Folding then
Stainless to stained, with arms about him wound,
In sacred silence mouth to mouth she pressed,
A long, long sister's kiss.   Like infant's flesh
The blighted and the blasted back returned :
That leper rose restored.

                      The legend saith
That Saint Cecilia by her stood that night :
' Once more I greet thee on thy dying day.'

   It came at last, that day.   Her convent grew
In grace with God and man : the pilgrim old
Sought it from far ; the gifts of kings enlarged :—
It came at last, that day.   There are who vouch
The splendour of that countenance never waned :
Thus much is sure ; it waxed to angels' eyes :—
Welcomed it came, that day desired, not feared.

By humbleness like hers those two fair deeds
Were long forgotten : each day had its task :
Not hardest that of dying.   Why should sobs
Trouble the quiet of a holy house
Because its holiest passes ?   Others wept ;
The sufferer smiled : ' Ah, little novices,
How little of the everlasting lore
Your foolish mother taught you if ye shrink
From trial light as this ! '   She spake ; then sank
In what to those around her seemed but sleep,
The midnoon August sunshine on her hair
In ampler radiance lying than that hour
When, danger near her yet to her unknown,
Beneath that forest tree her eyelids closed—
Her book upon her bosom. .

                Near her bed
Not danger now but heralds ever young,
Saint Catherine, Saint Cecilia, stood once more,
Linked hand in hand, with aureoles interwreathed :
One gazing stood as though on radiance far
With widening eyes : a listener's look intent
The other's, soft with pathos more profound.
The Roman sister spake : ' Rejoice, my child,
Rejoice, thus near the immeasurable embrace
And breast expectant of the unnumbered Blest
That swells to meet thee !   Yea, and on the earth

For thee reward remaineth.   Happy thou
Through prayer his sight restoring to thy foe,
Sole foe that e'er thou knew'st though more his own !
Child ! darkness is there worse than blindness far,
Wherein erroneous wanders human Pride ;
That prayer of thine from age to age shall guard
A realm against such darkness.   Where yon kine
Stand in mid ford, quenching their noontide thirst,
Thy footsteps crossed of old the waters.   God
In the unerasing current sees them still !
Close by, a nation from a purer flood
Shall quench a thirst more holy, quaffing streams
Of Knowledge loved as Truth.   Majestic piles
Shall rise by yonder Isis, honouring, each,
My clear-eyed sister of the sacred East
That won to Christ the Alexandrian seers,
Winning, herself, from chastity her lore :
Upon their fronts, aloft in glory ranged
With face to East, and cincture never loosed,
All Sciences shall stand, daughters divine
Of Him that Truth eterne and boon to man,
Holding in spotless hand, not lamp alone,
But lamp and censer both, and both alike
From God's great Altar lighted.'

                        Spake in turn
That Alexandrian with the sunlike eyes :

' Beside those Sciences shall stand a choir
As fair as they ; as tall ; those sister Arts,
High daughters of celestial Harmony,
Diverse yet one, that bind the hearts of men
To steadfast Truth by Beauty's sinuous cords ;
She that to marble changes mortal thought ;
She that with rainbow girds the cloud of life ;
She that above the streaming mist exalts
Rock-rooted domes of prayer ; and she that rears
With words auguster temples.   Happy thou
Healing that leper with thy virgin kiss !
A leprosy there is more direful, child !—
Therein the nations rot when flesh is lord
And spirit dies.   Such ruin Arts debased
Gender, or, gendered long, exasperate more.
But thou, rejoice !   From this pure centre Arts
Unfallen shall breathe their freshness through the land,
With kiss like thine healing a nation's wound
Year after year successive ; listening, each,
My sister's organ music in the skies,
Prime Art that, challenging not eye but ear,
To Faith is nearest, and of Arts on earth
For that cause, living soul.'
                         That prophecy
Found its accomplishment.   In later years,
There where of old the Oxen had their Ford,

The goodliest city England boasts arose,
Mirrored in sacred Isis ; like that flood
Its youth for aye renewing.   Convents first
Through stately groves levelled their placid gleam,
With cloisters opening dim on garden gay
Or moonlit lawn dappled by shadowing deer :
Above them soared the chapel's reverent bulk
With storied window whence, in hues of heaven,
Martyrs looked down, or Confessor, or Saint
On tomb of Founder with its legend meek
' Pro animâ orate.'   Night and day
Mounted the Church's ever-varying song
Sustained on organ harmonies that well
Might draw once more to earth, with wings outspread
And heavenly face made heavenlier by that strain,
Cecilia's Angel.   Of those convents first
Was Frideswida's, ruled in later years
By Canons Regular, later yet rebuilt
By him of York, that dying wept, alas,
' Had I but served my Maker as my king ! '
To colleges those convents turned ; yet still
The earlier inspiration knew not change :
The great tradition died not : near the bridge
From Magdalen's tower still rang the lark-like hymn
On May-day morn : high ranged in airy cells,
Facing the East, all Sciences, all Arts,

Yea, and with these all Virtues, imaged stood,
Best imaged stood in no ideal forms,
Craft unhistoric of some dreamer's brain,
But life-like shapes of plain heroic men
Who in their day had fought the fight of Faith,
Warriors and sages, poets, saints, and kings,
And earned their rest : the long procession paced,
Up winding slow the college-girded street
To where in high cathedral slept the Saint,
Singing its 'Alma Redemptoris Mater,'
On August noons, what time the Assumption Feast
From purple zenith of the Christian heaven
Brightened the earth.   That hour not bells alone
Chiming from countless steeples made reply :
Laughed out that hour high-gabled roof and spire ;
Kindling shone out those Sciences, those Arts
Pagan one time, now confessors white-robed ;
And all the holy City gave response,
' Deus illuminatio mea est.' [1]

[1] The motto of the University of Oxford.

THE BANQUET HALL OF WESSEX, OR THE KING WHO COULD SEE.

Kenwalk, King of Wessex, is a Pagan, but refuses to persecute Christians. He is dethroned by the Mercian King, and lives an exile in a Christian land. There he boasts that he never accords faith to what he hears, and believes only what he sees ; yet, his eye being single, he sees daily more of the Truth. Wessex is delivered, and a great feast held at which the Pagan nobles, priests, and bards all conspire for the destruction of the Faith. Birinus, the bishop, having withstood them valiantly, Kenwalk declares himself a Christian. Birinus prophesies of England's greatest King.

KING CYNEGILS lay dead, who long and well
Had judged the realm of Essex.   By his bier
The Christians standing smote their breasts, and said,
' Ill day for us :' but all about the house
Clustering in smiling knots of twos and threes,
The sons of Odin whispered, or with nods
Gave glad assent.   Christ's bishop sent from Rome,
Birinus, to the king had preached for years

The Joyous Tidings.   Cynegils believed,
And with him many ; but the most refrained :
With these was Kenwalk ; and, his father dead,
Kenwalk was king.

               A valiant man was he,
A man of stubborn will, but yet at heart
Magnanimous and just.   To one who said,
' Strike, for thine hour is come ! ' the king new-crowned
Made answer, ' Never !   Each man choose his path !
My father chose the Christian—Odin's I.
I crossed my father oft a living man ;
I war not on him dead.'

                   That giant hand
Which spared Religion ruled in all beside :
He harried forth the robbers from the woods,
And wrecked the pirates' ships.   He burned with fire
A judge unjust, and thrice o'er Severn drave
The invading Briton.   Lastly, when he found
That woman in his house intolerable,
From   bed   and   realm   he   hurled   her   forth,   though
    crowned,
Ensuing thence great peace.

                    Not long that peace :
The Mercian king, her brother, heard her tale
With blackening brow.   The shrill voice stayed at last,
Doubly incensed the monarch made reply :

' Sister, I never loved you ;—who could love?
But him who spurned you from his realm I hate :
Fear nought ! your feast of vengeance shall be full ! '
He spake ; then cried, ' To arms ! '

                              In either land,
Like thunders low and far, or windless plunge
Of waves on coasts long silent that proclaim,
Though calm the sea for leagues, tempest far off
That shoreward swells, thus day by day was heard
The direful preparation for a war
Destined no gladsome tournament to prove,
But battle meet for ancient foes resolved
To clear old debts ; make needless wars to come.
Not long that strife endured; on either side
Valour was equal ; but on one, conjoined,
The skill most practised, and the heavier bones :
The many fought the few.   On that last field
'Twas but the fury of a fell despair,
Not hope, that held the balance straight so long :
Ere sunset all was over.   From the field
A wounded remnant dragged their king, half dead :
The Mercian host pursued not.

                           Many a week
Low lay the broken giant nigh to death :
At last, like creeping plant down-dragged, not crushed,
That, washed by rains, and sunshine-warmed, once more

Q

Its length uplifting, feels along the air,
And gradual finds its 'customed prop, so he,
Strengthening each day, with dubious eyes at first
Around him peered, but raised at length his head,
And, later, question made.   His health restored,
He sought East Anglia, where King Anna reigned,
His chief of friends in boyhood.   Day by day
A spirit more buoyant to the exile came
And winged him on his way : his country's bound
Once passed, his darker memories with it sank :
Through Essex hastening, stronger grew his step ;
East Anglian breezes from the morning sea
Fanned him to livelier pulse : wild April growths
Gladdened his spirit with glittering green.   More fresh
He walked because the sun outfaced him not,
Veiled, though not far.   That shrouded sun had ta'en
Its passion from the wild-bird's song, but left
Quiet felicities of notes low-toned
That kept in tune with streams too amply brimmed
To chatter o'er their pebbles.   Kenwalk's soul
Partook not with the poet's.   Loveliest sights,
Like music brightening those it fails to charm,
Roused but his mirthful mood.   To each that passed
He tossed his jest : he scanned the labourer's task ;
Reviled the luckless boor that ploughed awry,
And beat the smith that marred the horse's hoof :

At times his fortunes thus he moralised :
' Here walk I, crownless king, and exiled man :
My Mercian brother lists his sister's tongue :
Say, lark ! which lot is happiest ? '

                        Festive streets,
Tapestries from windows waving, banners borne
By white-clad children chanting anthems blithe ;
With these East Anglia's king received his friend
Entering the city gate.   In joyous sports
That day was passed.   At banquet Christian priests
Sat with his thanes commingled.   Anna's court
Was Christian, and, for many a league around,
His kingdom likewise.   As the earth in May
Glistens with vernal flowers, or as the face
Of one whose love at last has found return
Irradiate shines, so shone King Anna's house,
A home of Christian peace.   Fair sight it was—
Justice and Love, the only rivals there,
O'er-ruled it, and attuned.   Majestic strength
Looked forth in every glance of Anna's eye,
Too great for pride to dwell there.   Tender-souled
As that first streak, the harbinger of dawn
Revealed through cloudless ether, such the queen,
All charity, all humbleness, all grace,
All womanhood.   Harmonious was her voice,
Dulcet her movements, undisguised her thoughts,

As though they trod an Eden land unfallen,
And needed raiment none.   Some heavenly birth
Their children seemed, blameless in word and act,
The sisters as their brothers frank, and they,
Though bolder, not less modest.   Kenwalk marked,
And marking, mused in silence, ' Contrast strange
These Christians with the pagan races round !
Something those pagans see not these have seen :
Something those pagans hear not these have heard :
Doubtless there's much in common.   What of that ?
'Tis thus 'twixt man and dog ; yet knows the dog
His master walks in worlds by him not shared—
Perchance for me too there are worlds unknown ! '

Thus God to Kenwalk shewed the things that bear
Of God true witness, seeing in his soul
Justice and Judgment, and, with these conjoined,
Valour and Truth : for as the architect
On tower four-square and solid plants his spire,
And not on meads below, though gay with flowers,
On those four virtues God the fabric rears
Of virtues loftier yet—those three, heaven-born,
And pointing heavenward.

To those worlds unknown,
Kenwalk ere long stood nigh.   In three short months
The loveliest of those children, and last born,

Lay cold in death. Old nurses round her wailed :
The mighty heart of Kenwalk shook for dread
Entering the dim death-chamber. On a bier
The maiden lay, the cross upon her breast :
Beside her sat her mother, pale as she,
Yet calm as pale. When Kenwalk near her drew
She lifted from that bier a slender book
And read that record of the three days' dead
Raised by the Saviour from that death-cave sealed,
A living man. Once more she read those words,
' I am the Resurrection and the Life,'
Then added, low, with eyes up cast to heaven,
'With Him my child awaits me.' Kenwalk saw ;
And, what he saw, believing, half believed—
Not more—the things he heard.

                       Yes, half believed ;
Yet, call it obduracy, call it pride,
Call it self-fear, or fear of priestly craft,
He closed his ear against the Word Divine :
The thing he saw he trusted ; nought beyond.
Three years went by. Once, when his friend had named
The Name all-blessed, Kenwalk frowned. Since then
That Name was named no more. O'er hill and dale
They chased the wild deer ; on the billow breathed
Inspiring airs ; in hall of joyance trod
The mazes of the dance. Then war broke out :

Reluctant long King Anna sought the field ;
Hurled back aggression.   Kenwalk, near him still,
Watched him with insight keener than his wont,
And, wondering, marked him least to pagans like
Inly, when like perforce in outward deed.
The battle frenzy took on him no hold :
Severe his countenance grew ; austere and sad ;
Fatal, not wrathful.   Vicar stern he seemed
Of some dread, judgment-executing Power,
Against his yearnings ; not despite his will.
Once, when above the faithless town far off
The retributive smoke leaped up to heaven,
He closed with iron hand on Kenwalk's arm
And slowly spake—a whisper heard afar—
' See you that town ?   Its judgment is upon it !
I gave it respite twice.   This day its doom
Is irreversible.'
                    The invader quelled,
Anna and Kenwalk on their homeward way
Rode by the grave of saintly Sigebert,
King Anna's predecessor.   Kenwalk spake :
' Some say the people keep but memory scant
Of benefits : I trust the things I see :
I never passed that tomb but round it knelt
A throng of supplicants !   King Sigebert
Conversed, men say, with prophet and with seer:

I never loved that sort :—who wills can dream—
Yet what I see I see.'
                              ' They pray for him,'
Anna replied, ' who perished for their sake :
Long years he lived recluse at Edmondsbury,
A tonsured monk : around its walls one day
Arose that cry, " The Mercian, and his host !
Forth, holy King, and lead, as thou wert wont,
Thy people to the battle, lest they die ! "
Again I see him riding at their head,
Lifting a cross, not sword.   The battle lost,
Again I see him fall.'   With rein drawn tight
King Kenwalk mused ; then smote his hands, and
        cried
' My father would have died like Sigebert !
He lacked but the occasion ! '   After pause,
Sad-faced, with bitter voice he spake once more :
' Such things as these I might have learned at home !
I shunned my father's house lest fools might say,
' He thinks not his own thoughts.'
                              Thus month by month,
Though Faith which 'comes by hearing' had not come
To Kenwalk yet, not less since sight he used
In honest sort, and resolute to learn,
God shewed him memorable things and great
Which sight unblest discerns not, tutoring thus

A kingly spirit to a kingly part :
Before him near it lay.

                        The morrow morn
Great tidings came : in Wessex war was raised :
Kenwalk, departing thus to Anna spake,
To Anna, and his consort : ' Well I know
What thanks are those the sole your hearts could prize : '
With voice that shook he added : ' Man am I
That make not pledge : yet, if my father's God
Sets free my father's realm——' again he paused ;
Then westward rode alone.

                            Well planned, fought well
(For Kenwalk, of the few reverse makes wise,
From him had put his youth's precipitance)
That virtuous warfare triumphed.   Swift as fire
The news from Sherburne and from Winbourne flashed
To Sarum, Chertsey, Malmsbury.   That delight
On earth the nearest to religious joy,
The rapture of a trampled land set free,
Swelled every breast : the wounded in their wounds
Rejoiced, not grieved : the sick forgat their pains :
The mourner dashed away her tear and cried,
' Wessex is free ! '   Remained a single doubt :
Christians crept forth from cave and hollow tree :
Once more the exiled monk was seen ; and one
Who long in minstrel's garb, with harp in hand,

Old, poor, haif blind, had sat beside a bridge,
And, charming first the wayfarer with song,
Had won him next with legends of the Cross,
Stood up before his altar.   Rumour ran
' Once more Birinus lifts his crosier-staff ! '
Then muttered priests of Odin, ' Cynegils
We know was Christian.   Kenwalk holds—or held,
Ancestral Faith, yet warred not on the new :
Tolerance means still connivance.'

Peace restored,

Within King Kenwalk's echoing palace hall,
The hall alike of council and of feast,
The Great Ones of the Wessex realm were met :
Birinus sat among them, eyed from far
With anger and with hatred.   Council o'er,
Banquet succeeded, and to banquet song,
The Saxon's after-banquet.   Many a harp
That day by flying hand entreated well
Divulged its secret, amorous, or of war ;
And many a warrior sang his own great deeds
Or dirge of ancient friend Valhalla's guest ;
Nor stinted foeman's praise.   Silent meanwhile
Far down the board a son of Norway sat,
Ungenial guest with clouded brows and stern,
And eyes that flashed beneath them : bard was he,
Warrior and bard.   Not his the song for gold !

He sang but of the war-fields and the gods;
He lays of love despised.   'Thy turn is come,
Son of the ice-bound North,' thus spake a thane :
'Sing thou !   The man who sees that face, already
Half hears the tempest singing through the pines
That shade thy gulfs hill-girt.'   The stranger guest
Answered, not rising : ' Yea, from lands of storm
And seas cut through by fiery lava floods
I come, a wanderer.   Ye, meantime, in climes
Balm-breathing, gorge the fat, and smell the sweet :
Ye wed the maid whose sire ye never slew,
And bask in unearned triumph.   Feeble spirits !
Endless ye deem the splendours of this hour,
And call defeat opprobrious !   Sirs, our life
Is trial.   Victory and Defeat are Gods
That toss man's heart, their plaything, each to each :
Great Mercia knows that truth—of all your realms
Faithfullest to Odin far ! '

                       ' Nay, minstrel, sing,'
Once more, not wroth, they clamoured.   He replied :
' Hear then my song ; but not those songs ye sing :
I have against you somewhat, Wessex men !
Ye are not as your fathers, when, in youth,
I trod your coasts.   That time ye sang of Gods,
Sole theme for manlike song.   On Iceland's shores
We keep our music's virtue undefiled :

While summer lasts we fight ; by winter hearths,
Or ranged in sunny coves by winter seas,
Betwixt the snow-plains and the hills of fire,
Singing we feed on legends of the Gods :
Ye sing but triumphs of the hour that fleets ;
Ye build you kingdoms : next ye dash them down :
Ye bow to idols !   O that song of mine
Might heal this people's wound ! '

                            Then rose the bard
And took his harp, and smote it like a man ;
And sang full-blooded songs of Gods who spurn
Their heaven to war against that giant race
Throned 'mid the mountains of old Jötunheim
That girdle still the unmeasured seas of ice
With horror and strange dread.   Innumerable,
In ever-winding labyrinths, glacier-thronged,
Those mountains raise their heads among the stars,
That palsied glimmer 'twixt their sunless bulks,
O'er-shadowing seas and lands.   O'er Jötunheim
The glittering car of day hath never shone :
There endless twilight broods.   Beneath it sit
The huge Frost-Giants, sons of Örgelmir,
Themselves like mountains, solitary now,
Now grouped, with knees drawn up, and heads low bent
Plotting new wars.   Those wars the Northman sang ;
And thunder-like rang out the vast applause.

That hour Birinus whispered one close by :
' Not casual this !   Ill spirits, be sure, this day,
And impious men will launch their fiercest bolts
To crush Christ's Faith for ever ! '

                                 Jocund songs
The bard sang next : how Thor had roamed disguised
Through Jötunheim, and found the giant-brood
Feasting ; and how their king gave challenge thus :
' Sir, since you deign us visit, show us feats !
Behold yon drinking horn ! with us a child
Drains it at draught.'   The God inclined his head
And swelled his lips ; and three times drank : yet lo !
Nigh full that horn remained, the dusky mead
In mockery winking !   Spake once more the king :
' Behold my youngest daughter's chief delight,
Yon wild-cat grey ! She lifts it : lift it thou ! '
The God beneath it slipped his arm and tugged,
And tugging, ever higher rose and higher ;
The wild cat arched her back and with him rose ;—
But one foot left the ground !   Last, forward stept
A haggard, lame, decrepìd, toothless crone,
And cried, ' Canst wrestle, friend ? '   He closed upon
    her :
Firm stood she as a mountain : she in turn
Closed upon Thor, and brought him to one knee :
Lower she could not bend him.   Thor for rage

Clenched both his fists until his finger-joints
Grew white as snow late fallen !

      Loud and long
The laughter rose : the minstrel frowned dislike :
' I have against you somewhat, Wessex men !
In laughter spasms ye reel, or shout applause,
Music surceased. Like rocks your fathers sat ;
In every song they knew some mystery lay,
Mystery of man or nature. Greater God
Is none than Thor, whom, witless, thus ye flout.
That giant knew his greatness, and, at morn,
While vexed at failure through the gates he passed,
Addressed him reverent : ' Lift thy head, great Thor !
Disguised thou cam'st ; not less we knew thee well :
Brave battle fought'st thou, seeming still to fail :
Thy foes were phantoms ! Phantasies I wove
To snare thine eyes because I feared thy hand,
And pledged thy strength to tasks impossible.
That horn thou could'st not empty was the sea !
At that third draught such ebb-tide stripp'd the shore
As left whole navies stranded ! What to thee
Wild-cat appeared was Midgard's endless snake
Whose infinite circle clasps the ocean round :
Then when her foot thou liftedst, tremour went
From iron vale to vale of Jötunheim :
Hadst thou but higher raised it one short span,

The sea had drowned the land !   That toothless crone
Was Age, that drags the loftiest head to earth :
She bent thy knee alone.   Come here no more !
On equal ground thou fight'st us in the light :
In this, our native land, the stronger we,
And mock thee by Illusions ! '

                                After pause,
With haughty eye cast round, the minstrel spake :
' Now hear ye mysteries of the antique song,
Though few shall guess their import ! '   Then he sang
Legends primeval of that Northern race,
And dread beginnings of the heavens and earth,
When, save the shapeless chaos, nothing was :
Of Ymer first, by some named Örgelmir,
The giant sire of all the giant brood :—
Him for his sins the sons of Bör destroyed ;
Then fashioned of his blood the seas and streams,
And of his bones the mountains ; of his teeth
The cliffs firm set against the aggressive waves ;
Last, of his skull the vast, o'er-hanging heaven ;
And of his brain the clouds.

                          'Sing on,' they cried :
Next sang he of that mystic shape, earth-born,
The wondrous cow, Auhumla.   Herb that hour
Was none, nor forest growth ; yet on and on
She wandered by the vapour-belted seas,

And, wandering, from the stones and icebergs cold
That creaked forlorn against the grey sea-crags,
She licked salt spray, and hoary frost, and lived ;
And ever where she licked sprang up, full-armed,
Men fair and strong !

                  Once more they cried, 'Sing on !'
Last sang the minstrel of the Night and Day :
Car-borne they sweep successive through the heaven :
First rides the dusky maid by men called Night ;
Sleep-bringing, pain-assuaging, kind to man ;
With dream-like speed cleaving the starry sphere :
Hrimfaxi is her horse : his round complete
Foam from his silver bit bespangles earth,
And mortals call it ' Morn.' Day follows fast,
Her brother white : Skinfaxi is his horse :
When forth he flings the splendours from his mane
Both Gods and men rejoice.

                    Thus legends old
The Northman sang, till, fleeting from men's eyes,
The present lived no longer.   In its place
He fixed that vision of the world new formed,
Which on the childhood of the Northern mind
Like endless twilight lay ;—spaces immense ;
Unmeasured energies of fire and flood ;
Great Nature's forces, terrible yet blind,
In ceaseless strife alternately supreme,

Or breast to breast with dreadful equipoise
In conflict pressed.   Once more o'er those that heard
He hung that old world's low, funereal sky :
Before their eyes he caused its cloud to stream
Shadowing infinitude.   He spake no word
Like Heida of that war 'twixt Good and Ill ;
That peace which crowns the just ; that God unknown :
Enough to him his Faith without its soul !
With glorying eye he marked that panting throng ;
Then, sudden, changed his note.   Again of war
He sang, but war no more of Gods on Gods ;
He sang the honest wars of man on man ;
Of Odin, king of men, ere yet, death past,
He flamed abroad in godhead.   Field on field
He sang his battles ; traced from realm to realm
His conquering pilgrimage : then ended, fierce :
' What God was this—that God ye honoured once ?
What man was this—your half-forgotten king ?
Your law-giver he was ! he framed your laws !
Your poet he : he shaped your earliest song !
Your teacher he : he taught you first your runes !
Your warrior—yours !   His warfare consummate,
For you he died !   Old age at last, sole foe
Unvanquished, found him throned in Gylfi's land :
Summoning his race around him thus he spake :
" My sons, I scorn that age should cumber youth !

Ye have your lesson—see ye keep it well !
I taught you how to conquer; how to live ;
Now learn to die !" His dagger high he raised;
Nine times he plunged it through his bleeding breast,
Then sheathed it in his heart. Ere from his lips
The kingly smile had vanished, he was dead !'

So sang the bard and ceased ; his work was done :
Abroad the tempest burst. 'Twas not his songs
Alone that raised it ! Memories which they waked,
Memories of childhood, fainter year by year,
Tripled his might. Meantime a Saxon priest
Potential there, bent low, with eye-brow arched,
O'er Eardulf's ear, Eardulf old warrior famed,
And whispered long, and as he whispered glanced
Oft at Birinus. Keen of eye the King,
The action noting well, the aim divined,
And thus to Offa near him spake, low-toned :
' The full-fed priest of Odin sends a sword
To slay that naked babe he'hates so sore,
The Faith of Christ !'
                              Rising with fiery face
And thundering hand that shook the banquet board
Eardulf began : ' " Ye are not what ye were !"
So saith our stranger kinsman from the north,
A man plain-tongued ; I would that all were such !

R

Lords, and my King, this stranger speaks the truth !
I tell you too, we are not what we were :
Nor lengthened trail he hunts who seeks the cause.
Lo, there the cause among us !   Man from Rome !
I ask who sent thee hither?   From the first
Rome and our native races stand at war ;
Her hope was this, to make our sons like hers
Liars and slaves, our daughters false and vile,
And, thus subverted, rule our land and us.
Frustrate in war, now sends she forth her priests
In peaceful gown to sap the manly hearts
Her sword but manlier made.   Ho, Wessex men !
Ye see your foe !   My counsel, Lords, is this :
The worm that stings us tread we to the earth,
Then spurn it from our coasts !'

                           Ere ceased the acclaim
Subdued and soft the Pagan pontiff rose,
And three times half retired, as one who yields
His betters place ; and thrice, answering the call,
Advanced, and leaning stood : at last he spake,
Sweet-voiced, not loud ; ' Ye Wessex Earls and Thanes,
I stand here but as witness, not as judge ;
Ye are the judges.   Late ye heard—yea, twice—
Words strange and new ; " Ye are not what ye were ! "
I witness this ; things are not what they were ;
For round me as I roll these sorrowing eyes,

Now old and dim—perchance the fault is theirs—
They find no longer, ranged along your walls
Amid the deep-dyed trophies of old time,
That chiefest of your Standards, lost, men say,
In that ill-omened battle lost which wrecked
But late our Wessex kingdom.   Odin's wrath—
I spare to task your time and patience, Lords,
Enforcing truth which every urchin knows—
'Twas Odin shamed his foe !   Ah Cynegils !
What made thee Odin's foe ?   Our friend was he !
Base tolerance first, connivance next, then worse,
Favoured that Faith perfidious !   Stood and stands
A bow-shot hence that church the strangers built ;
Their church, their font !   The strangers, who are they ?
Snake-like and supple, winding on and on
Through courtly chambers darkling still they creep,
Nor dare to face a people front to front ;
Let them stand up in light, and all is well !
And who their converts ?   Late, to please a king,
They donned his novel worship like a robe ;
When dead he lay they doffed it !   Earls and Thanes,
A nobler day is come ; a sager king ;
In him I trust ; in you ; in Odin most,
Our nation's strength, the bulwark of our throne.
I proffer nought of counsel.   Ye have eyes :
The opprobrium sits among you !'

From the floor
The storm of iron feet rang loud, and swords
Leaped flashing from their sheaths.   In silence some
Waited the event : the larger part by far
Clamoured for vengeance on the outlandish Faith,
The loudest they, the apostates of past time.
Then stately from his seat Birinus rose,
And stood in calm marmorean.   Long he stood,
Not eager, though expectant.   By degrees
That tumult lessening, with a quiet smile
And hand extended, noticing for peace,
Thus he addressed that concourse.

' Earls and Thanes,
Among so many here I stand alone,
Why peaceful ? why untroubled ?   In your hands
I see a hundred swords against me bent :
Sirs, should they slay me, Truth remains unpierced.
A thousand wheat ears swayed by summer gust
Affront one oak ; it slights the mimic threat :
So slight I, strong in faith, those swords that err—
Your ignorance, not your sin.   The truth of God,
The heart of man against you fight this day,
And, with his heart, his hope.   In every land,
Through all the unnumbered centuries yet to come,
The cry of women wailing for their babes
Restored through Christ alone, the cry of men

Who know that all is lost if earth is all,
The cry of children still unstained by sin, .
The sinner's cry redeemed from yoke of sin,
Thunder against you. Pass to lesser themes.

'Eardulf, that raged against me, told you, Lords,
That Rome was still the hater of your race,
And warred thereon. She warred much more on mine,
Roman but Christian likewise ! Ye were foes ;
Warring on you she warred on hostile tribes :
In us she tore her proper flesh and blood :
Mailed men were you that gave her blow for blow ;
We were her tender children ; on her hearths
We dwelt, or delved her fields and dressed her vines.
What moved her hatred ? that we loved a God
All love to man. With every God beside
Rome made her traffic : fellowship with such
Unclean we deemed : thenceforth Rome saw in us
Her destined foe.

            Three centuries, Earls and Thanes,
Her hand was red against us. Vengeance came :
Who wrought it ? Who avenged our martyred Saints
That, resting 'neath God's altar, cried, " How long ?"
Alaric, and his, the Goths ! And who were they.?
Your blood, your bone, your spirit, and your soul !
They with your fathers roamed four hundred years

The Teuton waste ; they swam the Teuton floods,
They pointed with the self-same hand of scorn
At Rome, their common foe !   In Odin's loins
Together came ye from the shining East :—
True man was he : ye changed him to false god !
That Odin, when the destined hour had pealed,
Beckoned to Alaric, marched by Alaric's side
Invisibly to Rome !

               Ye know the tale :
Her senate-kings their portals barred ; they deemed
That awe of Rome would drive him back amazed ;
And sat secure at feast.   But he that slew
Remus, his brother, on the unfinished wall,
A bitter expiation paid that night !
The wail went up : the Goths were lords of Rome !—
Alaric alone in that dread hour was just,
And with his mercy tempered justice.   Why ?
Alaric that day was Christian : of his host
The best and bravest Christian.   Senators
In purple nursed lived on, 'tis true, in rags ;
To Asian galleys and Egyptian marts
The rich were driven ; the mighty.   Gold in streams
Ran molten from the Capitolian roofs :
The idol statues choked old Tyber's wave :
But life and household honour Alaric spared ;
And round the fanes of Peter and of Paul

His soldiers stood on guard. Upon the grave
Of that bad Empire sentenced, nay of all
The Empires of this world absorbed in one,
In one condemned, they throned the Church of Christ ;
His Kingdom's seat established.

                         Since that hour
That Kingdom spreads o'er earth. In Eastern Gaul
Long since your brave Burgundians kneel to Christ ;
Pannonia gave Him to the Ostro-Goths,
Barbaric named ; and to the Suevi Spain :
The Vandals o'er the Mauritanian shores
Exalt His Cross with joy. Your pardon, sirs :
These lands to you are names ; but Odin knew them ;
A living man he trod them in his youth ;
Hated their vices ; bound his race to spurn
Their bait, their bond ! That day he saw hath dawned ;
O'er half a world the vivifying airs
Launched from your northern forests chaste and cold
Have blown, and blow this hour ! The Saxon race
Alone its destiny knows not. Ye have won
Here in this Isle the old Roman heritage :
Perfect your victory o'er that Pagan Rome
With Christian Rome partaking !

                         Earls and Thanes,
But one word more. Your pontiff late averred
That kings to us are gods ; through them we conquer :

I answer thus : That Kingdom God hath raised
Is sovereign and is one ; kingdoms of earth,
How great soe'er, to it are provinces
In spiritual things.   If princes turn to God
They save their souls.   If kingdoms war on God
Their choice is narrow, and their choice is this :
To break, like that which falleth on a stone ;
Or else, like that whereon that stone doth fall,
To crumble into dust.'

                    The Pagan priest
Whispered again to Eardulf, 'Praise to Thor !
He flouts our king ! The boaster's chance is gone !'
Then rose that king and spake in careless sort :
'Earls and my Thanes, I came from exile late :
It may be that to exile I return :
Not less my arm is long ; my sword is sharp :
Let him that hates me fear me !

                       Earls and Thanes,
I passed that exile in a Christian realm :
There of the Christian greatness, Christian right,
I somewhat heard, and hearing, disbelieved ;
Saw likewise somewhat, and believed in part :
Saw more, till nigh that part had grown to whole :
I saw that war itself might be a thing
Though stern, yet stern in mercy ; saw that peace
Might wear a shape dearest to manliest heart,

Peace based on fearless justice militant
'Gainst wrong alone and riot.   Earls and Thanes,
Returned, this day and in this regal hall
A spectacle I saw, if grateful less,
Not therefore less note-worthy—countless swords
In judgment drawn against a man unarmed ;
Yea, and a man unarmed with brow unmoved
Confronting countless swords.   These things I saw ;
Fair sight that tells me how to act, and when ;
For I was minded to protract the time,
Which strangles oft best purpose.   At the font
Of Christ—it stands a bow-shot from this spot,
As late we learned—at daybreak I and mine
Become henceforth Christ's lieges.

                                        Earls and Thanes,

I heard but late a railer who affirmed
That kings were tyrants o'er the faiths of men
Flexile to please them : thus I make reply ;
The meanest of my subjects, like his king,
Shall serve his God in freedom : if the chief
Questions the equal freedom of his king
That man shall die the death !   Through Christian
        Faith—
I hide not this—one danger threats the land :
It threats as much, nay more, my royal House :
That danger must be dared since truth is truth :

That danger ye shall learn tomorrow noon :
Till comes that hour, farewell ! '

                         The matin beam,
God's wingèd messenger from loftier worlds,
Through the deep window of the baptistery
Glittered on eddies of the bath-like font
Not yet quiescent since its latest guest
Had thence arisen ; beside its marge the king
In snowy raiment stood ; upon his right,
Alfred, his first-born, boy of seven years old,
And, close beside, in wonder not in dread,
Mildrede, his sister, younger by one year,
Holding her brother's hand.   From either waist
Flowed a white kirtle to the small snow feet
With roses tinged.   Above it all was bare,
And with the fontal dew-drops sparkling still ;
While from each head with sacred unction sealed
Floated the chrismal veil.   That eye is blind
Which sees not beauty save on female brows :
On either face that hour the lustre lay ;
But hers was lustre passive, lustre pale ;
The boy's was active, daring, penetrating—
The lily she ; but he the Morning Star,
Beaming thereon from heaven !   With dewy eyes
The strong king on them gazed, and inly mused,

'To God I gave them up : yet ne'er till now
Seemed they so wholly mine !'

                       Birinus spake :
'Ye have been washed in baptism, though no sin
Hath yet been yours save Adam's, and confirmed ;
And houselled ye shall be at Mass seven days,
Since Christ in infant bosoms loves to dwell.
Pray, day by day, that Christ would keep you pure :
Pray for your Father : likewise pray for me,
Old sinner soon to die.' · Then raised those babes
Their baptism tapers high, and fixing eyes
That moved not on their backward-fluttering flames,
Led the procession to their palace home,
Their father pacing last.

                     That day at noon
The monarch sat upon his royal throne,
Birinus near him standing : at his feet
His children played ; while round him silent thronged
Warriors and chiefs.   The king addressed them thus :
'Birinus, and the rest, I hold it meet
A king should hide his secret from his foes,
But with his friends be open.   Yestereve
I, Christian now, unfaulteringly avouched
That in the victory of the Christian Faith,
True though it be, one danger I discerned :

That danger, and its root, I now divulge.
Saw ye the scorn within that Northman's eye
Last eve, when, praising Thor, in balance stern
He weighed what now we are with what we were
When first he trod our shores !   He spake the truth :
His race and ours are kin ; but his retain
Stronglier their manly virtue, frost and snow
Like whetstones sharpening still that virtue's edge.
We soften with the years.   Beggars this day
Sue us for bread !   Sirs, in a famine once
I saw, then young, a hundred at a time
That, linking hand in hand, loud singing rushed,
Like hunters chasing hart, to sea-beat cliffs,
And o'er them plunged !   Now comes this Faith of
     Christ ;
That Faith to which, because that Faith is true,
I pledged this morn my word, my seal, my soul,
The fate and fortunes of our native land
And all my royal House, well knowing this,
The king who loves his kingdom more than God,
Better than both loves self—no king at heart.
Now comes this Christian Faith !   That Faith, be sure,
Is not a hardening faith : gentle it makes.:—
I told you, Lords, we soften day by day ;
I might have added that with growing years
Hardness we doubly need.   When Rome was great

Our race, however far diffused, was one,
Blended by hate of Rome.   When Rome declined
That bond dissolved. · A second bond remained
In Odin's Faith :—Northmen alone retain it.
In them a new Rome rises !   Earls and Thanes !
The truth be ours though for that truth we die !
Hold fast that truth ; yet hide not what it costs.
Through fog and sea-mist of the days to come
I see huge navies with the raven flag
Steering to milder borders Christian half,
Brother 'gainst brother ranging.   Kingdoms Seven
Of this still fair and once heroic land,
I say, beware that hour !   If come it must,
Then fall the thunder while I walk this earth,
Not when I skulk in crypts !'

                        The others mute,
From joy malicious some, some vexed with doubt,
Birinus made reply : ' My Lord and King,
Inly this day I gladden, certain now
That neither fancy-drawn, nor anger-spurred,
Nor seeking crowns, for others or thyself,
Nor shunning woes, the worst that earth can know,
For others or thyself, but urged by faith,
God's greatest gift to man, thou mad'st this day
Submission true to Christ.   So be it, King !
So rest content !   God with a finger's touch

Could melt that cloud which threats thy realm well-
    loved;
(That threat I deem nor trivial nor obscure)
Not thus He wills.   Danger, distress, reverse,
Are heralds sent from God, like peace and joy,
To nations as to men.   Happy that land
Which worketh darkling; worketh without wage;
And worketh still for God !   If God desired
A people for His sacrificial lamb,
Happiest of nations should that nation be
Which died His willing victim !'

                              'King, and Son,'
With voice a moment troubled he resumed,
'Thy future rests with God !   Yet shake, Oh shake
One boding grief—'tis causeless—from thy breast,
Deeming thy race less valiant than the North :
Faithfuller they stand and nearer to their sires !
Remorseless less to others and to self
I grant them ; that implies not valiant less :
The brave are still in spirit the merciful ;
Far down within their being stirs a sense
Of more than race or realm.   Some claim world-wide,
Whereof the prophet is the wailing babe,
Smites on their hearts—a cradle decks therein
For Him they know not yet, the Bethlehem Babe.
That claim thy fathers felt !   Through Teuton woods

(Dead Rome's historian saw what he records [1]),
Moved forth of old in cyclic pilgrimage
Thick-veiled, the sacred image of the Earth,
All reverend Mother, crowned Humanity !
Not war-steeds haled her car, but oxen meek ;
And, as it passed oppugnant bounds, the trump
Ceased from its blare ; the lance, the war-axe fell ;
Grey foes shook hands ; their children played together :
Beyond the limit line of dateless wars
Looked forth the vision thus of endless peace.
Think'st thou that here was lack of manly heart?
King, this was manhood's self ! '

$$\text{While thus he spake,}$$

Alfred, and Mildrede, children of the King,
That long time, by that voice majestic charmed,
Had turned from distant sports, upon their knees
Softly and slowly tô Birinus crept,
Their wide eyes from his countenance moving not,
And so knelt on ; Alfred, the star-eyed boy
Supported by his father's sceptre-staff,
His plaything late, now clasped in hands high-held.
Him with a casual eye Birinus marked
At first; then stood, with upward brow, in trance—
Sudden, as though with Pentecostal flame,

[1] Tacitus.

His whole face brightened ; on him fell from God
Spirit Divine ; and thus the prophet cried :

　‘ Who speaks of danger when the Lord of all
Decrees high triumph?　Victory's chariot winged
Up-climbs the frowning mountains of Dismay,
As when above the sea's nocturnal verge
Twin beams, divergent horns of orient light,
Announce the ascending sun.　Whatever cloud
Protracts the conflict, victory comes at last.

　‘ What ho ! ye sons of Odin and the north !
Far off your galleys tarry !　English air
Reafen, your raven standard, darkened long,
Woven of enchantments in the moon's eclipse :
It rains its plague no more !　The Kingdoms Seven
Ye came to set a ravening each on each :
Lo, ye have pressed and soldered them in one !

　‘ Behold, a Sceptre rises—not o'er Kent
The first-born of the Faith ; nor o'er those vales
Northumbrian, trod so long by crownèd saints ;
Nor Mercia's plains invincible in war:
O'er Wessex, barbarous late, and waste, and small,
The Hand that made the worlds that Sceptre lifts ;
Hail tribe elect, the Judah of the Seven !

' Piercing the darkness of an age unborn,
I see a King that hides his royal robe ;
Assumes the minstrel's garb. . Where meet the floods
That King abides his time. I see him sweep,
Disguised, his harp within the Northmen's camp ;
In fifty fights I see him victory-crowned ;
I· see the mighty and the proud laid low,
The humble lifted. God is over all.

' The ruined cities 'mid their embers thrill.:
A voice went forth : they heard it. They shall rise,
Their penance done, and cities worthier far
With Roman vices ne'er contaminate.
These shall not boast mosaic floor gem-wrought,
And trod by sinners. In the face of heaven
Their minster turrets these shall lift on high,
Inviting God's great angels to descend
And chaunt with them God's City here on earth.

' Who through the lethal forest cleaves a road
Healthful and fresh ? Who bridges stream high-swollen?
Who spreads the harvest round the poor man's cot ;
Sets free the slave ? On justice realms are built :
Who makes his kingdom great through equal laws
Not based on Pagan right, but rights in Christ,
First just, then free ? Who from her starry gates

Beckons to Heavenly Wisdom—her who played
Ere worlds were shaped, before the eyes of God?
Who bids her walk the peopled fields of men,
The reverend street with college graced and church?
Who sings the latest of the Saxon songs?
Who tunes to Saxon speech the Tome Divine?

   'Sing, happy land! The Isle that, prescient long,
Long waiting, hid her monarch in her heart,
Shall look on him and cry, "My flesh, my bone,
My son, my king!" To him shall Cambria bow,
And Alba's self. His strength is in his God;
The third part of his time he gives to prayer,
And God shall hear his vows! Hail, mighty King!
For aye thine England's glory! As I gaze,
Methinks I see a likeness on thy brow,
Likeness to one who kneels beside my feet!
The sceptre comes to him who sceptre spurned;
Through him it comes who sceptre clasped in sport;
From Wessex' soil shall England's hope be born
Two centuries hence; and Alfred is his name!'

EPILOGUE.

———◆———

BEDE'S LAST MAY.

———

Bede issues forth from Jarrow, and visiting certain villagers in a wood, expounds to them the Beatitudes of Our Lord. Wherever he goes he seeks records of past times, and promises in return that he will bequeath to his fellow-countrymen translations from divers Sacred Scriptures, and likewise a history of God's Church in their land. Having returned to his monastery, he dies a most happy death on the feast of the Ascension, while finishing his translation of St. John's gospel.

———

THE ending of the Book of Saxon Saints.
With one lay-brother only blessed Bede,
In after times 'The Venerable' named,
Passed from his convent, Jarrow. Where the Tyne
Blends with the sea, all beautiful it stood,
Bathed in the sunrise. At the mouth of Wear
A second convent, Wearmouth, rose. That hour

The self-same matin splendour gilt them both;
And in some speech of mingling lights, not words,
Both sisters praised their God.

'Apart, yet joined '—

So mused the old man gazing on the twain :
Then onward paced, with head above his book,
Murmuring his office.   Algar walked behind,
A youth of twenty years, with tonsured head,
And face, though young, forlorn.   An hour had passed ;
They reached a craggy height ; and looking back,
Beheld once more beyond the forest roof
Those two fair convents glittering—at their feet
Those two clear rivers winding !   Bound by rule,
Again the monk addressed him to his book ;
Lection and psalm recited, thus he spake :

'Why placed our holy Founder thus so near
His convents ?   Why, albeit a single rule,
At last a single hand, had sway o'er both,
Placed them at distance ?   Hard it were to guess :
I know but this, that severance here on earth
Is strangely linked with union of the heart,
Union with severance.   Thou hast lost, young friend,
But lately lost thy boyhood's dearest mate,
Thine earliest friend, a brother of thy heart,
True Christian soul though dwelling in the world ;

Fear not such severance can extinguish love
Here, or hereafter !   He whom most I loved
Was severed from me by the tract of years :
A child of nine years old was I, when first
Jarrow received me : pestilence ere long
Swept from that house her monks, save one alone,
Ceolfrid, then its abbot.   Man and child,
We two the lonely cloisters paced ; we two
Together chaunted in the desolate church :
I could not guess his thoughts ; to him my ways
Were doubtless as the ways of some sick bird
Watched by a child.   Not less I loved him well :
Me too he somewhat loved.   Beneath one roof
We dwelt—and yet how severed !   Save in God,
What know men, one of other?   Here on earth,
Perhaps 'tis wiser to be kind to all
In large goodwill of helpful love, yet free,
Than link to one our heart—
Poor youth ! that love which walks in narrow ways
Is tragic love, be sure.'
      With gentle face
The novice spake his gratitude.   Once more,
His hand upon the shoulder of the youth,
(For now they mounted slow a bosky dell)
The old man spake—yet not to him—in voice
Scarce louder than the murmuring pines close by ;

For, by his being's law he seemed, like them,
At times when pensive memories in him stirred,
Vocal not less than visible : ' How great
Was he, our Founder ! In that ample brow,
What brooding weight of genius ! In his eye,
How strangely was the pathos edged with light !
How oft, his churches roaming, flashed its beam
From pillar on to pillar, resting long
On carven imagery of flower or fruit,
Or deep-dyed window whence the heavenly choirs
Gave joy to men below ! With what a zeal
He drew the cunningest craftsmen from all climes
To express his thoughts in form ; while yet his hand,
Like meanest hand among us, patient toiled
In garden and in bakehouse, threshed the corn,
Or drave the calves to milk-pail ! Earthly rule
Had proved to him a weight intolerable ;
In spiritual beauty, there and there alone,
Our Bennett Biscop found his native haunt,
The lucent planet of his soul's repose :
And yet—O wondrous might of human love—
One was there, one, to whom his heart was knit,
Siegfried, in all unlike him save in worth.
His was plain purpose, rectitude unwarped,
Industry, foresight. On his friend's behalf
He ruled long years those beauteous convents twain,

Yet knew not they were beauteous! An abyss
Severed in spirit those in heart so near :
More late exterior severance came: three years
In cells remote they dwelt, by sickness chained :
But once they met—to die. I see them still :
The monks had laid them on a single bed ;
Weeping, they turned them later each to each :
I saw the snowy tresses softly mix ;
I saw the faded lips draw near and meet ;
Thus gently interwreathed I saw them die—
Strange strength of human love !'

                 Still **walked they on** :
As high the sun ascended, woodlands green
Shivered all golden ; and the old man's heart
Brightened like them. His ever active mind
Inquisitive took note of all it saw ;
And as some youth enamoured lifts a tress
Of her he loves, and wonders, so the monk,
Well loving Nature, loved her in detail,
Now pleased with nestling bird, anon with flower,
Now noting how the beech from dewy sheath
Pushed forth its silken leaflets fringed with down,
Exulting next because from sprays of lime
The little fledgeling leaves, like creatures winged,
Brake from their ruddy shells. Jesting, he cried :
'Algar ! but hear those birds ! Men say they sing

To fire their young, night-bound, with gladsome news,
And bid them seek the sun !'   Sadly the youth
With downward front, replied : 'My friend is dead ;
For me to gladden were to break a troth.'
Upon the brow of Bede a shadow fell ;
Silent he paced, then stopped : 'Forgive me, Algar !
Old men grow hard.   Yet boys and girls salute
The May : like them the old must have their maying ;
This is perchance my last.'
                              As thus he spake
They reached the summit of a grassy hill ;
Beneath there wound a stream, upon its marge
A hamlet nestling lonely in the woods :
Its inmates saw the Saint, and t'wards him sped
Eager as birds that, when the grain is flung
In fountained cloister-court of Eastern church,
From all sides flock, with sudden rush of wings,
Darkening the pavement.   Youths·and maids came first ;
Their elders followed : some his garments kissed,
And some his hands.   The venerable man
Stretched forth his arms, as though to clasp them all :
Above them next he signed his Master's cross ;
Then, while the tears ran down his aged face,
Brake forth in grateful joy ; ' To God the praise !
When, forty years ago, I roamed this vale
A haunt it was of rapine and of wars ;

Now see I pleasant pastures, peaceful homes,
And faces peacefuller yet. That God Who walked
With His disciples 'mid the sabbath fields
While they the wheat-ears bruised, His sabbath keeps
Within your hearts this day! His harvest ye!
Once more a-hungered are His holy priests;
They hunger for your souls; with reverent palms
Daily the chaff they separate from the grain;
Daily His Church within her heart receives you,
Yea, with her heavenly substance makes you one;
Ye grow to be her eyes that see His truth;
Her ears that hear His voice; her hands that pluck
His tree of life; her feet that walk His ways.
Honouring God's priests ye err not, O my friends,
Since thus ye honour God. In Him rejoice!'

So spake he, and his gladness kindled theirs;
With it their courage. One her infant brought
And sued for him a blessing. One, bereaved,
Cried out : 'Your promised peace has come at last;
No more I wish him back to earth!' Again
Old foes shook hands; while now, their fears forgot,
Children that lately nestled at his feet
Clomb to his knees. Then called from out that crowd
A blind man; 'Read once more that Book of God!
For, after you had left us, many a month

I, who can neither see the sun nor moon,
Saw oft the God-Man walking farms and fields
Of that fair Eastern land ! '   He spake, and lo !
All those around that heard him clamoured, ' Read ! '

  Then Bede, the Sacred Scriptures opening, lit
Upon the ' Sermon on the Mount,' and read :
' The Saviour lifted up His holy eyes
On His disciples, saying, Blessed they ; '
Expounding next the sense.   ' Why fixed the Lord
His eyes on them that listened ?   Friends, His eyes
Go down through all things, searching out the heart ;
He sees if heart be sound to hold His Word
And bring forth fruit in season, or as rock
Naked to bird that plucks the random seed.
Friends, with the heart alone we understand ;
Who doth His will shall of the doctrine know
If His it be indeed.   When Jesus speaks
Fix first your eyes upon His eyes divine,
There reading what He sees within your heart :
If sin He sees, repent ! '
        With hands upheld
A woman raised her voice, and cried aloud,
' Could we but look into the eyes of Christ
Nought should we see but love ! '   And Bede replied :
' From babe and suckling God shall perfect praise !

Yea, from His eyes looks forth the Eternal Love,
Though oft, through sin of ours, in sadness veiled ;
But when He rests them on disciples true,
Not on the stranger, love is love alone !
O great, true hearts that love so well your Lord !
That heard so trustingly His tidings good,
So long, by trial proved, have kept His Faith,
To you He cometh—cometh with reward
In heaven, and here on earth.'
                    With brightening face,
As one who flingeth largess far abroad,
Once more he raised the sacred tome, and read,
Read loud the Eight Beatitudes of Christ ;
Then ceased, but later spake : ' In ampler phrase
Those Blessings ye shall hear once more rehearsed,
And deeplier understand them.   Blessed they
The poor in spirit ; for to humble hearts
Belongs the kingdom of their God in heaven ;
Blessed the meek—nor gold they boast, nor power ;
Yet theirs alone the sweetness of this earth ;
Blessed are they who mourn, for on their hearts
The consolation of their God shall fall ;
Blessed are they who hunger and who thirst
For righteousness ; they shall be satisfied ;
Blessed the merciful, for unto them
The God of mercy mercy shall accord ;

Blessed are they, the pure in heart ; their eyes
Shall see their God : Blessed the peacemakers ;
This title man shall give them—Sons of God ;
Blessed are they who suffer for the cause
Righteous and just : a throne is theirs on high :
Blessed are ye when sinners cast you forth,
And brand your name with falsehood for my sake ;
Rejoice, for great is your reward in heaven.'

   Once more the venerable man made pause,
Giving his Master's Blessings time to sink
Through hearts of those who heard.   Anon with speech
Though fervent, grave, he shewed the glory and grace
Of those majestic Virtues crowned by Christ,
While virtues praised by worldlings passed unnamed ;
How wondrously consentient each with each,
Like flowers well sorted, or like notes well joined :
Then changed the man to deeper theme ; he shewed
How these high virtues, ere to man consigned,
Were warmed and moulded in the God-Man's heart ;
Thence born, and in its sacred blood baptized.
' What are these virtues but the life of Christ ?
The poor in spirit ; must not they be lowly
Whose God is One that stooped to wear our flesh ?
The meek ; was He not meek Whom sinners mocked ?
The mourners ; sent not He the Comforter ?

Zeal for the good ; was He not militant ?
The merciful ; He came to bring us mercy ;
The pure in heart ; was He not virgin-born ?
Peacemakers ; is not He the Prince of Peace ?
Sufferers for God ; He suffered first for man.
O Virtues blest by Christ, high doctrines ye !
Dread mysteries ; royal records ; standards red
Wrapped by the warrior King, His warfare past,
Around His soldiers' bosoms !   Recognise,
O man, that majesty in lowness hid !
Put on Christ's garments.   Fools shall call them rags—
Heed not their scoff !   A prince's child is man,
Born in the purple ; but his royal robes
None other are than those the Saviour dyed,
Treading His Passion's wine-press all alone :
Of such alone be proud ! '

                       The old man paused ;
Then stretched his arms abroad, and said : ' This day,
Like eight great angels making way from Heaven,
Each following each, those Eight Beatitudes,
Missioned to earth by Him who made the earth,
Have sought you out !   What welcome shall be theirs ? '
In silence long he stood ; in silence watched,
With faded cheek now flushed and widening eyes,
The advance of those high tidings.   As a man
Who, when the sluice is cut, with beaming gaze

Pursues the on-rolling flood from fall to fall,
Green branch adown it swept, and showery spray
Silvering the berried copse, so followed Bede
The progress of those high Beatitudes
Brightening, with visible beams of faith and love,
That host in ampler circles, speechless some
And some in passionate converse.   Saddest brows
Most quickly caught, that hour, the glory-touch,
Reflected it the best.

                  In such discourse,
Peaceful and glad the hours went by, though Bede
Had sought that valley less to preach the Word
Than see once more his children.   Evening nigh
He shared their feast ; and heard with joy like theirs
Their village harp ; and smote that harp himself.
In turn become their scholar, hour by hour
Forth dragged he records of their chiefs and kings,
Untangling ravelled evidence, and still
Tracking traditions upward to their source,
Like him, that Halicarnassean sage,
Of antique history sire.   ' I trust, my friends,
To leave your sons, for lore by you bestowed
Fair recompense, large measure well pressed down,
Recording still God's kingdom in this land,
History which all may read, and gentle hearts
Loving, may grow in grace.   .Long centuries passed,

If wealth should make this nation's heart too fat,
And things of earth obscure the things of heaven,
Haply such chronicle may prompt high hearts
Wearied with shining nothings, back to cast
Remorseful gaze through mists of time, and note
That rock whence they were hewn. From youth to age
Inmate of yonder convent on the Tyne,
I question every pilgrim, priest, or prince,
Or peasant grey, and glean from each his sheaf :
Likewise the Bishops here and Abbots there
Still send me deed of gift, or chronicle
Or missive from the Apostolic See :
Praise be to God Who fitteth for his place
Not only high but mean ! With wisdom's strength
He filled our mitred Wilfred, born to rule ;
To saintly Cuthbert gave the spirit of prayer ;
On me, as one late born, He lays a charge
Slender, yet helpful still.'
        Then spake a man
Burly and big, that last at banquet sat,
' Father, is history true ? ' and Bede replied ;
' The man who seeks for Truth like hidden gold,
And shrinks from falsehood as a leper's touch
Shall write true history ; not the truth unmixed
With fancies, base or high ; not truth entire ;
Yet truth beneficent to man below.

One Book there is that errs not : ye this day
Have learned therefrom your Lord's Beatitudes :
That Book contains its histories—like them none,
Since written none from standing point so high,
With insight so inspired, such measure just
Of good and ill ; high fruit of aid divine.
The slothful spurn that Book ; the erroneous warp :
But they who read its page, or hear it read,
Their guide, God's Spirit, and the Church of God,
Shall hear the voice of Truth for ever nigh,
Shall see the Truth, now sunlike, and anon
Like dagger-point of light from dewy grass
Flashed up, a word that yet confutes a life,
Pierces, perchance a nation's heart : shall see
Far more—the Truth Himself in human form,
Walking not farms and fields of Eastern lands
Alone, but these our English fields and farms ;
Shall see Him on the dusky mount at prayer ;
Shall see Him in the street and by the bier ;
Shall see Him at the feast, and at the grave ;
Now from the boat discoursing, and anon
Staying the storm, or walking on its waves ;
Thus shall our land become a holy land
And holy those who tread her !' Lifting then
Heavenward that tome, he said, ' The Book of God !
As stands God's Church, 'mid kingdoms of this world

Holy alone, so stands, 'mid books, this Book !
Within the " Upper Chamber " once that Church
Lived in small space ; to-day she fills the world :—
This Book which seems so narrow is a world :
It is an Eden of mankind restored ;
It is a heavenly city lit with God :
From it the Spirit and the Bride say " Come : "
Blessed who reads this Book ! '
                                        Above the woods
Meantime the stars shone forth ; and came that hour
When to the wanderer and the toiling man
Repose is sweet.   Upon a leaf-strewn bed
The venerable man slept well that night :
Next morning young and old pursued his steps
As southward he departed.   From a hill
O'er-looking far that sea-like forest tract
And many a church far-kenned through smokeless air,
He blessed that kneeling concourse, adding thus,
' Pray still, O friends, for me, since spiritual foes
Threat most the priesthood :—pray that holy death,
Due warning given, may close a life too blest !
Pray well, since I for you have laboured well,
Yea, and will labour till my latest sigh ;
Not only seeking you in wilds and woods
Year after year, but in my cell at night
Changing to accents of your native tongue

T

God's Book Divine.   Farewell, my friends, farewell ! '
He left them ; in his heart this thought, ' How like
The great death-parting every parting seems ! '
But deathless hopes were with him ; and the May ;
His grief went by.

              So passed a day of Bede's ;
And many a studious year were stored with such ;
Enough but one for sample.   Two glad weeks
He and his comrade onward roved.   At eve
Convent or hamlet, known long since and loved,
Gladly received them.   Bede with heart as glad
Renewed with them the memory of old times,
Recounted benefits by him received,
Then strong in youth, from just men passed away,
And preached his Master still with power so sweet
The listeners ne'er forgat him.   Evermore,
Parting, he planted in the ground a cross,
And bade the neighbours till their church was built
Round it to pray.   Meanwhile his youthful mate
Changed by degrees.   The ever varying scene,
The biting breath and balmy breast of spring,
And most of all that old man's valiant heart
Triumphed above his sadness, fancies gay
Pushing beyond it like those sunnier shoots
That gild the dark vest of the vernal pine.
He took account of all things as they passed ;

He laughed; he told his tale. With quiet joy
His friend remarked that change. The second week
They passed to Durham; next to Walsingham;
To Gilling then; to stately Richmond soon
High throned above her Ouse; to Ripon last:
Then Bede made pause, and spake; 'Not far is York;
Egbert who fills Paulinus' saintly seat
Would see me gladly: such was mine intent,
But something in my bosom whispers, "Nay,
Return to that fair river crossed by night,
The Tees, the fairest in this Northern land:
Beside its restless wave thine eye shall rest
On vision lovelier far and more benign
Than all it yet hath seen."' Northward once more
They faced, and, three days travelling, reached at eve
Again those ivied cliffs that guard the Tees:
There as they stood a homeward dove, with flight
Softer for contrast with that turbulent stream,
Sailed through the crimson eve. 'No sight like that!'
Thus murmured Bede; 'ever to me it seems
A Christian soul returning to its rest.'
A shade came o'er his countenance as he mused;
Algar remarked that shade, though what it meant
He knew not yet. The old man from that hour
Seemed mirthful less, less buoyant, beaming less,
Yet not less glad.

At dead of night, while hung
The sacred stars upon their course half way,
He left his couch, and thus to Egbert wrote,
Meek man—too meek—the brother of the king,
With brow low bent, and onward sweeping hand,
Great words, world-famed : ' Remember thine account !
The Lord's Apostles are the salt of earth ;
Let salt not lose its savour ! Flail and fan
Are given thee. Purge thou well thy threshing floor !
Repel the tyrant ; hurl the hireling forth ;
That so from thy true priests true hearts may learn
True faith, true love, and nothing but the truth ! '

Before the lark he rose the morrow morn,
And stood by Algar's bed, and spake : ' Arise !
Playtime is past ; the great, good work returns ;
To Jarrow speed we ! ' Homeward, day by day,
Thenceforth they sped with foot that lagged no more,
That youth, at first so mournful, joyous now,
That old man oft in thought. Next day, while eve
Descended dim, and clung to Hexham's groves,
He passed its abbey, silent. Wonder-struck
Algar demanded, ' Father, pass you thus
That church where holy John [1] ordained you priest ?
Pass you its Bishop, Acca, long your friend ?

[1] St. John of Beverley.

Yearly he woos your visit ; tells you tales
Of Hexham's saintly Wilfred ; shows you still
Chalice or cross new-won from distant shores :
Nor these alone :—glancing from such last year
A page he read you of some Pagan bard
With smiles ; yet ended with a sigh, and said :
" Where is he now ? " ' The man of God replied :
' Desire was mine to see mine ancient friend ;
For that cause came I hither :—time runs short ' :—
Then, Algar sighing, thus he added mild,
' Let go that theme ; thy mourning time is past :
Thy gladsome time is now.' As on they walked,
Later he spake : ' It may be I was wrong ;
Old friends should part in hope.'

                       On Jarrow's towers,
Bright as that sunrise while that pair went forth
The sunset glittered when, their wanderings past,
Bede and his comrade by the bank of Tyne
Once more approached the gates. Six hundred monks
Flocked forth to meet them. ' They had grieved, I know,'
Thus spake, low-voiced, the venerable man,
' If I had died remote. To spare that grief
Before the time intended I returned.'
Sadly that comrade looked upon his face,
Yet saw there nought of sadness. Silent each
Advanced they till they met that cowlèd host :

But three weeks later on his bed the boy
Remembered well those words.

                      Within a cell
To Algar's near that later night a youth
Wrote thus to one far off, his earliest friend :
' O blessed man ! was e'er a death so sweet !
He sang that verse, " A dreadful thing it is
To fall into the hands of God, All-Just ;"
Yet awe in him seemed swallowed up by love ;
And ofttimes with the Prophets and the Psalms
He mixed glad minstrelsies of English speech,
Songs to his childhood dear !

                        ' O blessed man !
The Ascension Feast of Christ our Lord drew nigh ;
He watched that splendour's advent ; sang its hymn :
" All-glorious King, Who, triumphing this day,
Into the heaven of heavens didst make ascent,
Forsake us not, poor orphans !   Send Thy Spirit,
The Spirit of Truth, the Father's promised Gift,
To comfort us, His children : Hallelujah."
And when he reached that word, " Forsake us not,"
He wept—not tears of grief.   With him we wept;
Alternate wept ; alternate read our rite ;
Yea, while we wept we read.   So passed that day,
The sufferer thanking God with labouring breath,
" God scourges still the son whom He receives."

' Undaunted, unamazed, daily he wrought
His daily task ; instruction daily gave
To us his scholars round him ranged, and said,
" I will not have my pupils learn a lie,
Nor, fruitless, toil therein when I am gone."
Full well he kept an earlier promise, made
Ofttimes to humble folk, in English tongue
Rendering the Gospels of the Lord.   On these,
The last of these, the Gospel of Saint John,
He laboured till the close.   The days went by,
And still he toiled, and panted, and gave thanks
To God with hands uplifted ; yea, in sleep
He made thanksgiving still.   When Tuesday came
Suffering increased ; he said, " My time is short ;
How short it is I know not." Yet we deemed
He knew the time of his departure well.

' On Wednesday morn once more he bade us write :
We wrote till the third hour, and left him then
To pace, in reverence of that Feast all-blest,
Our cloister court with hymns.   Meantime a youth,
Algar by name, there was who left him never ;
The same that hour beside him sat and wrote :
More late he questioned : " Father well-beloved,
One chapter yet remaineth ; have you strength
To dictate more ? "   He answered : " I have strength ;

Make ready, son, thy pen, and swiftly write."
When noon had come he turned him round and said,
" I have some little gifts for those I love ;
Call in the Brethren ;" adding with a smile,
"The rich man makes bequests, and why not I ? "
Then gifts he gave, incense or altar-cloth,
To each, commanding, " Pray ye for my soul ;
Be strong in prayer and offering of the 'Mass,
For ye shall see my face no more on earth :
Blessed hath been my life ; and time it is
That unto God God's creature should return ;
Yea, I desire to die, and be with Christ."
Thus speaking, he rejoiced till evening's shades
Darkened around us.　That disciple young
Once more addressed him, " Still one verse remains ; "
The master answered, " Write, and write with speed ; "
And dictated.　The young man wrote ; then said,
" 'Tis finished now."　The man of God replied :
" Well say'st thou, son, ' 'tis finished.'　In thy hands
Receive my head, and move it gently round,
For comfort great it is, and joy in death,
Thus, on this pavement of my little cell,
Facing that happy spot whereon so oft
In prayer I knelt, to sit once more in prayer,
Thanking my Father."　" Glory," then he sang,
" To God, the Father, Son, and Holy Ghost ; "

And with that latest Name upon his lips
Passed to the Heavenly Kingdom.'

                          Thus with joy
Died holy Bede upon Ascension Day
In Jarrow Convent.   May he pray for us,
And all who read his annals of God's Church
In England housed, his great bequest to man !

NOTES.

———◦•◦———

Page xxxvi. *The Irish Mission in England during the seventh century was one of the great things of history.*

THE following expressions of Dr. von Döllinger respecting the Irish Church are more ardent than any I have ventured to use :—

'During the sixth and seventh centuries the Church of Ireland stood in the full beauty of its bloom. The spirit of the Gospel operated amongst the people with a vigorous and vivifying power : troops of holy men, from the highest to the lowest ranks of society, obeyed the counsel of Christ, and forsook all things that they might follow Him. There was not a country in the world, during this period, which could boast of pious foundations or of religious communities equal to those that adorned this far distant island. Among the Irish the doctrines of the Christian religion were preserved pure and entire ; the names of heresy or of schism were not known to them ; and in the Bishop of Rome they acknowledged and venerated the Supreme Head of the Church on earth, and continued with him, and through him with the whole Church, in a never interrupted communion. The schools in the Irish cloisters were at this time the most celebrated in all the West. . . . The strangers who visited the island, not only from the neighbouring shores of Britain, but also from the most remote nations of the Continent, received from the Irish people the most hospitable reception, a gratuitous entertainment, free instruction, and even the books that were necessary for the studies. . . . On the other hand, many holy and learned Irish-

men left their own country to proclaim the Faith, to establish or
to reform monasteries in distant lands, and thus to become the
benefactors of almost every country in Europe. . . . The founda-
tion of many of the English Sees is due to Irishmen. . . . These
holy men served God, and not the world ; they possessed neither
gold nor silver, and all that they received from the rich passed
through their hands into the hands of the poor.   Kings and nobles
visited them from time to time only to pray in their churches, or
to listen to their sermons ; and as long as they remained in the
cloisters they were content with the humble food of the brethren.
Wherever one of these ecclesiastics or monks came, he was received
by all with joy ; and whenever he was seen journeying across the
country, the people streamed around him to implore his benediction,
and to hearken to his words.   The priests entered the villages only
to preach or to administer the Sacraments ; and so free were they
from avarice, that it was only when compelled by the rich and noble
that they would accept lands for the erection of monasteries.'

Page xliii.   *For both countries that early time was a period of*
wonderful spiritual greatness.

I cannot deny myself the pleasure of quoting the following
passage illustrating the religious greatness both of the Irish and the
English at the period referred to :—

'The seventh and eighth centuries are the glory of the Anglo-
Saxon Church, as the sixth and seventh are of the Irish.   As the
Irish missionaries travelled down through England, France, and
Switzerland, to Lower Italy, and attempted Germany at the peril
of their lives, converting the barbarian, restoring the lapsed,
encouraging the desolate, collecting the scattered, and founding
churches, schools, and monasteries as they went along ; so amid
the deep pagan woods of Germany, and round about, the English
Benedictine plied his axe, and drove his plough, planted his rude
dwelling, and raised his rustic altar upon the ruins of idolatry ; and
then, settling down as a colonist upon the soil, began to sing his
chants and to copy his old volumes, and thus to lay the slow but

sure foundations of the new civilisation. Distinct, nay antagonistic, in character and talents, the one nation and the other, Irish and English—the one more resembling the Greek, the other the Roman —open from the first perhaps to jealousies as well as rivalries, they consecrated their respective gifts to the Almighty Giver, and, labouring together for the same great end, they obliterated whatever there was of human infirmity in their mutual intercourse by the merit of their common achievements. Each by turn could claim pre-eminence in the contest of sanctity and learning. In the schools of science England has no name to rival Erigena in originality, or St. Virgil in freedom of thought ; nor (among its canonised women) any saintly virgin to compare with St. Bridget ; nor, although it has 150 saints in its calendar, can it pretend to equal that Irish multitude which the Book of Life alone is large enough to contain. Nor can Ireland, on the other hand, boast of a doctor such as St. Bede, or of an apostle equal to St. Boniface, or of a martyr like St. Thomas ; or of so long a catalogue of royal devotees as that of the thirty male or female Saxons who, in the course of two centuries, resigned their crowns ; or as the roll of twenty-three kings, and sixty queens and princes, who, between the seventh and the eleventh centuries, gained a place among the saints.'—Cardinal Newman, *Historic Sketches*, ' The Isles of the North,' pp. 128-9.

Page 16.

Instant each navy at the other dashed
Like wild beast, instinct-taught.

This image will be found in the description of a Scandinavian sea-fight in a remarkable book less known than it deserves to be, *The Invasion*, by Gerald Griffin, author of *The Collegians.*

The Saxons were, however, in early times as much pirates as the Danes were at a later.

Page 18. The achievement of Hastings had been rehearsed at a much earlier period by Harald.

Page 39. *At Ely, Elmham, and beside the Cam.*

In the reign of Sigebert, Felix, Bishop of East Anglia, founded schools respecting which Montalembert remarks : ' Plusieurs ont fait remonter à ces écoles monastiques l'origine de la célèbre université de Cambridge.'

Page 44. *How beautiful, O Sion, are thy courts !*

The following hymns are from the Office for the Consecration of a Church.

St. Fursey.   Page 67.

How one with brow .
Lordlier than man's, and visionary eyes.

' Whilst Sigebert still governed the kingdom there came out of Ireland a holy man named Fursey, renowned both for his words and actions, and remarkable for singular virtues, being desirous to live a stranger for Our Lord, wherever an opportunity should offer. . . . He built himself the monastery (Burghcastle in Suffolk) wherein he might with more freedom indulge his heavenly studies. There falling sick, as the book about his life informs us, he fell into a trance, and, quitting his body from the evening till the cock-crow, he was found worthy to behold the choirs of angels, and hear the praises which are sung in heaven. . . . He not only saw the greater joys of the Blessed, but also extraordinary combats of Evil Spirits.'—Bede, *Hist.* book iii. cap. xix. ' C'était un moine irlandais nommé Fursey, de très-noble naissance et célèbre depuis sa jeunesse dans son pays par sa science et ses visions. . . . Dans la principale de ses visions Ampère et Ozanam se sont accordés à reconnaître une des sources poétiques de la *Divine Comédie.*' —Montalembert, *Les Moines d'Occident,* tome iv. pp. 93–4.

Page 116. ' *None loveth Song that loves not Light and Truth.*'

This is one of the poetic aphorisms of Cadoc, a Cambrian

prince and saint, educated in the Irish monastery of Lismore, and afterwards the founder of the great Welsh monastery of Llan-carvan, in which he gave religious instruction to the sons of the neighbouring princes and chiefs.

Page 120.

True life of man
Is life within.

This thought is taken from one of St. Teresa's beautiful works.

Page 141. *Ceadmon, the earliest bard of English song.*

'A part of one of Ceadmon's poems is preserved in King Alfred's Saxon version of Bede's *History*.' (Note to Bede's *Ecclesiastical History*, edited by Dr. Giles, p. 218.)

Page 180. *Who told him tales of Leinster Kings, his sires.*

'L'origine irlandaise de Cuthbert est affirmé sans réserve par Reeves dans ses *Notes sur Wattenbach*, p. 5. Lanigan (c. iii. p. 88) constate qu'Usher, Ware, Colgan, en ont eu la même opinion. . . . Beaucoup d'autres anciens auteurs irlandais et anglais en font un natif de l'Irlande.'—Montalembert, *Les Moines d'Occident*, tome ii. pp. 391-2.

Page 191. *The thrones are myriad, but the Enthroned is One.*

Oft as Spring
Decks on thy sinuous banks her thousand thrones,
Seats of glad instinct, and love's carolling.'
Wordsworth (addressed to the river Greta).

Page 208. *Saint Frideswida, or the Foundations of Oxford.*

Saint Frideswida died in the same year as the venerable Bede, viz. A.D. 735. Her story is related by Montalembert, *Les Moines d'Occident*, vol. v. pp. 298-302, with the following references, viz.

Leland, *Collectanea*, ap. Dugdale, t. I. p. 173; cf. Bolland, t. viii. October, p. 535 à 568. I learn from a Catholic prayer book published in 1720 that the Saint's Feast used to be kept on the 19th of October. Her remains, as is commonly believed, still exist in the Cathedral of Oxford.

Page 240. *Your teacher he: he taught you first your Runes.*

'The Icelandic chronicles point out Odin as the most persuasive of men. They tell us that nothing could resist the force of his words; that he sometimes enlivened his harangues with verses, which he composed extempore; and that he was not only a great poet, but that it was he who first taught the art of poesy to the Scandinavians. He was also the inventor of the Runic characters.' —*Northern Antiquities*, p. 83. Mallet asserts that it was to Christianity that the Scandinavians owed the practical use of those Runes which they had possessed for centuries:—'nor did they during so many years ever think of committing to writing those verses with which their memories were loaded; and it is probable that they only wrote down a small quantity of them at last. . . . Among the innumerable advantages which accrued to the Northern nations from the introduction of the Christian religion, that of teaching them to apply the knowledge of letters to useful purposes is not the least valuable. Nor could a motive less sacred have eradicated that habitual and barbarous prejudice which caused them to neglect so admirable a secret.'—P. 234. Mallet's statement respecting the Greek emigration of the Northern 'Barbarians' from the East is thus confirmed by Burke. 'There is an unquestioned tradition among the Northern nations of Europe importing that all that part of the world had suffered a great and general revolution by a migration from Asiatic Tartary of a people whom they call Asers. These everywhere expelled or subdued the ancient inhabitants of the Celtick or Cimbrick original. The leader of this Asiatic army was called Odin, or Wodin; first their general, afterwards their tutelar deity. . . . . The Saxon nation believed themselves the descendants of those conquerors.' Burke, *Abridgment of English History*, book ii. cap. i.

Page 252. *Like hunters chasing hart, to sea-beat cliffs.*

This is recorded by Lingard and Burke.

Page 259. *Bede's Last May.*

This narrative of the death of Bede is closely taken from a letter written by Cuthbert, a pupil of his, then residing in Jarrow, to a fellow-pupil at a distance. An English version of that letter is prefixed to Dr. Giles's translation of *Bede's Ecclesiastical History.* (Henry G. Bohn.) The death of Bede took place on Wednesday, May 26, A.D. 735, being Ascension Day.

Page 265. *They hunger for your souls; with reverent palms.*

' But in a mystical sense the disciples pass through the cornfields when the holy Doctors look with the care of a pious solicitude upon those whom they have initiated in the Faith, and who, it is implied, are hungering for the best of all things—the salvation of men. But to pluck the ears of corn means to snatch men away from the eager desire of earthly things. And to rub with the hands is, by examples of virtue, to put from the purity of their minds the concupiscence of the flesh, as men do husks. To eat the grains is when a man, cleansed from the filth of vice by the mouths of preachers, is incorporated amongst the members of the Church.'—Bede, quoted in the *Catena Aurea. Commentary on St. Mark*, cap. ii. v. 23.

LONDON : PRINTED BY
SPOTTISWOODE AND CO., NEW-STREET SQUARE
AND PARLIAMENT STREET